Dear Mom,

I'm writing this to you just in case.

I know you understand why I have to go undercover and find the murderer, Mom. For Dad. For Wayne. For you and me. I also know you don't like it, but if I don't find the guilty one, who will?

I can't forget the promise I made the day they buried Dad. I looked into Reies Coulter's dark, dangerous eyes and vowed that I would make the killer pay. I even wondered if *he* was the one. Undoubtedly Coulter didn't believe me, probably put it to hot words from a smart-mouthed teenager. But I never forgot, and now I regret that I didn't act sooner, before we lost Wayne.

As you know, with each day that passes and I do nothing, my guilt grows. So, to live with myself, I'm keeping that promise to Dad now.

I hope that I'll be able to tell you everything in person. But if you are reading this, Mom, it means I didn't succeed and you'll be hearing the details from the captain.

It'll mean that the murderer got me, too.

Just know how sorry I am, and that I wanted one last chance to tell you how very much you mean to me.

All my love,

Libby

Ranch Rogues
1. Betrayed by Love
   Diana Palmer
2. Blue Sage
   Anne Stuart
3. Chase the Clouds
   Lindsay McKenna
4. Mustang Man
   Lee Magner
5. Painted Sunsets
   Rebecca Flanders
6. Carved in Stone
   Kathleen Eagle

Hitched in Haste
7. A Marriage of Convenience
   Doreen Owens Malek
8. Where Angels Fear
   Ginna Gray
9. Mountain Man
   Joyce Thies
10. The Hawk and the Honey
    Dixie Browning
11. Wild Horse Canyon
    Elizabeth August
12. Someone Waiting
    Joan Hohl

Ranchin' Dads
13. Ramblin' Man
    Barbara Kaye
14. His and Hers
    Pamela Bauer
15. The Best Things in Life
    Rita Clay Estrada
16. All That Matters
    Judith Duncan
17. One Man's Folly
    Cathy Gillen Thacker
18. Sagebrush and Sunshine
    Margot Dalton

Denim & Diamonds
19. Moonbeams Aplenty
    Mary Lynn Baxter
20. In a Class by Himself
    JoAnn Ross
21. The Fairy Tale Girl
    Ann Major
22. Snow Bird
    Lass Small
23. Soul of the West
    Suzanne Ellison
24. Heart of Ice
    Diana Palmer

Kids & Kin
25. Fools Rush In
    Ginna Gray
26. Wellspring
    Curtiss Ann Matlock
27. Hunter's Prey
    Annette Broadrick
28. Laughter in the Rain
    Shirley Larson
29. A Distant Promise
    Debbie Bedford
30. Family Affair
    Cathy Gillen Thacker

Reunited Hearts
31. Yesterday's Lies
    Lisa Jackson
32. Tracings on a Window
    Georgia Bockoven
33. Wild Lady
    Ann Major
34. Cody Daniels' Return
    Marilyn Pappano
35. All Things Considered
    Debbie Macomber
36. Return to Yesterday
    Annette Broadrick

Reckless Renegades
37. Ambushed
    Patricia Rosemoor
38. West of the Sun
    Lynn Erickson
39. A Wild Wind
    Evelyn A. Crowe
40. A Deadly Breed
    Caroline Burnes
41. Desperado
    Helen Conrad
42. Heart of the Eagle
    Lindsay McKenna

Once A Cowboy...
43. Rancho Diablo
    Anne Stuart
44. Big Sky Country
    Jackie Merritt
45. A Family to Cherish
    Cathy Gillen Thacker
46. Texas Wildcat
    Lindsay McKenna
47. Not Part of the Bargain
    Susan Fox
48. Destiny's Child
    Ann Major

Please address questions and book requests to: Harlequin Reader Service
U.S.: 3010 Walden Ave., P.O. Box 1325, Buffalo, NY 14269
Canadian: P.O. Box 609, Fort Erie, Ont. L2A 5X3

RECKLESS RENEGADES

WESTERN *Lovers*™

PATRICIA ROSEMOOR

AMBUSHED

Harlequin Books

TORONTO • NEW YORK • LONDON
AMSTERDAM • PARIS • SYDNEY • HAMBURG
STOCKHOLM • ATHENS • TOKYO • MILAN
MADRID • WARSAW • BUDAPEST • AUCKLAND

To Edwardo, the desperado
who ambushed this lady's heart

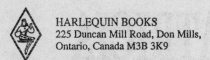

HARLEQUIN BOOKS
225 Duncan Mill Road, Don Mills,
Ontario, Canada M3B 3K9

ISBN 0-373-88537-7

AMBUSHED

Copyright © 1988 by Patricia Pinianski

Printed in U.S.A.

Prologue

A pair of watchful eyes pinned on the road observed the state patrol car as it left the lawless town called Sidewinder.

The vehicle wouldn't get far.

A rifle was slipped from its saddle holster, the metal cool in direct contrast to the blazing heat of the July day. The sun sat high in the sky, bathing the New Mexican hillside with color. The earth glowed deep red brown as if washed with blood.

Not yet. Soon.

The horse moved out and began its descent, picking its way between the scrub and cacti. When the patrol car came within range, the rider wordlessly signaled the mount to stop, then raised the rifle, took careful aim—a single shot would do it—and squeezed the trigger.

The front tire exploded; shredded black rubber immediately curled along the road. The patrol car swerved and came to a screeching halt as violent as the death that would claim its driver. But then, the cop had asked for it with his poking and prying. After thirteen years, he should have left well enough alone, should have let the dead stay buried.

The door swung open, and the man in the black-and-gray uniform stepped out and moved toward the rear of the vehicle. Good. By the time he realized his tire hadn't blown out by itself it would be too late.

While the lawman busied himself with the contents of the trunk, the rider urged the horse downward, not because the job couldn't be done from this distance, but out of fascination with any form of violence. The closer seen, the better.

A moment later, the unsuspecting dolt stepped out from behind the trunk hood, carrying a jack in one hand and wheeling a spare tire with the other. His gun remained an impotent weapon, secured in the holster at his hip. Suddenly he realized he wasn't alone. Eyes narrowed, mouth grim, he dropped the tool and let the tire go spinning off to the side of the road.

The rifle was already in position, trained on him.

"You!" the cop cried as he reached for his gun. "I was right!"

The first blast tore into the soft flesh of the cop's side, making his hand hesitate mere inches from his holster. His features were drawn but determined. He reached again until the second bullet shattered his collarbone. His expression changed to one of bewilderment, as if he had at that second realized he was about to die.

"You should have done something about what you thought you knew while you had the chance."

The third shot tore through the uniformed stomach, sending the lawman spinning. He fell face down and lay still.

The rifle slid back into its holster. The horse's neck quivered and the animal whinnied as if fearing death. The hand holding the reins was steady.

"Settle down."

Turning the mount away, the rider felt invigorated by this newest victory, yet at the same time disappointed that it had been so incredibly easy.

Chapter One

The green Jaguar sped west, bringing Libby Tate to the edge of the town so aptly named after the small, pale rattlesnake of the southwestern desert.

Sidewinder.

Treacherous. Violent. Lawless. A town without conscience.

She remembered all too well.

As she approached the town limits, Libby slowed the car; her heartbeat accelerated.

Though the twentieth century had rudely invaded northwestern New Mexico—abandoned adobe structures, and pastures nearly empty of horses lined the road into Sidewinder, while trailer homes and satellite dishes perched in the hills—the two-block main street itself hadn't changed much in thirteen years. Blending in perfectly with the old, newer buildings were camouflaged by the dust and aura of dilapidation that Libby had always associated with this small, godforsaken place.

Anglos strolled the street beside the natives—Indians, Hispanics and, most frequently, mestizos, people who represented a mixture of the two cultures. She wondered if the anglos were truly welcome or merely tolerated in this insular part of New Mexico. She suspected the latter. Here, true change would probably take centuries. Not to mention the strong hand of the law, Libby noted, glancing at the boarded-up jail.

Libby meant to drive right through town, to keep going until she arrived at Rancho Velasquez. She'd barely passed the main intersection when a man came flying into the street mere yards in front of the Jaguar, impressing on her that fate—and Sidewinder—had other plans. The screech of her brakes competed with the man's cry as he leaped to his feet, using the car's hood as a springboard.

"Whoreson!" yelled another man, followed by an explosion of Spanish in a dialect she only partly understood. Something about his woman. More implicit and even more threatening was the wicked-looking knife in his hand.

Libby's pulse surged and she almost leaped from the car. No. She mustn't get involved. Doing so would ruin everything. She watched, a helpless captive by the frightening spectacle, as the opponents circled each other in front of the Jaguar. Would no one try to stop them? Passersby turned their heads and entered nearby doorways. The street quickly became deserted.

The first man furtively pulled a knife from his boot.

"Angel, no!" Out of nowhere, a young, pretty woman ran between them. Her expression wild, she confronted the stockier of the two men and held out her arms. "Bobby, please, stop."

Knife-hand leading, Bobby tried to lunge around the woman. When she tried to interfere further, he threatened to hit her. As if she were used to such treatment, she grabbed onto his arm and wouldn't let go.

"Bobby, please. I told you I have done nothing with Angel."

"I saw you together."

"Talking, nothing else."

"Leave before the bastard hurts you more, Nina," Angel insisted. "I can take care of myself."

Bobby heaved her aside and Nina fell to the pavement. Libby gripped the steering wheel to stop herself from jumping out into the fray. But she had to do something. Thinking quickly, she slammed her palm onto her horn and didn't stop until the raucous sound got their attention. The swarthy faces of the two men turned in her direction, their expressions surprised as if they were only now noting her presence.

Libby's mouth went dry as the one called Bobby stepped toward her menacingly. What did he plan on doing? More importantly, what was *she* going to do? She locked her door and quickly rolled up her window. By then, Nina was off the ground, pulling at Bobby's arm, and two other men surrounded Angel as if protecting him. Relatives, perhaps.

The fight was over as quickly as it had begun, but not before both Bobby and Angel aimed chilling glares at Libby. She got the message. As soon as they moved out of the way, she shifted the Jaguar into gear and zoomed out of town.

What would they have done had they known her purpose for being there?

REIES COULTER RODE toward the hacienda-style building that had been his home for most of his life. Ensconced in a hand-carved wooden chair on the front porch, Emilio Velasquez posed for a portrait that would commemorate his upcoming seventy-fifth birthday. Reies stopped his horse at the edge of the porch, but didn't dismount.

"Grandfather. Victor."

The white-haired man immediately came to life. "Ah, Reies, there you are."

"Reies." Victor Duprey didn't take his blue-eyed gaze from the brush that continued to stroke the canvas. "Checking on my progress?"

"I don't need to check up on you, Victor. I know you'll finish in time. It's my mother you'll have to worry about pleasing." Reies turned to his grandfather. "So where's this reporter of yours? I expected her to be plying you with questions by now. Hasn't she arrived from Santa Fe?"

"Elena said she showed the young woman to her quarters earlier this afternoon, but that she saw Miss Tate walking up the west hill with her camera an hour or so ago."

"And Elena didn't have the sense to keep her from going?"

"Elena is a housekeeper, Reies, not a jailer. But you are right to be worried. Miss Tate does not know this country. Perhaps you should go find her and escort her back."

"I still have work to do."

"You will always have more work to do around here."

Feeling the pressure of his grandfather's firmly issued words, Reies gave in to the old man out of love and respect, just as he always did. "All right, Grandfather. I'll bring her back if that's what you want."

The true patriarch, Emilio merely inclined his head before returning his full attention to the artist and his portrait. Reies signaled Sangre to back off, then turned the horse toward the west trail. He glanced toward the bungalow he'd given up for their guest and noted the Jaguar, a dark green older model, parked there. He cursed to himself, exasperated that Libby Tate hadn't stayed put once she had what she wanted—the opportunity to snoop around his family's ranch. What kind of a story had the reporter expected to find here on the range anyway?

She shouldn't have been allowed to set one foot on the ranch, but his grandfather had been flattered by her interest. If it had been up to Reies . . .

But respecting his grandfather's wishes even if he didn't agree with them, Reies had voiced his opposition and then backed off. Through the years, the old man had been stripped of everything but his pride, and Reies was not about to take that away from him, even if he himself was now running the ranch. So, Libby Tate had been allowed to come to snoop and pry. Reies could only hope he could curtail her activities so she wouldn't do permanent damage. If she became discouraged enough, she might even go away.

"Magnificent!" Libby brought the still camera to her eyes, the scenario on the mesa enthralling her in spite of her somber thoughts. She adjusted the lens. The distant mountains fuzzed while a roan stallion preening amidst the sparse juniper and sagebrush came into sharp focus. Standing silent guard scant yards above a wobbly-legged foal rooting for its mother's milk, the animal glanced her way and froze as if he were posing.

Click.

Unused to the weight and awkwardness of the telephoto lens, Libby hoped she'd held the camera steady enough. She had to shoot some professional-looking photos to make her cover convincing. Since she had no idea of how long her investigation would take, she assumed she'd have to come up with some evidence of her ongoing work before she was through. Though she was an amateur when it came to cameras and lenses, taking pictures would be the easiest part of her job.

Libby was ready to head back for the adobe bungalow that would be her quarters for the next week or so, yet she aimed the camera one last time. She was thankful the wind held southwesterly. Had she been upwind, her scent would have panicked the wild horses, and the herd would have scattered immediately. She zoomed in to frame the proud father alone. But before she could check her focus, the stallion reared and trumpeted a warning to his brood. Tails arched, they were off in a flash of hooves and a spray of sandy earth.

Libby turned to seek the source of their fear and found it heading straight for her.

"Ye-e-ha-a!"

A dust-covered cowboy riding a sturdy blood bay broached the peak of the hill directly behind her. His mount was galloping across the rise at breakneck speed.

Libby sensed her danger. A shot of adrenaline impelled her body in a desperate lunge to the right. Rolling to the ground, she sheltered the camera with her arms. The metal housing bit into her breasts, and she stopped mere inches from impaling herself on a wicked-looking cholla cactus.

Seemingly without command from the rider, the horse braked in a crouching, sliding movement, ending a short foot from where she had stood only seconds ago.

Her heart pounded irregularly, informing her she was still alive. "Are you crazy?" she demanded as the man dismounted.

In answer, he removed his hat and slapped it against his jeans, sending an obnoxious cloud of reddish-brown dust directly at her. Coughing, Libby was forced to cover her mouth and nose and squeeze her eyes shut. She opened

them rapidly enough when strong hands gripped her upper arms and she was pulled to her feet in a none-too-
gentle fashion. He did it easily, though she was a tall
woman with her center of gravity smack in the middle of
her full hips. He was taller, his shoulders broad and well
muscled.

Libby blinked rapidly to dissipate the gritty feel in her
eyes, determined to give the man the tongue-lashing he
deserved, whether or not he understood English. Many
inhabitants in this insular northwestern part of New
Mexico spoke only an archaic Spanish dialect. Others
spoke Athabascan or another Indian tongue. She found
it impossible to utter a word when her vision cleared,
however, for in the midst of a grime-covered face, above
a thick, drooping mustache, black eyes glittered down at
her.

She freed her arms and stepped backward.

"You must be Libby Tate," the man drawled in ac-
centless English.

Reies Coulter. "You have the advantage," she lied.

An amused smile pulled at his drooping mustache.
"You don't recognize the grandson of the owner of
Rancho Velasquez? What kind of a photojournalist are
you?"

"Oh, Lord, the camera!" Libby quickly inspected the
borrowed piece of equipment. Satisfied that it hadn't
been damaged, that its owner wouldn't skin her alive, she
said, "I'm a hardworking one, or I was, before you interrupted me."

She gave him an impersonal once-over, though she was
far from detached. Well-worn leather chaps covered his
jeans and outlined thighs thick with muscle, developed
from years of sitting on a horse. His midnight hair was
pulled back and tied with a strip of rawhide, where it

curled over the collar of a faded, blue work shirt stained with perspiration.

"You must be Reies Coulter." Wayne had put the description together with the name for her. She held his gaze steadily, adding, "I thought your work with horses was skilled, not reckless."

"I trained this bay myself. As we demonstrated, Sangre can stop on a dime."

"Then I'm thankful I'm considerably larger, so he didn't mistakenly stop on me."

He didn't apologize. Libby strode off in the general direction of the hacienda's grounds. Knowing what she did about the lawless town of Sidewinder and many of its dangerous citizens, she figured rudeness could well be the least of the man's offenses. The saliva in her mouth suddenly felt thick, but she told herself it was because she'd run out of the candies she'd brought to suck on rather than a nervous reaction. She had to begin somewhere and Coulter was as good a start as any. She glanced over her shoulder as, still standing at the horse's neck, he turned a stirrup outward while urging the mount forward and swinging into the saddle in one fluid motion.

"If you hold out your thumb, I'll let you hitch a ride behind me."

She whipped her head away from him. The last thing in the world she intended to do was to get cozy with a murder suspect.

"I walked out here. My legs will take me back."

"We can ride together. It'll be faster." Coulter paced his mount to match her long-legged stride. "And your camera will be safer tied to the saddle horn than dangling over your shoulder."

"Forget it."

He reached down and looped his hand in the strap. Rather than struggle and chance damaging the equipment, she let go. He lifted the camera and wound the strap around the horn, then secured the housing by tying it to the leather saddle-strings.

"Now come on up here. I wouldn't want you to get lost, or step in a snake hole." He freed his booted left foot from its stirrup and held out a hand, which seemed as demanding as the tone he used. "My grandfather is worried enough already."

"I find that hard to believe, since the only person who met me when I drove in from Santa Fe was your housekeeper."

"Believe what you want."

He shoved his open hand practically in her face. Libby looked up into eyes that seemed to bore through her. Their expression was assessing...yet impersonal. And formidable. If she continued to refuse, she sensed he was capable of doing anything. She wouldn't put it past him to consider tying her up and throwing her over the saddle.

Her stomach tightened in fear at the thought of making this man act in anger, not that she would let things come to that. Not yet. She was a smart woman who was not only able to take care of herself, but others as well. She'd been trained to deal with men like Reies Coulter.

But then, so had Wayne.

Fingers suddenly stiff, Libby retrieved her hat from where it had fallen to her back. She set it on her head and tightened the leather strap under her chin. A delaying tactic. She didn't need the hat now. The sun was already low in the western sky.

"Do you think you could put some speed into it?" His expression was a study in impatience. "I have work to finish around the ranch."

"Then it was your mistake to come after me."

With bravado that was half real, half manufactured—she'd be plain stupid to be overconfident—she slid the toe of her boot through the freed stirrup and took Coulter's hand. The palm and fingertips were well callused, attesting to the fact that his work was hard and physical. She bounced upward and grabbed onto the cantle to steady herself as she rose. Then, as he edged forward to make room for her, she swung her leg over the horse's flank and settled herself in back of the dust-caked man. Though the saddle was a large one, probably Mexican, rather than American-made, it was too tight a squeeze for her comfort.

"Hold on."

"I am."

Though she gripped his belt with both hands, Libby leaned back from him as far as she dared. The only problem was that the position brought their bottoms into even snugger contact.

"Tighter. Put your arms around my waist."

"I'm comfortable as I am," she lied.

"It's your pretty little behind if you land in the cholla."

She might have taken the description as a compliment if a touch of sarcasm hadn't backed the words. "Like you said, it's my behind. I'll chance it."

What she couldn't chance was his knowing that her elaborately tooled leather vest concealed a shoulder holster and a small handgun, which he'd surely feel if she pressed up against his back. In trying to get a better grasp on his belt, Libby brushed her left hand against a knife sheath. She hated knives. Reies signaled his horse—she felt the backs of his thighs tighten against hers—and Sangre moved out smoothly.

"I understand you brought an entire herd of horses up from Mexico," she said. "I've only seen a few of them out here."

"Most of them are still wild. They don't like to socialize with strangers."

Libby pretended to misunderstand the implication that he didn't, either. She decided to keep up her probing as any good reporter would. If she was lucky, she'd get something of value out of the man, whether he wanted to give it or not.

"How big exactly is this new herd of yours?"

"Big enough."

"Have you sold many of your specially trained horses?"

"A few."

This wasn't getting her anywhere. Maybe being confrontational would work. She took a steadying breath and plunged ahead. "Do you dislike questions in general, or just ones by reporters?"

In answer, he tightened his thighs once more, making Libby fidget when Sangre switched from a walk to an easy lope, the new gait pressing her even closer to the man.

Reies Coulter was amused in spite of the initial irritation he'd felt upon agreeing to look for Libby Tate. Good thing he'd caught up with her before she got herself lost.

Now he found himself entertained by her efforts to keep her distance from someone she probably considered a dangerous character. The way she was trying to balance herself behind him, he wouldn't be surprised if she fell off the damned horse and took him with her. Wouldn't that be a sight to behold—one he'd never live down if any of his *vaqueros* saw. He should have had the sense to bring a second mount. Then he could be studying those unusual, dark, cactus-green eyes of hers—he swore he'd seen them before and he was determined to remember where—rather than feeling her soft thighs squirming against him.

And yet a little discomfort might be worth the information he could glean from the woman while she was off balance, Reies told himself.

"What gave you the burning desire to write an article about Rancho Velasquez?" he asked smoothly.

"Horse ranches have always had a certain mystique for the general public. Why do you think the Santa Fe area has so many visitors every year?"

"This ranch isn't a tourist attraction. It's too small, we don't offer trail rides, and sixty-five miles from Santa Fe is too far for curiosity seekers to go for a little local color."

"But it's a working ranch, even if it's not a large one. Besides, think of the positive angle: local man returns home after more than twelve years to give small town shot in economy." She paused, and her tone changed slightly as she added, "Twelve years is a long time. What made you come back?"

"Like you said, it's home."

Reies had worked his way through New Mexico, Arizona, Texas, and finally Mexico, but everywhere he'd roamed, he'd felt like an outsider. Fit justice, perhaps, since along with the other citizens of Sidewinder, he'd never trusted nor had any use for outsiders.

"You're not a man who likes to talk much about himself."

"I thought I made my point."

"What is your point?" she persisted. "That you don't approve of my being here?"

"It's what my grandfather wants."

"But not you."

No. He didn't. He had enough problems without worrying about the media getting on his back again. Who knew what Libby Tate was really after—or what she would unearth? She might get curious about the murders. Not that killings were unusual in a town like Sidewinder—feuds were common and long-lived, and people believed in taking "an eye for an eye."

"You don't belong," he finally told her.

"But I'm going to write an article that'll give you and your ranch publicity. Your business will benefit."

"We're doing all right now."

"What's wrong with doing better?"

"What's wrong with doing all right?"

"Nothing, I guess, if you're not ambitious."

"I'm just interested in making sure the ranch survives, Miss Tate—if that meets with your approval."

Reies couldn't keep the annoyance and sarcasm out of his voice. She was wearing designer jeans, an obviously expensive leather vest and new-looking boots. Her short, copper hair had been cut in a high-fashion style, cropped close at the sides with curls tumbling onto her forehead and one long curl decorating the back of her neck. She should be writing for a fashion magazine, not cruising around a dusty, working ranch. What the hell did a woman who owned a Jaguar know about survival?

Her silence annoyed Reies as much as her questions. He signaled Sangre to move out, and the horse's powerful muscles propelled him from the easy lope into a spirited gallop. The reporter's thighs tightened behind his, and she leaned forward, yet didn't thrust herself onto him. Her seat and balance were excellent, especially under the circumstances. A horsewoman. He shouldn't be surprised. She probably had a horse of her own to go with the jeans and vest.

Not wanting to continue pushing the horse with the weight of two riders on his back, Reies brought Sangre to a trot when he passed a supply shack at the edge of some broken-down fencing. He'd been home and doing repair work for almost six months, but there was still so much to do.

Libby felt the subtle change in tension in Coulter's body as the silence stretched between them. His comment about the survival of his family's ranch still rankled her. She'd seen the signs of neglect—broken fences, weather-worn outbuildings in disrepair—but she'd noted the improvements, as well. Wayne had told her about the money Coulter had been pumping into the place. At least he'd been able to save his heritage, she thought, remembering with renewed bitterness what had happened to hers.

She was thankful when they crested a small rise within sight of the grounds where her quarters lay. At the bottom of the hill stood several outbuildings—horse barn, toolshed, bunkhouse for the hired men, and two different-size corrals. A hundred yards farther on stood the small adobe guest bungalow where she was staying, and directly to the left was the hacienda itself, the sprawling, Spanish-style house.

She was surprised when, rather than heading for the barn or one of the corrals, Coulter guided Sangre past them and toward her bungalow. Libby wondered if she should object, but before she could make up her mind, he was pulling the horse up in front of her door.

"Curb service, just like a taxi."

Libby dismounted, thankful to be free of the unwanted contact and to be on her own legs once more. Still, she frowned up at the man who'd seemed so anxious to bring her back. "I thought everyone was waiting for me."

"I'll let the family know you're safe."

"I can tell them myself."

"At dinner." Keeping his eyes on her, he pulled a thin, black cheroot from his shirt pocket and lit it. "Come up to the hacienda a little before seven."

Though Libby was used to taking orders, she did so only on her job. With difficulty, she smiled. "But I'd like to meet Mr. Velasquez as soon as possible."

"All in good time."

"I thought I could get started on my story."

"But isn't that why you toured the place on your own? To get your bearings?" He puffed on the cheroot and returned her smile, his expression as fake as her own. "So you see, you've already begun."

"Look, it can't be more than four o'clock—"

"Four-thirty," he corrected without consulting a watch.

Frustrated at the waste of time—she desperately wanted to get going on this case—Libby asked, "What do you suggest I do until seven?"

Coulter's dark eyes roamed down her body in an assessing way that made her strangely self-conscious. For the first time he was looking at her the way a man does a woman. The difference was subtle, but it didn't escape her.

"Get yourself cleaned up. You're pretty dusty from that roll on the ground. And change into something more appropriate. Grandfather thinks being civilized means dressing for dinner."

"I didn't bring anything formal."

"A skirt and blouse will do." Before she could protest, he quickly added, "My grandfather's preference."

"Are you trying to tell me he doesn't approve of women in pants?"

"I'd say he thinks of himself as a man still young enough to appreciate a shapely set of legs."

Libby crossed her arms, wondering if she'd ever gain an inch or pry a grain of information from Reies Coulter. "I'll make you a deal. I'll cooperate if you will."

His black eyes hooded, he asked, "How?"

"I'll wear a skirt if you'll talk to me like a human being rather than like something that slithered out from under a rock."

His scarred eyebrow shot upward. He couldn't hide his surprise at the direct confrontation. "What makes you think I'm treating you any differently than anyone else?"

"Call it instinct," Libby said wryly. She'd have to be blind, deaf and plain stupid not to realize that he was far from enchanted by her presence and that it had nothing to do with whether or not she belonged there. Was he afraid she'd find out something she shouldn't? Aloud she asked, "So, do we have a deal?"

"Wear the skirt and find out."

Without waiting for her response, he stuck the cheroot in his mouth and wheeled Sangre in a tight half circle. Horse and rider set off for the barn in a relaxed lope. She watched for a moment, then, remembering she wasn't there to admire the view, turned away and entered the bungalow.

Inside, Libby leaned against the door, her knees weak, the enormity of her self-imposed mission suddenly threatening to overpower her. She was in this alone. Without backup. She took a deep breath and reprimanded herself. She was no ordinary woman who would run at the first taste of fear. She was a professional. A cop.

She untied the string at the front of her vest and removed her Beretta automatic from its shoulder holster. The feel of the cold, blue metal against her palm was reassuring, gave renewed strength to her knees. She knew how to use the piece. As a matter of fact, she was still the best shot in her division. She'd been trained to use weapons, trained to work undercover, trained to find and bring lawbreakers to justice.

Only it had never been personal before.

And she'd never had to do it alone.

Pushing herself from the door, she wandered across the small living area toward the bedroom. The bungalow had been decorated simply—the furniture, area rugs and wall hangings in colors and patterns typical of the southwest. The sand-colored paint on the walls was fresh, and the floor had been recently refinished. Odd that the guest quarters had been given priority over some of the work areas.

In the bedroom, she went straight to the camera bag she'd left on the dresser. Setting down her gun, she unloaded lenses, light meter and flash from the bag. Then she undid the Velcro fastenings that divided the interior into compartments and felt for the loose flap at the bottom. She lifted it and slipped out the hidden five-by-eight-inch envelope, then backed up until her legs felt the edge of the bed.

Libby sat and removed the black-and-white glossies from the envelope. She took a deep breath and spread them in front of her across the coral- and sand-colored quilt. In the first photograph, the officer lay chest down, sprawled on the ground at the side of the road, not far from his patrol car. The next was a shot from the waist up and gave a clearer view of his face. Even from that distance, the casual observer could tell the officer was young.

She was no casual observer. She knew exactly how old he'd been when he died: twenty-four.

Her eyes stung. She wouldn't cry. If she did her face would get puffy. *He'd* be able to tell, even hours later. Nothing escaped Coulter's intense black gaze. She squeezed her eyes shut and swallowed hard. When the lump in her throat eased, she opened her eyes and continued her perusal of the photographs with the professional eye of a law officer.

The next two photos were close-ups, one of his right hand, palm down in the dirt, the other of what that hand hid: something he'd carved into the earth before he'd died. An S.

She traced the S as she mouthed the word Sidewinder.

The final photograph was almost her undoing. His body had been turned to show where the bullets had entered. Three dark gray spots stained his uniform: shoulder, side, stomach...

His eyes were still open.

Blank.

Wayne had been so full of life.

Her forefinger stroked the familiar face. "Oh, Wayne, why? Why didn't you listen to me?" she whispered as though he could hear her. Maybe he could. She'd never thought much about what came after death, but now she had to believe there was something.

Holding onto the photograph, she lay back on the bed and closed her eyes, remembering the first time she'd seen the godforsaken town and the pitiful graveyard where her father's body still rested. Had anyone put flowers on his grave in thirteen years? she wondered. If not, the flowers would have to wait a little while longer. She didn't dare arouse suspicion by going there.

Squeezing her eyes tighter, she remembered the vacation she and Wayne had taken with their mother, aunt and cousins. They'd driven to Sedona, Arizona, an artists' town. When they'd returned home, a message awaited them: Oliver Reardon had been murdered several days before, sixty miles from home. The county authorities had tried to reach the family numerous times for instructions on disposal of the remains.

Remains. That's all that was left of the father Libby had idolized.

If Mrs. Reardon didn't respond in the required time, Oliver Reardon would be buried in a county cemetery.

Libby remembered everything about that awful day....

THE OLD CHEVY NOSED its way into the decrepit town and stopped in front of the gas station. Gloria Reardon hit the horn with the flat of her hand. No response. Opening the door, she stepped out. "Hello! Is anyone here?" She was almost hysterical.

Sixteen-year-old Libby shaded her eyes and looked around, past the rundown post office and gray, cinder-block grocery toward the ancient adobe church with its peeling beige paint. No one. Nothing but a tumbleweed ambling down the middle of the street. She wanted to yell that the message had been a mistake, but she knew her mother wouldn't leave. Movement caught her eye as the door of the gas station opened and two young men strolled out.

"Can we help you, sweet thing?" the younger of the two, a tall, sandy-haired man, asked her mother.

"I—I'm looking for the sheriff."

The statement was met with rude, mocking laughter. "Ain't no sheriff, lady," the swarthy, dark-eyed man assured her. He pulled his stocky body to its full height as he advanced on Gloria. "Ain't no law in this town at all."

"But I received a message from the county—"

"The last lawman assigned to Sidewinder met with an accident." The sandy-haired man stepped forward, practically pinning her against the side of the car. "A fatal accident."

He reached out to stroke her shoulder and Gloria flinched. Raw fear snaked out and gripped Libby. About to lunge out of the car to protect her mother, she stopped when the creep let go and pointed west toward the hillside.

"What you're looking for is over there, sweet thing."

With a cry of distress, Gloria jumped back into the car while the two men snickered and exchanged comments in Spanish. She slammed the door in their grinning faces.

"My God, we're too late," she whispered while throwing the car into gear. "Not Oliver! Oh, God, not like this!"

Libby sat in silence, fingers twining together tighter and tighter as though she could physically constrain her emotions in her thin body. Her mother pressed the Chevy on, through the town, across the creek and onto the rocky road that ran parallel to the irrigation ditch. She tried to ignore the muffled sobs next to her and the sniffles coming from her brother in the back seat. She tried to ignore the dust that curled into the open windows, threatening to choke her.

Unreal. All so unreal.

Before them, the desert plain rose steeply. Beyond were the mountains. Her pulse thudded in long, jagged strokes as her gaze settled on the gathering at the top of the hill.

Silhouetted against the deep blue sky were altar boys and
a priest in ceremonial garments, women of every age
shrouded in black, men beside them, white straw hats in
hand.

Her mother continued to push the Chevy, and Libby
had to clench her jaw to keep her teeth from clacking.
Dust clouded around them, settling when they stopped
only yards away from the townspeople, unable to go farther because of a rotting picket fence. Heads turned as
Gloria flew out of the car. People moved aside for her
and for eleven-year-old Wayne, who followed close on
her heels.

Libby took her time. Dry eyed, she trailed her mother
and brother at a slower pace, one that belied the pulse
racing through her. She focused on the sea of mourners,
on her sobbing mother and brother in their midst, on the
coffin being lowered into the ground as the priest
mouthed meaningless words.

The hot wind blew long strands of fine hair in her eyes.
She looked through them at the knot of people who immediately surrounded the grave that surely had been dug
for Oliver Reardon.

One of them? she wondered. Had one of them killed
her father?

The police didn't know.

That was why she committed each of them to memory: a tall, distinguished-looking man with a thick head
of white hair; a striking woman at his side who looked
more Indian than anything else; a young man with a cleft
in his chin, who could be her son; a beautiful Hispanic
girl with unusual light brown eyes; an anglo, one of only
a few in this gathering, his blond hair and blue eyes setting him apart from the others; a slender, wiry Hispanic

with perfect, almost feminine features, except for cruel lips, which seemed to taunt her with unspilled laughter.

"Honey, over here," came a broken cry.

Libby's gaze strayed, not to her mother, but to the last of those immediately surrounding the grave. His straight, black hair hung to his shoulders and a mustache drooped over a full lower lip. He had an angular face, hollow cheeks accenting prominent cheekbones, and a straight blade of a nose. A scar slashed through his left brow. His black eyes were closed and devoid of emotion as they locked with her own.

Dark, dangerous-looking eyes, she thought, shivering despite the scorching heat that had outlasted the setting August sun.

The braces on her teeth making her words sound slurred and awkward to her own ears, she made her brave promise directly to him. "You won't get away with it. The police will find the guilty one." She tried to swallow the feeling of desperation that threatened to suffocate her. "And if they don't, I will. One of you will pay for my father's murder."

SHE'D NEVER FORGET Reies Coulter's eyes. She'd never forget anything about that day, about what she'd felt.

But old wounds heal and old vows weaken. At least they did for her. She'd been too busy surviving to stay wrapped up in the past. Even while she and Wayne had talked about becoming law-enforcement officers and pursuing their father's murderer on their own when they grew up, she and her mother had been trying to save their ranch. They'd failed miserably. They hadn't had the livestock Oliver Reardon had come to Sidewinder to buy from Emilio Velasquez. They hadn't had the money her father had withdrawn to do so, leaving them only a meager bank account. The money had simply disappeared, as had their entire way of life.

Except for her mother everything Libby loved had been taken from her. No more. The time had come for the taker to pay.

Still lying on the bed, she held the glossy photo of her brother above her. This time when she made the promise, it was to Wayne's sightless eyes. "I swear to you, I'll find the murderer. For your sake—" in spite of her determination not to cry, tears spilled down her cheeks "—and for my own."

Chapter Two

Reies didn't realize Libby's camera was still tied to his saddle horn until he was at the barn. His first thought was to turn Sangre around and take it to her at once; his second was to keep the camera, at least for the moment.

He dismounted. When his full weight bore down on his right leg, the automatic tightening of his thigh made his teeth clench. He dropped the cheroot and ground the lighted tip with his boot heel. Then, as best he could through the leather covering, he massaged the flesh above his knee all the way up to his hip. The cramped feeling eased. After all these years, he thought his long-healed muscles would have been inured to the rigors of the hours he spent on horseback, but it wasn't always so. He had his good days and his bad.

Maybe the tension of this one had gotten to him.

After flipping the reins over a rail and patting Sangre's neck, Reies undid the leather ties that held the camera fast. He thought quickly. Getting a sneak preview of what the reporter deemed of interest around the ranch might give him a needed advantage. Libby Tate had been on her own for the better part of the afternoon. Who knew what she had been into or what she had photographed? Instincts humming from their encounter, he decided getting the contents of the camera developed himself was a smart idea.

Though the reporter had made the overtures to his grandfather about doing the article, she had seemed put out—or put off—by him. True, he hadn't exactly greeted her in a cordial manner, but then he hadn't been trying to make friends. Even so, her reactions had surprised him. She'd been wary, yet collected, as if she'd been expecting hostility and had prepared herself to deal with it.

Why would the woman have assumed anyone would be hostile to her... unless she wasn't really planning on doing the story she said she was? Reies had checked out her request to do the article with Bob Gulley, the features editor at the *Santa Fe Sun*. But the man could have been covering for her, he thought, and Libby Tate could be an investigative reporter hoping to hit on something at Rancho Velasquez to advance her career. The public was always willing to read about murder.

"Hey, gringo, how's it going?" called Luis Salazar as the *vaquero* trotted his horse up to Sangre. "I hear you had to go after the reporter lady. Did she survive the ride back or did you dump her in the cactus?"

"She's intact. The cactus wouldn't have pierced her tough hide, anyway."

The stocky man laughed as he dismounted. Of the half-dozen hands Reies had brought to the ranch, Luis was the only one he really trusted. They'd worked together since Brownsville, Texas, almost seven years before. Though Luis, at forty-three, was ten years his senior, and the man's outgoing, fun-loving personality sometimes drove him crazy, theirs was the closest thing to friendship that Reies had ever known with someone not born and raised in Sidewinder.

"Taking up photography?" Luis asked.

"Maybe." Turning the camera over in his hands, Reies realized the thing was out of his line of expertise. It had been years since he'd even used a simple instant camera. He didn't have the faintest idea of how to rewind and remove the film, and he didn't want to make any wrong guesses and take the chance of ruining some potentially revealing photographs. "You know how to work one of these?"

Palms held out in a gesture of horrified denial, Luis said, "You know me. I'm a simple man with simple tastes. Wine...women...song." With that, the older man demonstrated by bursting into a Spanish love song.

"All right. I get the message," Reies growled, making Luis retreat into a mock hurt silence. "Listen, there's something you've got to do for me right away."

The other man sighed loudly. "For you, gringo, anything. Your words are so sweet, they are like music to my ears. How can I refuse?"

Ignoring the sarcasm, Reies said, "I want you to go into Santa Fe."

"What for? We short on supplies?"

"That's what I'll tell anyone who asks, but I want you to find one of those shops that can get film developed right away. Someone there should know how to get the film out of this camera properly."

"You have to have the pictures tonight?"

"As soon as possible. Why?"

Brown eyes twinkling, Luis puffed up his barrel of a chest and lifted his bearded chin. "A man has interests other than work and horses. If I'm going into Santa Fe..."

"I get the message. You're lonely and you want to stay the night with one of your women."

"Good thinking." Luis took the camera and held it as if the complex-looking piece of equipment might bite. "Besides, I doubt I'll be able to get your developed pictures back before tomorrow morning. So you see, your generosity works out for the best."

And in the meantime, Reies would have to figure out how he was going to keep Libby from making a scene about retrieving her camera.

"Get going. I'll take care of your horse."

"I'm already gone." But Luis stopped after taking a couple of steps. "You wouldn't want to tell me what you are looking for in these pictures?"

"No."

"I didn't think so." Shrugging, the stocky man continued on his way.

Reies undid Sangre's flank cinch, then the front cinch. The blood bay shifted restlessly as the weight was removed from his back. Thinking about the hunch that had made him keep the camera, Reies carried the heavy leather saddle into the tack room at the front of the barn.

The truth was that he didn't have the faintest idea of what he'd find in the photographs. He was merely paying attention to his finely honed survival instincts.

Libby Tate had been awfully interested in the fact that he'd been away from Sidewinder for the past twelve years. He wouldn't be at all surprised to learn that the reporter knew of the circumstances surrounding his departure.

Though the citizens of the small town invariably closed ranks against official investigations—even if the crime was as serious as murder—an outsider turning up gutshot in Reies Coulter's bed warranted speculation by everyone. Reies had taken a great deal of heat both from his friends and family, as well as from the press. He'd dealt with enough questions and curiosity on the subject of Oliver Reardon's demise to last him a lifetime.

And now the latest murder victim found a few miles southeast of town last month—another Reardon, this one a cop—had been enough to put him on his guard. Yet, other than questioning him as they had everyone else in this part of the county, the police hadn't made any unsubstantiated suppositions—the way they had before.

But who was to say that a persistent and clever reporter wouldn't try to connect both crimes to him?

He was right to worry about Libby Tate's purpose in being at the ranch, Reies assured himself. He only hoped the developed photographs would give him the edge he needed to drive her back to where she belonged.

THINKING SHE WAS ALONE when she entered the hacienda through the main doors, Libby admired the large central room with its high-beamed ceiling and shiny wood floor. Brightly colored native rugs accented seating and dining areas. Drawn by the warmth of the flames, which drove the evening mountain chill from the room, she wandered toward the stone fireplace. A comfortable-looking brown sofa and two overstuffed tan chairs with foot rests flanked the massive opening.

Neither chair was empty.

"Ah, Miss Tate." An elderly man with a thick shock of white hair and full, white mustache stood, his tall, gaunt form ramrod straight. "I am enchanted to meet you at last." He bent slightly from the waist. "Emilio Velasquez, at your service."

The introduction wasn't necessary. Libby would have recognized the family patriarch anywhere, just as she had his grandson. She kept her smile pleasant and neutral.

"Mr. Velasquez." Noting her host's deep brown suit with modestly embroidered bolero jacket, she realized Reies hadn't been pulling her leg about dressing for dinner. She took the hand the older man offered, only to find her own being kissed in a courtly European manner. "I'm sorry we missed each other when I arrived."

"I must apologize if you were offended by my absence."

"No, of course I wasn't."

"Good. Then let me introduce you to Sidewinder's own extraordinary artist, Victor Duprey."

Libby turned to the second chair, as its occupant stood up. He was the anglo who'd been at her father's grave. She hadn't expected to run into him so soon. Her pulse picked up a beat as his blue eyes narrowed in scrutiny, the skin around them crinkling like worn leather.

Did she detect a hint of recognition in their depths?

She rejected that possibility as quickly as it occurred to her. She looked nothing like the unsophisticated teenager who'd decided thirteen years ago she'd someday get retribution for her father's death. Her ex-husband, Harry Tate, owner of a busy resort ranch in the Santa Fe area, had been responsible for her image, as well as the name change.

Though Victor looked much the same, his blond hair was threaded with gray, and several extra pounds had settled around his waist. He wore silver and turquoise jewelry unusual enough that it might have been designed by another artist rather than a Pueblo Indian. The squash-blossom necklace was of the finest craftsmanship, as was the thick, silver snake bracelet that wrapped his wrist.

He took her hand. "What an interesting and vibrant addition you make to our humble little town." With the practiced eye of an artist used to absorbing details, he quickly scanned her cream silk blouse, pencil-thin skirt and bronze accessories. "You'll have to sit for me while you're here. In the afternoon, I think, when the sun will turn the copper of your hair to flame."

"I'm flattered, but I expect I'll be actively learning the ins and outs of a working ranch. I am being paid to work, after all."

"But surely not twenty-four hours a day."

"I'll see what I can do," Libby hedged, as her attention was drawn to the faint sound of leather soles whispering over bare wood.

She turned as Reies entered the room alongside a black-garbed woman who appeared to be in her late thirties, but surely had to be his mother. That would place the woman in her early fifties, though her striking features framed by a coronet of thick braids were as beautiful and ageless as they had been the last time Libby had seen her. There was little resemblance between mother and son other than their black hair and eyes.

"This is my mother, Inez Obregon," Reies said.

That confirmed the information Libby had gathered from a telephone conversation with Wayne. Her brother had fit the names with the descriptions for her, as well as explained the relationships within the Velasquez-Coulter-Obregon family. Inez was the daughter of Emilio Velasquez and his late Apache wife. Married first to Alex Coulter, an anglo, a second time to Frank Obregon, a mestizo like herself, Inez had two sons, half brothers Reies and Nick.

The older woman's expression remained neutral as she spoke. "Welcome to Rancho Velasquez."

The words were issued with graciousness, but without warmth, making Libby suspect Reies's mother wasn't exactly thrilled with her presence.

"Inez, tell Elena we are ready to be seated," Emilio requested in a pleasant voice.

"But Nick and Pilar aren't—"

"We have been over this many times." Emilio's voice grew firm. "If your son and daughter-in-law must choose the dinner hour to squabble with each other, they will have to make do with cold food."

"Yes, Father." Dark, flashing eyes the only indication that she was subverting her own wishes to follow the order, Inez complied.

As Emilio and Victor exchanged comments in hushed voices, Libby realized that Reies was inspecting her long legs.

"I see you took my advice."

"Good advice," she admitted, remembering the bargain she'd proposed. "I hope you'll be as wise."

He was more direct. "You certainly don't remind me of something that slithered out from under a rock."

"You gave me that distinct impression," she insisted.

"Then I must apologize."

Libby narrowed her eyes suspiciously. Reies certainly hadn't treated her with the slightest civility earlier. Now, noting the curve of his full lower lip under the mustache that seemed to droop a bit less than it had before, she realized he was smiling. Sort of.

Maybe the change in temperament came with the alteration of his appearance. Although not handsome, the man was definitely striking, a fact she hadn't discerned through the dusty cowboy trappings. His straight, blue-black hair, tied back by a leather thong, shone even in the dim light. His skin glowed with a healthy tan against a shirt that belied the tough image he'd projected to perfection. A single row of ruffles, embroidered with several shades of blue thread, decorated the white, full-sleeved garment.

She was so fascinated with the amazing transformation that she almost forgot to ask Reies about her camera. She hadn't even realized the equipment was still tied to his saddle until she'd returned the glossies of Wayne to their hiding place.

"Reies. My camera." Libby was sure his lower lip tensed slightly as she asked, "Where have you—?"

"The table awaits!" Emilio announced, interrupting her question. "Reies, please seat our guest."

"Of course."

Reies swiftly guided her to the long oak table. His hand was sure on her elbow, his arm warm as it grazed her back. A subtle fragrance of after-shave mixed with his masculine scent teased her imagination. Libby acknowledged the fleeting impression of Reies as a man who appealed to the senses . . . until she remembered that he'd been the prime suspect in her father's murder, even if he'd never been arrested. She immediately stiffened and gave him a swift look, which assured her he'd noted her reaction.

His dark eyes closed immediately. He seated her to the right of his grandfather before taking the chair on her other side. Her pulse threading through her in a rush, Libby decided it might be prudent to hold the camera issue until later when her own emotions were in better balance. She stared at the expensive table settings, which were not exactly a display of the near-poverty Wayne had described when he'd first seen the place shortly after Reies returned from Mexico.

Inez joined them, followed by Elena who carried a large soup pot to the sideboard. The housekeeper set the pot on the practical, ceramic-tiled surface. Victor pulled out the chair at the foot of the table for Inez before seating himself to her left. Only the two chairs on the opposite side of the table remained vacant.

"Miss Tate, I hope you'll enjoy Elena's cooking as we all do," Emilio said, as the housekeeper set the first bowl in front of her.

The piquant scent of jalapeño pepper wafted up from the soup, and Libby realized Elena was watching her closely. "I'm sure I will." She sipped at a spoonful. The fiery chicken broth warmed her. "Delicious."

Beaming, the rotund housekeeper went back to her task of serving the family.

"Victor, how is my father's portrait progressing?" Inez asked.

"I think you'll be pleased. I'd be happy to show it to you after dinner."

"I'd like that," Inez said.

"I will be seventy-five next week, Miss Tate," Emilio announced. "My daughter has commissioned Victor to paint my portrait, which will be unveiled at my birthday celebration. You must stay until then, at least."

"Grandfather, as a photojournalist for the *Santa Fe Sun*, Miss Tate is a busy woman," Reies protested. "I'm sure she has another assignment all lined up for next week."

Sensing he'd like her to be gone as soon as possible, Libby experienced an odd kind of triumph in being able to oppose him. "Actually, I haven't taken another assignment, because I didn't know now much time this one would involve. I don't like to rush my work. I'd rather be thorough," she said truthfully. Shifting her gaze past

Reies's scowl, she smiled at the family patriarch. "So, I probably will be staying through next week, Mr. Velasquez, if I don't wear out my welcome."

"Of course you will not. You will enjoy an extraordinary birthday party," Emilio insisted.

"Extraordinary how?"

"All of Sidewinder will turn out for music and food and entertainment provided by my grandson. Reies is putting together a modest *charreada*."

"Rodeo?"

"Yes. Mexican style," Reies added, his voice not hinting at his feelings about her possible presence. "My horses can show off their talents."

"Like stopping on a dime?"

"Exactly."

Ignoring the sound of voices arguing in Spanish coming from somewhere down the hall, Libby asked, "Are you performing in Santa Fe, then?" Although there was usually only one rodeo held in the summer, she'd seen several posters advertising another in mid-August.

"Yes," Reies said as a now-silent couple entered the room. "Several *charreada* clubs from around the United States will be competing for awards."

"I deserve the award around here!" claimed a voluptuous woman who gathered her full, red skirt and flounced into the chair opposite Libby. Her unusual light brown eyes sought Reies before adding, "For being married to your penny-pinching brother."

"Then perhaps you shouldn't have married Nick," Reies said calmly, paying more attention to his soup than to his sister-in-law.

Pilar Obregon.

Her husband, Nick, muttered something low and threatening in Spanish as he took the seat next to Pilar,

while Elena scurried forward with their bowls of soup.
Libby stared in silent fascination as the petulant woman
ignored the food and defiantly tossed her loose, sable hair
over a bared shoulder. She'd worn her peasant blouse
pulled as low as possible, revealing the tops of her full
breasts. A long, copper earring danced along her golden
flesh.

"I hope you will excuse the manners of these *children*, Miss Tate." Emilio's fierce expression reflected his
disapproval of the display.

"I am a woman, not a child—"

"Then act like one!" Nick exclaimed.

"As I was saying," Pilar continued, her light brown
eyes narrowing, "I am a woman with a woman's needs."
Again, she turned to Reies. "And what I need right now
is a new dress that Nick refuses to buy me. Your selfish
brother says we can't afford anything but the necessities." Her tone changed into liquid silk as she pleaded,
"That's not true anymore, Reies, is it? Tell him."

Face contorted with fury, Nick grabbed a handful of
Pilar's hair close to her scalp and yanked her head around
to his. "I am your husband. I will say what we can afford and what we cannot." He released her. "Reies divorced you. Remember that."

Libby swallowed hard and tried not to stare. Pilar was
once married to Reies? This was news that either Wayne
hadn't known or had seen no reason to share with her.
She glanced at Reies, but if she expected a reaction, she
was sorely disappointed. His expression was as closed as
his emotionless eyes. Flustered, Libby turned away.

Across the table, Pilar pouted as prettily as a woman
her age could manage. When no one paid her any mind,
she reached for her spoon and toyed with her soup, while
Nick attacked his bowl as if he were a man possessed.

Libby studied him, looking for any likeness to his older half brother. There was none. Except for the dark brown hair and eyes and cleft in his chin, Nick closely resembled his mother.

No further outbursts interrupted the dinner conversation, which Emilio eventually picked up. As if she knew exactly how far she could go without earning the ire of the other members of the household, Pilar remained silent for the rest of the meal.

Amazing that after thirteen years she remembered each of these people, Libby thought during a quiet moment between courses. Their faces were still etched in her memory as if her father's burial had been the previous week. Only one of those mourners around the grave was missing—the beautiful young Hispanic man with the cruel mouth.

As for Pilar...

She'd known her father had been found in Reies's bed and that the police had surmised Reies might have killed him out of jealousy. What she hadn't remembered was the wife's name, and she hadn't believed then that the supposition was true. Now she was sure it wasn't. Oliver Reardon would have had no use for a spoiled, self-centered woman, no matter how alluring. Of that, Libby was certain.

She should feel triumphant that her mission had begun so well, yet a subtle tension had begun its work tightening the muscles between her shoulder blades, and a dull throb was making itself known at the base of her skull. She was relieved when she finished dessert and coffee and felt free to leave the table. A couple of aspirins and a hot shower would do wonders.

As she rose, Emilio stopped her from making her excuses and retiring. "I would be honored if you would join

us at the fire for a brandy, Miss Tate. This was once a
custom reserved for men, but even I must give in to
change.''

"Hah!" Pilar spat. "Nothing of any importance
changes around here." Red skirt swirling around full
hips, she rose and left the room. Nick quickly followed
and their bickering began anew.

Before the elderly man could again apologize for
something that wasn't his fault, Libby said, "I'll join you
by having another cup of coffee if that's all right." She
had nothing against brandy except that alcohol tended to
fuzz her mind and reflexes, and she wanted to remain
clearheaded and in control.

"Whatever you wish."

"It will give us all a better chance to get acquainted,"
Reies said agreeably. "Perhaps you can tell us more
about the stories you write."

Sensing an attempt by Reies to discredit her, Libby
smiled at his grandfather and directed her request to him.
"Actually, I would rather discuss Rancho Velasquez.
That's why I'm here, after all."

"Father, you'll excuse us?" Inez looked up at Victor.
"I am anxious to see the progress on your portrait."

"Of course, since you commissioned it."

The artist took her arm and led Inez out of the room,
while Emilio, Reies and Libby moved toward the fire.
Libby sat, and the men remained standing. Elena followed and served coffee and brandy.

"This land has been in the Velasquez family since the
early nineteenth century, long before Mexico ceded the
territory to the United States." Swirling his brandy, Emilio stood even straighter than usual. "My ancestor who
settled this land was Juan Velasquez, a man of noble

birth, but a fifth son with no hopes of a substantial inheritance. He made his own inheritance here.''

"He built this house?''

Emilio nodded proudly. "His first home was more modest, but he built the hacienda shortly before he died. These walls echo with New Mexican history. A Velasquez has always lived here, but alas, I am the last in the line. My two sons died in unfortunate incidents before they had the chance to marry.'' He didn't explain further but looked pointedly at Reies when he said, "I hope my heir will honor me by allowing the Velasquez name to live on through the land.''

"You'll have to speak to Nick about that, Grandfather.''

"You are the older and should be my heir.''

"He stayed while I left.''

"But you brought life back here when there was little hope of saving anything,'' Emilio insisted.

"I think this discussion should be private.''

Both men fell silent.

Knowing the old man's last reference was to the mysteriously gotten money Reies had been pumping into the ranch, Libby took the opportunity to get some of the information she wanted. "I'd like to hear more about the changes you've made since your return, Reies.''

Placing his drink on the stone mantel, he leaned back and pulled out a cheroot. "I thought you wanted to know more about the ranch itself.''

"But your grandfather makes your involvement sound so intriguing.'' She didn't see how he was going to get out of that one.

In the process of lighting a match, Reies lifted his head and stared at the front windows. "Something's coming. A truck.''

"I don't hear anything," Libby said, figuring he was trying to change the subject.

"Trust him," Emilio told her. "His sharpened senses are his heritage from my late wife. She was Apache."

"How interesting."

A few seconds later, the sound of a vehicle stopping a short distance from the house brought Elena from the kitchen. She opened the door before the visitor could knock.

"I gotta see Reies," an impatient male voice insisted.

Reies moved away from the fire. "It's Johnnie Madrigal, Grandfather. I'll take care of him while you keep our guest entertained."

The brief glance Libby caught of the visitor startled her. His was the missing face!

Reies took the door from Elena and barred the slender man from entering. "Johnnie, let's go for a walk."

Before he departed, Reies glanced quickly at Libby. One look at his expression convinced her he was unhappy leaving her alone with his grandfather. And she was equally certain he didn't want her to know the purpose of Johnnie's visit, which made her determined to find out.

Just as he closed the door behind him, Inez and Victor returned from the north wing of the house.

"Father, the likeness is wonderful!" Inez gushed. "Victor has outdone himself."

"Yes," Emilio said with a pleased laugh. "He has even managed to remove a decade from this old face."

"Emilio, I paint only what I see," Victor insisted. He looked toward the dining area where Elena was straightening up. "I would like that glass of brandy now."

When the housekeeper turned around, Inez said, "Don't bother. I'll get Victor's drink myself."

Seeing her opportunity to leave, Libby yawned and rose. "You'll all have to excuse me. I'm afraid that walk I took this afternoon did me in."

"Sleep well, Miss Tate." Emilio bowed stiffly from the waist. "The morning begins early on the ranch."

"Thank you. Good night."

Libby escaped out the front door with no intention of heading directly for her bungalow. Instead, she followed the distinctive scent of Reies's cigar smoke toward the back of the horse barn. If her luck held, she hoped to overhear something of importance to her investigation.

Not wanting the men to be aware of her presence, she skirted the building on tiptoe, careful to make no noise as she settled herself behind a scrawny bush where she had a fragmented view of the two men by moonlight. His lithe body in constant motion, Johnnie paced in front of the much larger man.

"The Coalition is meeting tomorrow night. We need men like you, now more than ever."

The Coalition. Though the name sounded vaguely familiar, Libby couldn't quite place it.

"I was wondering how long it would take you to get to that." Leaning against a corral post with his right leg lifted, his boot heel hooked on the wood behind him, Reies puffed on his cheroot. "The thing is...I don't need the Coalition."

"You don't know that until you've been."

"I know I don't need any more trouble."

"Trouble?" Johnnie stopped in front of Reies, but even then, his muscles seemed to quiver. "Since when have you been afraid of trouble?"

"We're not kids anymore. I grew up a long time ago."

"You grew up or away from this town? Why'd you come back, then?"

"This is still my home."

Libby shifted her stance, grazing her hip on the rough barn board. A horse inside neighed softly as if it sensed her presence. She froze and wished herself invisible as Reies's head turned in her direction. Adrenaline rushed through her as she held her breath.

If only she could see his expression... but from this distance, the men were barely visible, silhouettes in the moonlight. And they were in the open, Libby told herself, not hiding behind a bush. Reies couldn't possibly see her. When he turned back to his companion a few seconds later, she allowed herself to breathe again.

"It's the money, isn't it, Reies?"

Johnnie was moving again, yet he never turned his back on Reies, never took his eyes off him. Libby watched in rapt fascination while acknowledging the reference to money.

"You don't need us anymore," Johnnie continued when he didn't get his answer. "You're not the same person, Reies. You used to be one of us until you made those big bucks on the outside. It's changed you."

"The money hasn't changed my attitude. I was opposed to the Coalition before I left Sidewinder. I still am."

"That's it, then?"

"That's how I feel," Reies agreed, pushing away from the corral.

He began walking toward the barn, Johnnie behind him. Bush or no bush, he'd surely see her. Trapped! Libby's mind frantically raced for an excuse, a reason to be there, until she realized he was heading to the other side of the building.

"Reies, you think things over, all right? When you see things straight, you let me know."

Reies's faint, "Don't count on it," were the last words Libby heard before she sneaked away from her hiding place.

Ears and eyes attuned to the sights and sounds around her, she guardedly crossed to the corral fence. She skirted it in a crouch and made for her bungalow. A stitch pulled at her side and her breath was coming in irregular spurts by the time she arrived at her door. With a last look around to assure herself no one had seen her furtive movements, she slipped inside.

Libby barely had time to kick off her shoes and congratulate herself on a day full of positive accomplishments when a fist vigorously attacked her front door. Eyes wide, she whipped around.

Reies.

Her heart thudded in an odd rhythm. She knew he'd be standing there, his face closed, anger tight inside him. She should have taken Emilio's warning to heart. Reies was part Apache. He'd heard the truck. He'd heard her, too. She'd been foolish to believe otherwise.

The knocking resumed.

"All right," she muttered. Delay would make him angrier. She jerked open the door while her mind spun along, looking for a way to put him off guard. "Reies."

Light from inside the bungalow washed over him. His expression was as closed as she'd expected it to be, but his dark eyes glittered down at her. The impression of danger hit her hard. Her mouth went dry.

"You don't seem surprised to see me." With a last puff on his cheroot, he dropped it in front of her door and ground the glowing tip under his heel. "Have you had your fill?"

In a show of bravado, she crossed her arms over her chest and blocked his entrance. "Pardon me?"

He leaned against the left side of the doorjamb and propped his right hand on the other side, effectively barring her escape. "Of me? And Johnnie Madrigal? Did our conversation make your reporter's ears burn?"

"I don't know what you're talking about," she bluffed.

"People in Sidewinder like their privacy. They stick together, protect their own. They don't take kindly to interference from outsiders."

"Is this some kind of warning?"

He stared at her until she squirmed inside. "Your nose for sniffing out news could land you in big trouble in these parts."

Veiled threats. Anger replaced fear. "Ears. Nose. What about my eyes? Do you have something to say about them, too? I know," she said, turning the tables on him. "I should keep my eyes, and my camera lens, closed. Great advice." She held out her hand. "So where is it?"

For once it was Reies who seemed startled. Libby could have sworn he was scrambling for a clever answer. She even thought a hint of admiration crossed his features. But when his response came, she didn't like it any better than the threat.

"You can have your camera back. When you pay the proper ransom."

Libby stiffened. "What kind of ransom?"

He allowed his dark gaze to roam down her cream-clad body in lazy exploration. "I'll bet you could think of something to make returning it worth my while."

She saw red. Literally. The haze in front of her eyes provoked Libby to action. Resisting the urge to hit him, she stepped back and slammed the door in Reies Coulter's face. The soft laughter on the other side only made her more furious. She bolted the door against him lest he get any ideas.

His laughter trailed away.

She knew he'd left.

"Damn!"

She shouldn't have let her anger get to her. She should have been more clever, played his game, gotten more information.

But she'd done enough for one day. She needed a hot shower, a couple of aspirins and a good night's sleep. She needed to let her mind rest.

Unfortunately, her brain wouldn't cooperate and shut down. As Libby undressed, it replayed the day, scanning for anything she might have missed. She saw each of the suspects as clearly as if they stood before her.

Suspects.

Seven of them.

She'd always perceived her father's murderer as being one of the mourners around the grave. What better place to hide than in the open? The conviction had come from instinct and emotion, rather than the kind of logic she'd use to pinpoint the guilty one, but her opinion hadn't changed.

One face and voice stood out from the rest. Reies Coulter's. Though never arrested, because of a lack of evidence, he'd been the prime suspect in her father's murder. Now he'd gone out of his way to make her feel unwelcome, to warn her. That didn't mean he was the guilty one, but he might be trying to protect someone. His statement about sticking together echoed through her mind. So the citizens of Sidewinder protected their own. That hadn't been news to her. She'd known what she was up against at the outset. The fact didn't make her investigation impossible, merely more difficult.

Stripping off her panty hose and underwear, Libby thought about dinner and the scene Pilar had created. Reies's family might close ranks against outsiders, but obviously they weren't as in tune with one another as they might lead one to believe. Something told her Pilar might be the weak link at Rancho Velasquez, and if there was one weak link in Sidewinder, there were bound to be others.

All she had to do was pinpoint them without raising too many suspicions.

Naked and feeling undeniably vulnerable, Libby climbed on a chair and pulled her gun and holster down from the top of the wardrobe where she'd stashed them before dinner. Her clothing had kept her from hiding the weapon on her person. She'd dressed with the certainty that she would be safe for a few hours surrounded by so many people. But now, clearly imagining Reies's dark eyes glittering down at her as they had a few minutes ago, a chill swept through Libby that had nothing to do with her nudity.

She could not forget for a moment the dangerous situation in which she'd placed herself. Though her captain knew why she'd insisted on taking vacation time and understood her need to pursue the murderer, he'd been powerless to help her. Sidewinder was sixty-five miles out of his jurisdiction. No one was staked outside of her bungalow in case she ran into trouble.

Libby carried the holster into the bathroom and hung it on a peg next to the shower stall. Wayne had been driven but careless, and in the end he'd faced the murderer at the wrong end of a gun. She wouldn't be so foolish as to go unprotected again.

Chapter Three

"Hey, little brother, take over here for a while, would you?" Reies asked.

His bronzed face splitting into a sardonic grin, Nick Obregon straightened from where he'd been checking a newly repaired section of the fence.

"Sure thing." Nick tilted his hat higher on his forehead. "Will you be back soon?"

"As soon as I see if Luis is back from Santa Fe."

Reies couldn't wait any longer to examine the developed film. He only hoped the photos would give him the ammunition he needed to convince his grandfather Libby Tate was planning to do a hatchet job on their family rather than a complimentary feature on the workings of the ranch.

"What did you send Luis in for, anyway?"

"Some vitamins we're running short on," Reies hedged, hoping Nick wouldn't hear the lie in his words. The two brothers had grown up so close they'd sometimes known what the other was thinking before he thought it. "I'd better get going." He checked Sangre's cinch before mounting the horse. "I have a few things I want to discuss with Luis about varying the diet for the colts, anyway."

"We'll do our best without you," Nick assured him wryly, turning his attention to the *vaqueros*.

Reies's glance lingered on the younger man. He wondered how good an actor his brother was. If Nick resented him, he couldn't tell. He wouldn't blame him if he did, though. He hadn't planned to usurp his brother upon returning to Rancho Velasquez after a twelve-year absence, but things had just seemed to fall into old patterns, and the power of running the spread had shifted to Reies.

But in reality the ranch had been in dire straits less than a year ago, the near-failure due to bad luck and lack of funds rather than neglect. Nick had worked his butt off to keep the family off welfare and the land out of government hands, and now he was working with Reies as hard as ever to build the place back up to the ranch it had once been. That morning, he'd been the one actually supervising the fence repair despite his older brother's presence.

Reies had been otherwise occupied with thoughts of the redhead and his supposition that she was an investigative reporter.

Why else would she have been spying on him and Johnnie the night before?

He urged Sangre into a smooth lope. As much as he wanted to, Reies thought as he took the trail south toward the hacienda's grounds, he wouldn't tell Libby to pack her bags without his grandfather's consent. He had too many memories of the past when Emilio had been the only father he'd known, treating Reies like one of his beloved sons. Now it was his turn to protect his grandfather, but he had to do so with care and tact, allowing the old man to make ousting the reporter his decision.

Libby sure as hell wasn't going to turn tail and run on her own. He'd done his best to intimidate her with that comment he'd thought up on the spur of the moment, and she'd merely slammed the door in his face. No woman, not even Pilar, had ever dared do that before. To his annoyance, Reies found himself smiling and, though there was no one to see, forced the expression into a grimace.

Being around the reporter got him edgy. She rubbed him the wrong way, not only because of what she might want but because of who she was: an outsider. An attractive outsider—he would have to be blind and a liar not to admit it—but an outsider nevertheless, and one who was well-heeled.

He was back to that again, as if it made any difference to why the woman was there.

Besides, to be fair, Reies supposed he shouldn't be so critical of Libby's financial circumstances. He had money himself now. Not an enormous amount, and certainly not enough to impress a woman who drove a Jaguar, even an old one. But to anyone in Sidewinder—including his grandfather who'd barely been able to hang on to his land—Reies had brought back a fortune, both in money and breeding stock. And as far as he himself was concerned, he had enough. He could look as well-heeled as the woman if he so desired.

If he didn't have more important priorities.

The truth of the matter was that he'd been around the rodeo circuit long enough to be turned off by wealthy women who were turned on by cowboys with their dust and sweat and perverse sexual allure. He'd been tempted into the trap a few times early on, out of loneliness and need, but he hadn't liked the bitter taste the short-lived encounters had left in his mouth. He wasn't a man to be used by anyone.

Reies suddenly realized he was thinking in personal terms, but of course there was nothing personal about his feelings for the redhead. Besides, other than that brief moment before dinner the night before, she hadn't given him the slightest sign that she thought him anything but a desperado whose presence she barely tolerated.

He was still thinking about her reactions to his appearance at her door when he crossed the summit of the hill and spotted the woman herself. She was walking on the east side of the large corral with his grandfather. After checking to make sure Luis had not yet arrived—his truck was nowhere in sight—Reies slowed Sangre to an easy trot and caught up to the couple in no time.

"Grandfather. Miss Tate. So, you're out and investigating already?" he asked her pointedly.

Squinting slightly, she tilted her head to meet his eyes. Though she wasn't wearing a hat to protect her from the midmorning sun, her copper curls tumbled over her forehead like a fiery visor. "Your grandfather warned me ranch life begins in the early morning. I left the house shortly after you did last night. I wanted to be well rested, so I went to bed almost immediately."

"Really." Reies kept his tone conversational. Obviously she was trying to hide the fact that she'd been spying on him from his grandfather. He decided to play along for the moment. "I hope you slept well."

"There's nothing on the ranch to disturb me—at least nothing I've run into yet."

Brows raised in silent debate, Reies stared down at the reporter who boldly glared at him in return.

"I was just telling Miss Tate that she deserves a proper tour of the ranch," Emilio interjected, looking from one to the other, his expression cagey. "I would be pleased if you would see to it personally, Reies."

Reies unclenched his jaw and forced himself to smile. Libby was studying him closely through those deep, cactus-green eyes of hers. Where had he seen them before? That he still couldn't remember plagued him, but he'd get it eventually. Realizing his grandfather was waiting for his response, Reies sensed Libby assumed he would refuse. He figured she hoped he would. But then, Reies had rarely been one to do the expected, unless the matter involved family honor.

"I'd be delighted, Grandfather." He didn't look away from her when, deliberately reminding her of their first uncomfortable encounter, he added, "I assume the lady can handle a horse on her own?"

"If the horse isn't as difficult as some of the men I've been meeting lately," she returned.

Emilio chuckled appreciatively, making Reies wonder what his grandfather found so amusing. "I'm sure I can choose a suitable mount for you, Miss Tate."

"Good." Her lips curved in satisfaction. "Because while we're touring the ranch, I'd like to photograph—"

Reies cut her off before she could mention the camera. "Tomorrow morning, then."

Without waiting for her reaction, he rode back the way he came. Curse Luis! Where was the man? Reies told himself to calm down. Luis would undoubtedly arrive at the ranch at any moment. He'd check back in an hour or so. Then he wouldn't have to worry about carrying out the commitment to show the reporter around the ranch, not if the photos came through for him.

Then Libby Tate could take herself and her damned camera right back where they both belonged.

Annoyed that he'd gotten away again without revealing the whereabouts of her camera, fascinated by the way he seemed to become one with his horse, Libby stared after Reies longer than she'd meant to.

"You and my grandson...you find each other... sympathetic?"

Libby's head whipped around and her eyes connected with Emilio's. "Sympathetic?"

"Attractive."

"No, of course not!" she said quickly and with what she thought of as the proper amount of vehemence.

Emilio laughed good-naturedly and patted her arm. "The young, they are so stubborn. They do not want to admit what is right under their noses for others to see."

"You're wrong, Mr. Velasquez." Libby's pulse surged as she stated, "There's nothing to admit."

"I was young once. I remember the looks, the altered tone of voice, the carefully chosen words, the pretended indifference."

Libby felt herself flush under the elderly man's close scrutiny. She wasn't attracted to Reies Coulter. She couldn't be, not when he might have been responsible for the deaths of her father and her brother, although she had to admit that she sensed Reies was innocent, at least of murder.

"You could do worse than my grandson," Emilio went on. "He can be difficult at times, this I grant. But he is a loving man to his family, and his loyalty is unquestionable."

And he could be an accessory, protecting a loved one from the law, Libby thought grimly. "Is that why he abandoned the ranch and his beloved family for a dozen years?"

Emilio blanched. Libby hadn't meant to upset him. After spending the past few hours with the elderly man, she decided she liked the family patriarch and couldn't conceive of him being guilty of anything but getting too wrapped up in the past...and perhaps of loving his family too well. She felt a rush of guilt when she noted the hurt in his faded brown eyes.

"My grandson's reasons for leaving are not mine to discuss with an outsider," Emilio said stiffly. "If and when he grows to trust you, he will explain."

"I'm sorry. I didn't mean any—"

"I am sorry also. And, I'm afraid I have business to attend to before Victor arrives, so I will have to leave you on your own for the rest of the morning."

"I understand."

Libby watched Emilio walk away, pride keeping his back straight. Sighing, she only hoped she wouldn't have to destroy the old man by revealing an awful truth about one of those he loved so dearly.

But hurting him wouldn't ease the ache of loss that haunted her days. Hurting him wouldn't bring back her own loved ones.

What now? Strolling toward her bungalow, Libby realized it was time to take a closer look around Sidewinder, time to use her cover as a reporter to ferret out the weak links.

THE SOLITARY HORSE stopped at the top of the hill overlooking the piñon- and juniper-studded terrain. An unexpected sight caught its rider's attention: a dark green Jaguar on the ribbon of winding road below.

Dust billowed around and behind the small car that sped its way toward Sidewinder. So the woman was going to town, was she? Why?

And why was the Jaguar stopping directly across from the county cemetery?

The watchful eyes narrowed as the redhead spilled from the front seat, quickly catching onto the door frame for support. She didn't step away from the car, merely took a quick look around and stared toward the graveyard as though looking for something or someone. The distance was too great to read her expression, but if the rider knew anything about reporters, it was that they were always suspicious of something.

Luckily, however, they could be manipulated just like any of the other fools in the world.

Before there was time to speculate further about her motives, the woman climbed back into her car and tore down the road as if the demons from hell were after her.

Perhaps she had good reason.

The rider cursed, the harsh sound alarming the horse into side-stepping nervously.

If necessary, the demons would take care of her....

AFTER HER LAST SWEEP through the lawless town, Libby didn't relish returning to Sidewinder—not that she had a choice. She only hoped the place could stay incident-free for a few hours. Standing by and watching the confrontation the day before had been frustrating, but her purpose was to find and bring to justice a killer, not to break up fights. She would never succeed if anyone guessed her identity or occupation. Being there at all had been a risk. She'd undoubtedly turned at least three of the town's citizens against her.

Libby pulled into an open spot in the middle of the first block. Surrounded by pickups and cars that could be described kindly as junkers, the Jaguar stuck out as much as she did. And no one could have missed her when she'd leaned on the horn the day before!

She was convinced of the fact when she got out of the car. Either the townspeople stopped and stared at her, or they made a point to avoid looking at her altogether—like the woman who dragged her two toddlers by so quickly she made one of them trip over a break in the sidewalk when Libby merely smiled at them. The child screamed and the mother glared at her.

Feeling heat rise along her neck, Libby moved down the street, barely able to prevent herself from checking the county-office window to make sure she didn't have "outsider" tattooed across her forehead. She was being too sensitive, probably because of the second stupid thing she'd done in two days, this time on the way into town— even if she had only stopped for a minute.

She hadn't been able to prevent her emotions from overriding her common sense when she'd passed the cemetery. She'd had to take one quick look at her father's final resting place. No one had been around to see. She'd checked. Still, at the first sign of weakness, she should have stepped on the accelerator rather than on the brake. That minute had been one of the most painful in her life. She'd felt as if she could have reached out and touched her father's spirit.

She wouldn't take any more foolish chances, Libby promised herself as she entered the post office. Not until this ordeal was over.

The grimy, green-walled room was empty except for a man hunched over a mail cart behind the counter. A brass plaque in front of the old-fashioned scale identified him as Daniel Kilkenny. Libby's spirits brightened at the pleasant looks of the paunchy, middle-aged man who turned toward her. Maybe she was in luck.

"Good morning, Mr. Kilkenny."

"Help you?"

Her smile wasn't returned, but Libby wasn't about to give up hope yet. "Ten stamps, please."

The postmaster dutifully pulled a fresh sheet from a stamp drawer and counted out two rows of five. He seemed to study the dotted lines as he split the sheet along them. "That'll be two-fifty."

Libby handed him a ten so he'd have to take the time to make change. "Interesting little town. Have you lived here long, Mr. Kilkenny?"

His hands stopped over the change drawer and he looked at her directly. "You're that reporter woman, aren't you?"

"Yes. I'm doing a piece on Rancho Velasquez." Libby took a deep breath. "I was hoping to get some information on the town itself to go with the article."

"Not from me, you won't. Don't want no trouble."

"But—"

"No buts, missy. I mind my own business like smart folks around here do. No one bothers me. I aim to keep it that way. Here's your change. You can be on your way."

His invitation to leave couldn't be more clear. Libby smiled again as she scooped up the change, but Kilkenny's back was already to her.

Her foray at the local grocery wasn't any more successful. Sal and Maria Zuno, proprietors, watched her suspiciously as she chose a tube of toothpaste she didn't need and a pack of gum she did. Her single pleasantry at the cash register ignored, Libby left the store without trying to further the conversation.

She was getting nowhere fast. Now what? Of all the buildings on the opposite side of the street, one popped out at her. Literally. The brightly painted pink cinder blocks of Ada's Cafe stood out among the grays and beiges of the rest of the town. Libby checked her watch. Almost noon. She wasn't sure she wanted to eat in the place, but she could have a cup of coffee. If she were lucky and everyone didn't go silent at her entry, maybe she could listen to a conversation or two. It was worth a try.

She crossed the street and slipped through the door quietly, hoping the dozen or so diners wouldn't notice her entrance. But conversation slacked off by the time she got to the counter, and one by one, heads turned. Every eye in the place was on her by the time she slid onto a pink, vinyl-and-chrome stool.

The fortyish blonde at the grill turned toward Libby. Her ample curves were squeezed into a pink uniform that was a size too small. Pink-and-purple eye shadow decorated lively blue eyes that took in every detail of Libby's appearance.

"Hi, honey. I'm Ada Fry, owner, cook and waitress of this joint. You must be the Tate gal who's got everyone talking." She looked out over the counter and raised her voice a notch. "And staring real rude like, too."

Slowly voices returned to normal as did the sound of forks scraping plates. Libby grinned at the slightly blowsy woman who gave her a genuinely friendly smile.

"Thanks. Being the center of attention isn't my cup of tea," she admitted.

"Your line of work brings others to the center," Ada said with conviction, making Libby realize everyone in town must know who she was. "So what'll you have, honey? We can talk while the chow's cooking."

Though she hadn't meant to eat in the place, Libby immediately asked, "What do you recommend?"

"Nothing," Ada admitted with good humor. "Anything I cook is bound to be questionable. But some folks say even I can't ruin a hamburger."

"Sounds good. A burger and a cup of coffee."

"Coming up."

Ada flipped a patty onto the grill and took a minute to serve another. Then, pouring the coffee, she placed the cup in front of Libby, leaned over the counter and rested her elbows on the cracked, pink linoleum surface.

"So, you're going to make Rancho Velasquez famous."

"Maybe." She just might, Libby thought, if one of the family members turned out to be the murderer.

"I envy you, honey—getting to cozy up to Reies Coulter."

Libby tried to hide her surprise. "You're partial to Reies?"

"In a friendly sort of way, same as every available woman in these parts." The blue eyes inspected her as if Ada couldn't believe she was immune. "And some of the unavailable ones, come to think of it. We're all out of luck. Reies doesn't give any of us a second look. Pays more attention to his horses."

"He's been back here quite a while to go without female companionship."

"Yeah, well, probably had to do with the divorce..." Ada's voice trailed off. When she spoke again, her voice was low. "Strange situation, if you ask me. One brother divorces his wife just before he does a long-term disappearing act. Then the other brother marries her within months. Well, I shouldn't flap my jaw about it since I wasn't around at the time. I'm new in these parts, going on six years."

"Hey, Ada, you gonna take my money or do I get lunch on the house?"

"Keep your shirt on."

The blonde sauntered to the other end of the counter where she took care of the customer. For the next several minutes her attention was split between the grill and other people who'd finished eating. Finally, she placed the promised hamburger in front of Libby and leaned forward on her elbows.

"I can't imagine Reies is still carrying a torch for Pilar," Ada murmured as Libby took a cautious bite of hamburger.

"He divorced her, didn't he?"

"For cattin' around. From what I hear, she hasn't changed, either. She'd better watch her step. Nick's crazy about her, but his temper is a lot hotter than his brother's."

"Ada, where's my pie?"

The blonde threw her hands up. "Sorry, honey, but I have to keep these folks happy."

"Go ahead."

While she ate, Libby thought about and stored away the bits of information that might be important. The divorce and Reies's departure had gone hand in hand; Pilar unfaithful, then and now; Nick jealous and hot tempered. Enough to kill if he thought Pilar was with another man? Passion was a prime motive for murder, Libby knew.

By the time she'd finished her hamburger, Ada was caught in the middle of the lunch rush, obviously too busy to dish out more information. Libby decided she could come back another time. She caught Ada's attention by waving her bill.

"They were right," Libby said when she and the blonde met at the register.

"What's that, honey?"

"You can't ruin a hamburger."

Ada's hearty laugh competed with the register ring. She made change and settled with Libby. "You come back now. Not too many women frequent this joint. It gets lonely sometimes."

Libby saw the truth of the statement reflected in the blue eyes, but only for a brief second before they sparkled with good humor once more.

"The people in this town aren't too friendly," Libby agreed.

"Yeah, but they're not as mean as they seem, leastwise not most of them. Don't judge us all by what happened yesterday. Every town has its troublemakers, this one more than its fair share, I guess. You were real brave, honey, but you be careful. There's no law in Sidewinder to protect you."

Libby's pulse picked up in response to the direction the conversation was taking. "Doesn't the state patrol the area?"

"For all the good it does. Didn't you read about that poor young patrolman who got himself shot last month? It happened a couple of miles outside of town. Nice kid, too."

"You knew him?"

"He came in for pie and coffee once in a while. Let me talk his ear off..." Suddenly looking uneasy, Ada muttered, "I have to go, honey."

"I'll be back."

Caught up in her thoughts, wondering what could have made an outgoing woman like Ada Fry move to a town like Sidewinder, wondering if Ada knew anything that could shed light on her brother's death, Libby didn't see the man squared off in front of her until she almost ran into him. Her gaze was caught by his heavy gold chain and the unusual medallion, a circle enclosing a C and an S, the abstract letters twisted together.

"Where you rushing off to, Red?" he asked, making her gaze travel upward.

Johnnie Madrigal's smile sent chills up Libby's spine. Though his face had matured, the features were as beautifully perfect as they had been the first time she'd seen them thirteen years before, the only exception his mouth, which seemed to taunt her even more.

Libby cocked her head and gave him an innocent expression. "Have we been introduced?"

"Does it matter? I know who you are."

Just as she knew who he was. Wayne had told her Johnnie Madrigal was the most feared man in town, and the sudden chilling silence confirmed her brother's words. The hoodlum's entrance must have been the reason Ada had clammed up so fast, Libby decided. He didn't look like much of a threat to anyone. Medium height, slender build, filled with nervous energy that made him seem to move even when he was standing still. But then, looks could be deceiving, as she'd found out the hard way many times on the job.

"Then you'll know I'm going back to Rancho Velasquez," Libby finally said. "I have business there."

"Yeah, I gotta take care of business, too." His brown eyes traveled down her length insolently in an obvious attempt at intimidation. "Me and the boys here have an important meeting that's gonna start any minute now."

Libby glanced at "the boys" who backed him up—one tall and sandy-haired, the other stocky, dark and wearing a threatening expression aimed directly at her. He was

the man named Bobby! Taking a better look at Johnnie's sidekicks together, she realized they were the same
pair she and her mother and brother had confronted at
the gas station on the day of her father's funeral.

Some of the fear she'd felt then rushed forward.
Smothering it, she attempted escape.

"Well, I won't hold you up then."

Johnnie's grip was strong, belying the slenderness of
the fingers that wrapped around her arm like a vise. They
stood eye to eye and, though she wanted to, Libby
couldn't look away, couldn't move, could only hope he
wouldn't feel the gun holster where the back of his arm
pressed against her vest. Her mouth went dry.

"I'll see you again, huh, Red? You can interview me.
I'm gonna be known around this state. You can say you
had the pleasure of my acquaintance when I was a big
fish in a small pond. I'll give you copy so hot it'll set that
dull rag of yours on fire."

"Another time."

Libby forced the words through gritted teeth as she
extricated her arm with a quick, expert twist. Johnnie
didn't like the fact that she was able to free herself. She
could see it in those eyes. She'd been wrong about them.
Despite their perfect almond shape and thick, long
lashes, they weren't beautiful. Johnnie's eyes reflected his
ruthlessness even as his cruel lips twisted into a grimace
of a smile.

"Another time," he echoed softly, his words filled with
unnamed promise.

No one else in the place spoke. Ada's patrons concentrated on their food as if their plates were filled with
gourmet cuisine. The blonde had turned her back on
them and was keeping herself busy at the grill. Avoiding
Bobby, whose animosity was palpable, Libby skirted the

sandy-haired anglo and strode out the door. She was in the Jaguar and heading for the ranch before she realized the blood was pumping through her system as fast as the car was accelerating.

And whether or not she wanted to admit it, the unpleasant taste of fear lingered in her mouth.

"WHERE IN HELL have you been, Luis?" Reies demanded when the truck finally pulled in front of the bunkhouse halfway through the afternoon.

"Hey, gringo, take it easy. I got here as fast as I could. The store didn't get the film in the morning delivery and the clerk had to track it down. I would have gone over to the processing plant myself to pick up the pictures, but they said the order was already on the way for the next delivery."

Not altogether sure the story was true, Reies let it slide as he took the packet and camera from Luis. The evidence was in his hands and that was the important thing. He opened the envelope and pulled out the prints.

"Thank you, Luis, for doing me this favor," the stocky man said in an imitation of Reies's voice. "You're welcome, gringo. No problem—"

"The hell there isn't!" Reies bellowed.

"What? Didn't they give me the right pictures?"

Luis tried to look, but Reies was already turning away from the other man. "They're right, but there's something very wrong here."

Without another word, he stalked off toward Libby's quarters. *His* quarters, damn it! She had some fast explaining to do.

Once there, Reies rapped on the door, but Libby didn't answer. He tested the handle. Locked. He always kept a key hidden on the *viga* which stuck out over the front window. Feeling along the wood, he found the key and used it to let himself in. The faint sound of the shower pinpointed her whereabouts. He stalked into the bedroom and dropped the camera onto the center of the bed. Another look through the envelope's contents only served to raise his temper. He threw the photos down so hard they flew across the quilt.

Then he sat in a straight-backed wooden chair to wait.

Each passing minute made him angrier, but the anger grew cold and calculating as he tried to make sense of things. By the time the sound of the water stopped, Reies was calm. Leaning back so that the chair rested on two legs, he propped his booted feet up on the edge of the bed and crossed them at the ankles in a show of indifference.

A few seconds later, the bathroom door opened and he could hear her humming. Humming! Reies felt his muscles tense as the anger warred with control. Control won as, continuing to hum, Libby stepped from the bathroom with one towel wrapped around her, another bunched in her hands.

And then, when she got to the middle of the room, she spotted him and went very still.

Her gaze flicked to the camera and the pictures spread across the quilt. She didn't say a word. Didn't order him to get out. Immobilized, she merely stared, her cactus-green eyes wide and vulnerable as little rivulets of water from her hair ran into them. She blinked silently.

"I thought it was time you and I had a heart-to-heart talk, Miss Tate." Voice laced with fury, Reies held her captive, transfixed by his steady gaze. She couldn't look away. "For starters, you can tell me who in the hell you really are and explain why you're here."

Chapter Four

A thread of alarm ran through her. His eyes were as cold as his voice. Had Reies discovered the truth? If so, could he possibly be as menacing as his scowl indicated? For the first time since she'd left Santa Fe, Libby was unsure of herself and afraid that she was unprepared to deal with the situation—or at least to deal with this man.

She thought quickly, deciding that taking the offense and putting him on the defense was her best tactic. Tightening her grip on the bundled towel for courage, she bluffed as well as a half-naked woman in her position could do.

"You know very well who I am and why I'm here."

She ignored the water sliding down her forehead and dripping off her nose, ignored the alternating hot and cold tingles along her bare skin. She drew on her deep-seated anger that had been festering since her father's murder, let it feed on the grief she was still feeling for Wayne, and cloaked the emotions around herself like armor.

"What the hell are you doing in my quarters, anyway?" she demanded to know. "And how did you get in? I distinctly remember locking the door."

She watched his face intently, noted how his jaw tightened. The rest of him was equally tense, as if he were a predator ready to spring at its prey.

At the moment, she made an easy target.

In spite of her determination to get the upper hand, Libby felt further threatened when Reies rose from the chair. Slowly. Deliberately. His eyes never leaving her face. She couldn't help herself. She backed away from him. Her pulse went berserk. She could feel it hammering in her throat, trying to choke her. Her fingers fumbled with the bundle in her hands, but she couldn't make the towel cooperate.

Then Reies turned away for a second to snatch a photograph from the bed, giving her a meager respite, a few seconds to calm down. She took a deep breath, drew herself together. Still, when he resumed stalking her, she retreated as far as she could, until her terry-covered backside pressed against the edge of the dresser.

"How do you explain this?"

Libby slid her eyes to the photo in his hand. The stallion. Out of focus. Damn! If only she'd had time to learn to use the equipment with some semblance of expertise.

"Explain what? That I shot too quickly?"

"That would do for this one, but what about the others?"

"What about them?"

"Nice work for an amateur, Libby. But a professional didn't take those photographs. Even I can see the difference. Who are you really?"

Ignoring the question, she hedged. "All right, so I'm not an expert photographer. I admit I'm new at the photo part of the job, but—"

"Don't try to con me, Libby. I'm not a trusting seventy-five-year-old man who wears rose-colored glasses so life won't be quite so grim. Why are you here?"

"You know why!" she insisted, refusing to back down now that she was on a roll. "I'm writing an article about this ranch. I had a hard time convincing Bob Gulley that it was a viable idea. That's why he didn't send a staff photographer. He told me I was on my own."

Though she was sure she could have convinced anyone else, Reies wasn't buying. Maybe she'd taken a few seconds too long to concoct the story. Or maybe he read the truth in her face despite her carefully schooled features.

"I don't think so. I think you're lying through your teeth. But I'm going to find out for sure. You can bet your Jaguar and your hand-tooled leather vest on that."

Noting the subtle sarcasm in his tone, Libby decided attack was still her best defense. She had to throw Reies Coulter off the scent. She pulled her head back with a defiant toss of wet curls. Fine droplets of water sprayed his face. He didn't even blink.

"Do I hear a note of envy in your voice, Reies? Is that your problem? You don't like successful women who drive cars more expensive than yours?"

She'd hit a nerve. The searing emotion that made his dark eyes flash exposed it as surely as if she'd peeled back his flesh. She wondered what he would think if he knew the Jaguar and the clothes had been all she'd agreed to accept as her part of the divorce settlement.

Reies moved closer until he was almost touching her. He did touch her—via the photograph. One corner rounded the curve of her shoulder and made her skin crawl.

"Do you have any idea of how violent some of Sidewinder's citizens can be?"

Her pulse was surging again, but she fought the instinct to bolt. She'd never escape him anyway, not even if she were fully clothed.

"I suppose you're going to tell me."

"In this part of the state, murder is what you'd call a fact of life." He trailed the scratchy edge of the photo along her collarbone. "People are often killed for simple reasons. Jealousy. Revenge. Saturday-night entertainment. Even imagined insults."

He was baiting her. She refused to react. At least not outwardly. Her stomach was knotting into a lump. "Is that a threat?"

"It doesn't take much for a man to die," Reies went on. "Or a woman, for that matter."

The sharp tip of the photograph pricked the delicate skin of her throat. She couldn't move, couldn't take her eyes from his. He might as well have been holding her at knife point.

"If someone had an ulterior motive in dealing with the locals, Libby..."

He shook his head and moved away. Only then did she realize she'd been holding her breath. She shuddered and gasped for air as she watched him throw the picture on the bed and move to the other room. He was leaving. Her fingers relaxed and she almost dropped the terry-wrapped bundle.

Reies paused in the doorway and gave her one last, searing look.

"Tomorrow, Libby. We'll finish this discussion out on the trail tomorrow. See you in the morning. Early."

Libby knew she'd have to be crazy to ride out alone with Reies where anything could happen, even a convenient accident. She'd be armed, she assured herself as he left the bungalow, slamming the front door behind him. Somehow the fact wasn't all that reassuring.

Glancing down, she unwrapped the bunched towel. Blue metal mocked her. The Beretta had lain between her hands during the entire altercation, and her having the weapon hadn't made her feel safe. For a short while, Reies Coulter had even made her forget its existence.

And, given the advantage of a few precious seconds, a dangerous man was capable of anything.

BY MORNING, Libby had her doubts back under control where they belonged. Reies Coulter might be a dangerous man, but he was no criminal, except perhaps by association. He might be guilty of many things, even of protecting someone else, but he was not capable of cold-blooded murder.

She was sure of it.

Eight years on the Santa Fe police force had honed her instincts to a fine edge. She was rarely wrong once she'd made up her mind about someone, though Reies had done his best to change her opinion the afternoon before. She wondered if he'd been born suspicious, or if living in Sidewinder had bred distrust in him. The latter was probably accurate. His performance had been pure intimidation, a flagrant attempt to scare her off if he couldn't get the truth from her.

Unbelievably, she was actually considering giving it to him. What would he do once he knew why she was here?

She'd be taking a big chance. He could use the truth against her, expose her cover, put her in even more danger. Yet Reies could make as powerful an ally as he could an enemy. Knowing that made her admit a grudging respect for the man, so why shouldn't she use the fact to her advantage? She needed all the help she could get.

Torn, Libby decided to adopt a wait-and-see attitude. She'd have the morning alone with Reies. Camera slung over her shoulder, she left her quarters and headed for the barn. Perhaps he would make up her mind for her.

REIES DIDN'T KNOW WHY he hadn't been surprised when Libby had shown up as if yesterday's scene in the bungalow hadn't happened. She'd even had the nerve to drag the camera along. She had guts, he'd say that for her.

They'd been riding for more than half an hour, the silence broken only by his occasional warning about the trail ahead or by his pointing out some feature of the land. Tired of doing all the talking, of wondering who the hell she was and what she was thinking, Reies moved Sangre to the right and slowed the horse until Libby and Incendiaria caught up with them.

"No questions?" he challenged her. "If you want me to believe you're a reporter you should be asking dozens of them."

From her expression, Reies decided Libby's guard was up.

"Sometimes a reporter learns as much from keeping her eyes open as she does from an interview. For example, I've seen a lot of improvements around the place. I was wondering where you got the money to make them."

She was trying to put him on the spot again. Annoyed, Reies snapped, "Maybe I robbed a couple of banks."

"Did you?"

"Would you believe me if I said yes?"

"I don't know. Try me."

"I'm a rancher, not a bank robber," he growled, noticing her only reaction was to continue probing.

"From what I understand, the economy has crippled the small, independent rancher just as it has the farmer. In light of that fact, I'm surprised you're willing to pour money into the place—wherever you got it."

Her logic was irrefutable. Reies decided no harm would come from a simple explanation. "I would like my grandfather to die happy, Libby. I want Rancho Velasquez to be a profit-making venture again, for his sake."

"Your grandfather's not ill, I hope?"

Recognizing the genuine note of concern in Libby's question made Reies uneasy. Her brows wrinkled above worried green eyes. He looked straight ahead. He didn't want to like her.

"Physically, Grandfather has always been in excellent health, still is for a man his age. Mentally, though, he was dying a slow death, just as the ranch was. When I came back from Mexico, his self-esteem was lower than I'd ever seen it. Poverty and hopelessness does that to a proud man."

She took a minute to digest his words before asking, "Why did you take so long to return?"

"Money may be green, but it's not a crop waiting to picked. I had a few short-lived jobs on a handful of the corporation ranches. The work didn't pay much. Wrangling never does." Knowing he couldn't avoid looking at her forever, Reies met her gaze. He felt an immediate discomfort he couldn't explain. "If you're good, the rodeo circuit can be more profitable."

"And more dangerous."

"I needed a stake so I could invest in good stock. The danger paid off."

"Considering the way you feel about your grandfather, I'm surprised you left in the first place," Libby went on, her probing making him tense. "You could have found work in Santa Fe."

"I don't like big cities."

"Santa Fe isn't exactly a metropolis."

"Big enough."

He wasn't about to admit that he'd felt guilty as hell about leaving Sidewinder and deserting not only his grandfather, but his mother and half brother. Even then, though he hadn't quite seen his twenty-first birthday, he'd felt the same sense of responsibility to his family that he felt now. But everything had been crumbling around him. The ranch. His joke of a marriage. And, after the circumstances of Oliver Reardon's murder, he'd had no choice when it came to divorcing Pilar or abandoning his home.

"So you traveled around a lot?"

"Some."

"Wasn't it difficult, having to make new friends every time you got settled, and then picking up and leaving again?"

Reies was beginning to regret ever starting this conversation. She was better than he was with words. Maybe she really was a reporter. He should have left well enough alone.

"I'm not a man who makes friends easily."

Libby laughed. "I can believe that. You're probably too suspicious of everyone's motives."

"Shouldn't I be?" he asked, giving her a penetrating look. Her smile faded; her expression became unreadable. "I can imagine what you and your kind think of me, of the people who live in this area of the state."

She sobered completely and he sensed she was annoyed.

"My kind. Really? Tell me."

"You think we're all desperadoes, lawless, exciting maybe, but certainly not to be trusted."

"Why should anyone trust you when you don't trust them?"

"Good point."

"Maybe that's why you kept moving, Reies. Still, twelve years is a long time. How did you survive outside?"

"By not letting anyone get too close."

With that, Reies pushed Sangre into a canter, putting some distance between himself and the irritating woman. She'd managed to do it again. He knew nothing more about her than he had when they'd started out. Libby kept Incendiaria in line several yards behind him. He wondered if she had gotten what she wanted from him. She'd better have. Turnabout was fair play, and the first opportunity she gave him, he would renew his own attack. Next time, he wouldn't let himself be distracted by a set of disturbing green eyes.

Libby studied the stiff back in front of her. Reies Coulter was vulnerable. Who would have thought it? What a contrast between this man and Johnnie Madrigal, a man who boasted of the misdeeds that had created his reputation. Reies cared that people thought badly of him—not that he'd ever admit it directly. Maybe that's why he held others at a distance. She'd heard the fine edge to his voice through his anger. He'd managed to strike a sympathetic chord in her.

Sympathy and trust were two different things, however, and Libby still was not sure she could trust Reies with the truth. And yet, how would she ever know if she didn't give him the opportunity to prove himself?

Reies slowed again and waited for her to catch up. He indicated a spot to the right, deeper in the valley, a gully cut by a creek and lined with cottonwood trees.

"Why don't we take a break down there?"

"Fine with me."

While Libby loved horses and rode when she could, she wasn't used to spending all day on horseback as she had during her growing-up years. Her body was definitely less supple. She would appreciate the opportunity to stretch her legs and back. Once more, she let Reies lead the way.

A few minutes later, they dismounted under the shade of a large old cottonwood. Working in silence, they looped their horses' reins over a couple of low branches and loosened their cinches. Reies drew the rifle from his saddle. Libby stiffened slightly until she realized he was using its barrel to poke the area around the felled tree that lay at the narrow creek's bank.

Checking for rattlers; she breathed easier.

Not exactly eager to join him—her thoughts about trusting Reies still had Libby in turmoil—she patted Incendiaria's neck. The chestnut's coat was darkened by sweat. A brilliant red brown from the tip of her nose to the end of her tail, the mare was a beautiful counterpart to Reies's more powerfully built and darker-colored blood bay with its black mane, tail and ears. Both horses were unusual in an area where palominos, patchwork pintos and Appaloosas were standard stock.

Libby spoke to her mount in low, soothing tones. Nickering, the mare lowered her head and pushed her nose into the leather vest, twitching her ears at exactly the right angle to be scratched. Libby laughed and complied, then gave the horse a last vigorous pat before joining Reies.

Puffing on a cheroot, he watched her closely from his seat on the log where he massaged his right thigh absently as though it bothered him. The rifle lay propped, barrel up, within arm's reach.

"You not only ride well, you know your way around horses," he said. "You must have one of your own."

"As a matter of fact, I don't. I wish I could afford the upkeep of one." From the way his scarred eyebrow rose, Libby knew he didn't believe that for a minute. Trying not to look at the rifle, she straddled the log, leaving a safe distance between them. She couldn't afford to make a mistake as Wayne had. "Don't let the Jaguar fool you. My ex-husband bought it for me as a birthday present when we were first married. It was what you'd call an impulse buy—the color reminded him of my eyes."

"Ex-husband?"

"Harry Tate. He owns a resort ranch outside of Santa Fe." The information was out of her mouth before Libby realized Reies could use it to find out who she really was—if she chose not to tell him herself.

"So that's where you learned so much about horses."

She raised her leg and draped her ankle over the log so she could alternately arch her spine and stretch her body forward to relieve some of the building tension.

"Actually," she finally said, "I learned about horses from my father, who was a real rancher."

"Was? I take it he was one of those small operators who lost his land."

"Not exactly." Wondering how far she was willing to let this conversation go, Libby switched legs and repeated the procedure. "My father is dead."

"I'm sorry."

"So am I."

She held his gaze steadily, didn't miss the flicker in his black eyes. But of what? Sympathy? She didn't think so. Recognition? Surely not.

"Who are you?" he asked as if that was exactly the case. "Why did you come to Rancho Velasquez?"

Her pulse shot through her as she automatically bluffed. "The name is Libby Tate—"

"Tate was your husband's name."

She took a deep breath. If she was ever going to tell Reies the truth, now was the time. Fear skittered along her nerves as she tried to make up her mind. She could continue the bluff, but Reies wouldn't believe her any more than he had the last time. And where would that get her? Certainly not his help. And yet, if he were the murderer, he could kill her right here, using that rifle. Or he could wait, play with her, ambush her somewhere along the trail and hide her body so no one would ever find it. Could she take the chance?

"Afraid to tell me the truth?" he asked.

"Afraid?" she echoed. Tough cop that she was, fear was still a frequent companion. Yes, she was afraid.

"Your eyes give you away. You'd make a rotten poker player." His forehead pulled together in a frown. "I've seen those eyes before. Care to tell me where? It'll come to me eventually."

Libby's mouth went dry and her heart bumped against her ribs. She let the words spill from her lips before she could change her mind. "Elizabeth Reardon."

"Damn! The funeral. You're Oliver Reardon's daugh ter."

She didn't say another word while Reies digested the information. And as he did so, she watched him closely and tried to determine if she could tell him the rest.

Something like pain flicked across his features. Pain? The murdered man had been *her* father. About to say so, she let the words die in her throat when he spoke.

"I didn't shoot him even if he was found in my bed. I respected and liked your father. Oliver was a good man. What about the cop named Reardon who was killed last month...?"

"My brother."

He swore again. For once he seemed unable to freeze her out, to hide his thoughts. "You're here because of them."

"Wayne was on to our father's murderer—"

"And you have some foolhardy idea that you're going to take up the investigation where he left off? Are you crazy, lady? Look where it got your brother—and he was trained for that kind of work."

"So am I!"

The words flew from her lips, lifting the burden of the last decision from her shoulders. Now she had no secrets from Reies Coulter.

"You're a cop?"

His voice didn't get louder, but its timbre made the hair rise at the back of her neck.

"And some insane state official agreed to let you go undercover alone?"

"I don't work for the state. I'm a detective for the city of Santa Fe," Libby told him with a calm she didn't feel. Straddling the log, she boldly leaned forward and anchored her tense fingers to the rotting wood. "No one agreed to anything. I'm using up vacation time and going undercover by my own choice."

Reies's next expletive was more vile than the last, making Libby relax slightly. He was shocked and angry, almost as if he was worried about her. Ridiculous as it sounded, she knew she was right. Actually, Reies seemed more horrified than worried. Drained of the adrenaline that had been holding her as stiff as rigor mortis gripping a corpse, she went limp with relief—though she wasn't quite sure she hadn't made the biggest mistake of her life.

"You came out here alone, with no backup—"

"I'm not stupid. My captain and my brother's friends on the state force know where I am and what I'm doing," she informed him, meaning the information as a warning.

"I assume you're armed."

His eyes strayed to her left breast; nothing personal in the inspection. That worried her.

"A Beretta doesn't take up much room, but it can be a deadly weapon in the right hands," she told him warily.

"I take that to mean yours are those hands."

She lifted them, fingers spread, and turned them palms forward. Amazing. They were steady. "I wouldn't be here if they weren't." She lowered her palms to her thighs and swore she could feel the rush of blood through her limbs; her fingers sought the inert steadiness of the log once more.

"You have to be able to get to that gun to use it."

Reies smashed the glowing ember from the cheroot against the tree bark. The searing glance he aimed at her gave Libby the distinct feeling that he'd be just as pleased to crush the stubbornness from her head. He whipped the cigar into the creek where it floated downstream like a tiny black war canoe.

Would her lifeless body move down the rock-strewn water so easily?

"You had me fooled," he went on with a calm that fed her renewed worry. "I'll have to give you that. I knew you were up to something, but I assumed you were an investigative reporter trying to dig up dirt on the murders to make a name for yourself."

"Now you know differently." She took a shallow breath. "What are you going to do about it?"

The sudden and absolute silence between them was palpable. She swallowed hard, clenched her teeth. He was the stronger, perhaps even the swifter, yet not necessarily the smarter. Only time would tell. Silence stretched between them so tautly that she imagined she could hear the cactus grow above the soft rush of creek water. His eyes, like cool obsidian, bore into hers.

Dark, dangerous eyes.

The familiar feeling crept along her spine.

Provoked too far, Reies Coulter could be an unpredictable, perhaps deadly man. She knew that. And he was armed. So why was she taunting him?

Studying him closely, Libby watched as the emotions flickering across Reies's features buried themselves deep inside the man where they would hide, tucked away, waiting for the thin muted wrapping paper to be peeled away, a layer at a time. This was one package she wished she didn't have to open.

"Why should I do anything?" he finally asked.

Her smile was forced, tense. "You might want to stop me."

"I might."

"Enough to kill me?"

"If I wanted to see you dead, I could kill you right now," he spat, his dark gaze shifting to his rifle before coming to rest on her face.

Cheeks warm, she returned both the haughty stare and the challenge. "If I didn't stop you first."

Her fingers itched to move away from the log and beneath her vest, to embrace the familiar Beretta, to remove it from its sheath, to test Reies's mettle when faced by blue steel. She did nothing. Waited. Retained eye contact.

An old Apache test of bravery if myths could be trusted.

And if the eyes were truly the windows of the soul, the instincts that made a man a cold-blooded killer—an ambusher—were nowhere to be found in Reies Coulter.

"We'll work together."

His words nearly knocked her off the log. She blinked in surprise and caught her balance. His easy acquiescence had been too much to hope for, and she didn't quite trust it.

"Let me get this straight." She kept her words devoid of emotion. "You're willing to help me?"

Reies studied the redhead thoughtfully. How could he have let her fool him? Elizabeth Reardon might be thirteen years older and calling herself Libby Tate, but she hadn't changed in the ways that counted. She embodied the same spirit he'd recognized that first time he'd seen her.

So determined.

This time, however, he felt no pity for her. Underneath all of Libby's bluffing and bravado, Reies recognized a strong and worthy opponent, who would put her life on the line to find the murderer.

Just as her brother had.

Reies not only respected that, he understood that neither Wayne nor Libby could have been prepared for Sidewinder. They hadn't been born here, hadn't been raised with danger and wiliness and the fight for survival their constant companions. Learning had come too late for Wayne; perhaps was already too late for Libby. How could Reies know what alarms she had already set off? Being an outsider automatically put her under suspicion.

Someone had to protect her pretty behind, and as little as he relished the thought, Reies appointed himself to do what would undoubtedly be a thankless task.

"We can help each other," he repeated.

She released the death grip she'd had on the log. Color returned to her whitened knuckles.

"Why?" she asked.

"I don't want the death of a third Reardon connected to me or to my family."

He wanted to find the murderer as much as she did, Reies assured himself. He had his own reasons, his own loved ones to protect. None of them could have been involved in the crimes, and he intended to make sure Libby didn't try to prove that they had.

As if she knew exactly what he was thinking, Libby asked, "But what if a member of your family...?"

"The only way you'll get to the truth is if I find it for you."

"You really are arrogant. *I'm* the one trained for this type of work."

She jumped up and cleared the tree trunk in one fluid motion, which made him think of other, more pleasurable dangers.... It was difficult to drive the unbidden image away.

"Your brother was trained for this type of work," he said. "Where did it get him?"

Libby's sun-kissed face paled. "Wayne was hot-headed. Too inexperienced. Too careless. Don't underestimate me. I'm none of those things."

"And how far have you gotten alone?"

He could see she was warring within herself. She knew she needed him. If not, she would never have exposed herself, never have told him the truth. Even so, even knowing that he could blow her cover, that his doing so could mean her death, she needed to be able to accept his help on agreeable terms—or on none at all.

"Give me time," Libby hedged. "I haven't even been here for forty-eight hours."

"It wouldn't matter if you'd been here forty-eight days. No one in Sidewinder who knows anything will talk to you, and you know that. You're an outsider. We protect our own."

Her eyes narrowed as she assessed him. "So how do I know you won't do the same?"

"You don't. You'll have to trust me, just as I'll have to trust you."

Reies rose and stepped toward her. He gave her credit; she stood her ground. Holding out his hand, he almost smiled when she stared at it as if he were offering her a rattlesnake, fangs exposed and tongue flicking at the artery in her wrist.

Without blinking, she slid her hand into his large callused one.

Her grip was strong, her palm damp.

Their eyes met and measured and seemed to find no fault.

And so, in the shade of an old cottonwood tree whose roots writhed through blood-red earth before snaking down into the gurgling vein of the narrow creek below, they sealed their uneasy alliance.

"WHAT HAVE YOU FOUND OUT about the reporter?" Bobby Aguirre asked his sister in their native Spanish.

Hitting the door of Incendiaria's empty stall with the flat of her hand, Pilar Obregon gave her younger brother a glare of contempt. Horses startled by the sudden noise backed away nervously as she stomped out of the stable.

"What makes you think I'm interested in her?"

"Because you want Reies. It's always been Reies!" he shouted, following close on her heels. "Always what you can't have. Men are toys to you. Even Nick, your *current* husband."

Pilar whirled on her brother so quickly her single braid barely missed his face. "Don't lecture me about my duties to my husband."

"You soiled the family honor once with the divorce and then this mockery of a remarriage."

"If marriage means so much to you, then why don't you bring your little Nina to the priest?" Pilar grinned, knowing the line of her straight white teeth would aggravate Bobby. "Or won't she marry you? Perhaps Angel has had her, after all, and she will choose him over you."

Bobby stepped forward, closed fist raised. Pilar quickly ducked him and climbed the fence of the corral, where she perched on the top rail, laughing.

"Mark me and you will be a dead man, brother mine. This I promise."

The fist lowered, but Bobby's eyes burned like hot coals in his swarthy face. Pilar licked her lips and held back the shiver that was a combination of excitement and knife-edged fear swirling through her depths. Someday she would push her little brother too far. The thought made her pulse race, her stomach tighten, her juices run. Push and push and then what? Blood had stained the

Aguirre line more than once over the decades, and Pilar was as every inch an Aguirre as Bobby....

Before she had time to reflect further on such intriguing notions, she heard the sound of approaching horses. She strained to see around the barn.

"It's them. The bitch is on my horse! Get out, now," Pilar spat, "before Reies gets suspicious."

"You'll do what I ask? Find out about her?"

"You know me, Bobby. I'll do anything if the price is right. There's that dress Nick won't buy me..."

Bobby was already on his way. He didn't have a job any more than Johnnie Madrigal or Doug Barron did, but the unholy trio that rode roughshod on Sidewinder always seemed to have enough money for their pleasures. Pilar knew she would get the dress just as her brother had gotten this souped-up four-wheeler after his last truck had been buried in a mud slide. Maybe someday she would find it profitable to learn what he'd done to earn his series of expensive vehicles, but right now she had other, more important things on her mind.

OVERWHELMED BY THE ENORMITY of what she had done, Libby remained silent during the return ride. That Reies was equally silent made her feel unsure. He would help her, so he said, but how?

They hadn't discussed a single detail.

And now, from the looks of things—a flurry of activity around the ranch grounds—they'd missed their opportunity to do so. A new four-wheeler cut in front of them, slowing long enough so its driver could glare at her through the open window. The man with the violent streak named Bobby. What was he doing there? Before she could speculate or ask Reies, Bobby accelerated, and the four-wheeler spewed dust and stones in their path.

From the other direction, the more modest, brown, open-backed truck she recognized as belonging to Victor ambled toward them.

Emilio left the house to greet them all. Artist, patriarch and riders arrived at the barn within seconds of one another.

"How was your ride?" the elderly man inquired as they dismounted.

"Quite interesting, thank you, Mr. Velasquez," said Libby.

With unconcealed interest, Victor eyed the camera she untied from the saddle horn and hung on an end post before working with the horse's tack.

"Take many pictures?"

Wondering if Reies would refute the lie, Libby said, "A few. This country tends to look alike in almost every direction. I would hate to get lost out there."

"That would not be difficult," Emilio admitted. "Not even for a native of these parts. The land can be a tricky and brutal taskmaster."

Not wanting to answer other, more direct questions Victor might pose, Libby freed the saddle in record time, braced herself for its weight as she slid it and the padding off the damp chestnut back and carried the tack into the barn.

"The people make the difference." While he remained outside, Victor continued the conversation. And when she passed him again, curry brush and hoof pick in hand, his eyes swept over her in a familiar fashion. "I enjoy ferreting out the hidden power in people and bringing the inner self to life on canvas."

"Making pictures with oils is Victor's special talent," Emilio agreed. "Yours is making them with the camera."

Libby tried not to wince at the assumption.

Reies's mustache twitched when he stated, "Actually, clever words are more her specialty."

Her pained expression turned to a guarded glare at the man, as he carried his own saddle to the tack room. It was only then she noted Pilar watching the scene through narrowed eyes. The sable-haired woman was perched on the top rail of the corral fence, taking in every detail of the conversation. Her silent presence unnerved Libby, who immediately set to work brushing Incendiaria.

"Well, enough talk about talent," Victor said from the back of his pickup where he removed a case smeared with different-colored paints. "Time to get to work, eh, Emilio?"

"Certainly." The elderly man turned to Libby. "And you must continue with your work as well, Miss Tate. You cannot have covered much in a few short hours."

"You might be surprised at the things we discussed, Grandfather," Reies said, returning from the tack room.

"Take as much time as Miss Tate needs to explore the ranch."

"As long as it's not on my horse!"

Pilar spoke with rancor as she jumped down from her perch. If her tone hadn't been enough to convey her dislike of Libby, her venomous glare spoke volumes.

Libby tried to pacify her. "I'm sorry. I didn't realize Incendiaria was your horse."

"She isn't." Reies looked pointedly at his ex-wife. "Go ahead with Victor, Grandfather. I'll take care of this. The horse belongs to me, as Pilar well knows."

Though the two men ambled off, they were still within hearing distance when Pilar grabbed the tools from Libby's hand and insisted, "I am the only one who rides Incendiaria!"

"Correction." Reies's tone had that fine, no-nonsense edge to it again. "I have allowed you to ride the mare. That can change."

Pilar switched the argument to rapid Spanish and Reies did the same. Libby looked from one to the other, trying to follow the conversation but only grasping words here and there. Uncomfortable, she stepped back from the argument.

Without looking at her, Reies said, "Go, Libby. I'll take care of this and find you later. We'll make plans to cover the rest of the ranch."

"Don't ride Incendiaria again!" Pilar shouted. Again Reies chastised her in Spanish.

Libby grabbed the camera and sauntered away. Was Pilar angry because she'd ridden the mare, or because she'd been with Reies? Libby remembered the way Pilar had tried to wheedle the new dress from her ex-husband. She'd obviously expected him to interfere. Was it because they still had feelings for one another, or because Reies had power over what took place on the ranch?

That made Libby wonder if Reies thought he now had power over her as well. She hadn't forgotten his remark about her getting to the truth only if he found it for her.

Perhaps she'd better plan her strategy before Reies could take charge of her investigation.

Chapter Five

Bringing up the investigation at all was a difficult enough task. Reies put her off easily at dinner, assuring her that a new dawn would bring with it renewed opportunities. Libby awoke feeling refreshed and ready for anything. After breakfast, she found him in the large corral working with a young stallion.

Quietly, so as not to disturb horse or trainer, she hiked herself up onto the fence, hooked her legs between the middle rails and made herself as comfortable as possible.

Without looking at her, Reies asked, "Interested in my methods?"

"Working with horses or solving murders? I had no idea you had equal experience with both."

"You're direct this morning."

He led the saddleless buckskin around the outside arena, keeping control over the animal by the use of a hackamore, which applied pressure on the horse's nostrils. Libby watched, entranced.

Reies spoke to the stallion in quiet tones, all the while touching him gently, running his hands over the horse's withers and flanks. The flesh under the horse's pale coat quivered, but the animal didn't move away.

The thought of what those hands running over her own skin would feel like made Libby quiver. Annoyed at herself, she asked, "Don't you think it's time we were both straightforward and got down to business? We need to decide how to proceed with our investigation."

"We only came to an agreement less than twenty-four hours ago." Reies stopped a few yards in front of her. "I needed some time to think about it."

"To change your mind?"

He looked at her steadily. She couldn't read his aloof expression.

"Maybe it's you who've had a change of heart about working with a—"

"Desperado?" she finished for him.

After watching Reies work so patiently and gently with the horse, she had formed a new regard for the man. His respect for life was so evident, at odds with the dangerous quality he usually projected. Libby wondered if the quality came to him naturally, or if it had been something he'd had to practice. The very idea made her grin, perhaps for the first time in days.

"So, you do have a sense of humor," he said.

She was sure his drooping mustache picked up in an answering smile.

"About some things." Her grin faltered slightly. "Not about murder."

"And not about these murders in particular. I understand—but this isn't the time to talk about them."

He tilted his head and rolled his eyes to the right making her turn and focus on the other side of the corral. Nick was climbing the fence almost directly opposite her. Settling with one leg hooked over a middle rail, he was almost directly in back of Reies. Reies couldn't possibly have seen him, but his instincts must have alerted him to the other man's silent arrival.

"Working hard, big brother?" Nick called, his tone teasing. "Or courting on the job?"

"It's too early for your complaints," Reies returned good-naturedly. In an aside to Libby, he whispered, "Be ready to go to town when I finish up here."

"I'm ready now. Just say the word and make our excuses."

"Soon."

Reies moved away to one end of the arena. He tied the horse between two posts, then effortlessly hefted himself to the crossbar above. Hanging from his hands, his arm muscles supporting his weight, he lowered himself until his boot tips barely touched the buckskin's sides. He lifted his body and repeated the procedure over and over, each time sliding first his feet, then his legs farther down the horse's flanks toward his abdomen, accustoming the animal not only to his touch, but to his weight.

And through it all, Reies treated the horse with more regard than some men treated human beings. Libby couldn't help but be impressed and fascinated.

Watching the gentling process, Libby wished she could see the man without the worn, blue work shirt that so effectively covered his arms and broad shoulders. Reies's hidden strength had to be formidable, and she wouldn't be adverse to exploring that musculature in closer circumstances.

Telling herself that her interest was nothing more personal than her admiration for the art in the gallery her mother managed in Santa Fe didn't wash. Paintings and sculptures didn't provide the excitement she'd experienced with this man.

She was watching Reies so raptly that she almost missed the way Nick was studying her from across the corral, as if he was trying to figure her out. She made sure her expression was blank and refocused her attention on Reies. The feeling of being scrutinized didn't dissipate. As a matter of fact, it grew stronger, and to some extent, Nick's sudden interest in her spoiled the pleasure she had observing Reies.

The reason for her being at Rancho Velasquez came back all too vividly.

The scuffle of boots against stone distracted her from visualizing the police photographs of her brother. She turned to find the ranch hand Luis behind her. The middle-aged, paunchy man gave her an exaggerated, appreciative macho once-over that made her laugh. He stepped through a couple of fence rails into the corral and headed for Reies.

"Aren't you done with Buckito, gringo? You've spent most of the morning working with him."

The horse sidestepped nervously as Reies pulled himself up and over to a side post, then dropped to the ground, landing with bent knees. "Your timing is excellent, my friend. I was just finishing up."

Libby took that as her cue to enter the corral, as did Nick. They stopped on opposite sides of the two men as Reies massaged his right thigh with both hands. He winced as if in pain.

"And, of course, you will give me the pleasure of taking care of the young one here, eh?" Luis ran his hand down the horse's glossy neck, then ruffled his forelock. "Who'll be next?"

"Why don't you work with Rayando?" Reies suggested. "I promised to take Libby into town for a couple of hours so she can take some photographs there."

"Then she'd better remember to bring her camera," Nick said pointedly staring at her empty hands.

"Don't worry," she said quickly. "I'm going to grab it before we leave."

"This afternoon I want to work with Zanaton," Reies said. "He's far more advanced," he told her, "and photogenic." His expression aimed at Libby was somewhat challenging. "Care to try some fancy riding yourself?"

"Why not? It sounds like fun."

"Luis, have Incendiaria saddled for the lady. We should be back about—"

"Do you think that's wise?" Nick interrupted. "Letting Libby ride the mare again will put Pilar in a temper. Who knows what she might do?"

Reies's eyes locked with his brother's. "That's your problem now, isn't it, Nick?"

The silence stretched between them perceptibly until Luis cleared his throat and began singing lustily in Spanish while he led Buckito right between the brothers toward the stable, as if purposely to break the tension between them.

Reies took Libby's arm, following Luis toward the corral gate. She glanced over her shoulder. Nick stood ramrod stiff and stared straight at her rather than at Reies. His curious half scowl made her wonder whether he was upset by the confrontation about Pilar...or whether he was worried for her.

"WHAT DO YOU THINK we're going to be able to learn in town?" Reies asked, noting that, although she was part of the "establishment," Libby well exceeded the speed limits. The way she took the car around the narrow sharp turns made him glad he was wearing his seat belt.

"I'm not sure. The last time I came in, the only one who was remotely friendly was Ada."

"She's an all-right lady. She hasn't lived here long enough to have known your father, but your brother must have stopped at her place for lunch or coffee a few times."

"So she said. We'll have to work backward, anyway, starting with Wayne's death. Trying to find clues to a thirteen-year-old murder is crazy...."

Libby's voice died off for a few seconds. Reies watched her hardened profile, the way she swallowed before she resumed what she'd been saying in a tone that belied the utterly personal nature of the topic.

"I tried telling Wayne that. If only he had listened to me. He proved me wrong, though. He found something, all right—the murderer."

Reies heard the slight catch in her voice, but her expression remained steady. Her knuckles, however, turned white on the steering wheel.

"What did Ada say about your brother?"

"Not much. She talked. He was willing to listen. That's all I know for sure."

"We'll have lunch at the diner and get the details. Ada's got a memory like a steel trap."

The corners of Libby's mouth turned up, softening the harsh set of her womanly features, which Reies found attractive, if not beautiful.

Her delicate nostrils flared when she said, "In case you weren't aware of the fact, Ada's burgers are safe."

Reies gave her a curious look, but didn't respond directly to the odd comment. "It's a little early for lunch. Maybe we can start by talking with some of the other townspeople."

"Good luck," Libby muttered. "I hope you can get more out of them than I did."

"Isn't that why you recruited me?"

Rounding a curve, she stepped on the accelerator, making Reies brace himself.

"Is that how you view it?" she asked. "As being recruited? I seem to remember your having volunteered."

"Bull. You wouldn't have admitted a thing if you'd thought you could conduct your investigation all on your own. You needed me. Correction. *Need* me. Admit it."

She had a stubborn chin. Reies hadn't noticed before the way it jutted slightly when she was irritated. Thinking he was going to have to really squeeze an admission out of her, he was surprised when she capitulated.

"All right. I do need help. I need someone to talk to so I don't go crazy. I need to feel that I'm not alone in this. I need someone these townspeople will open up to so I can solve my brother's and father's murders. I need *you*. Satisfied?" Before he could answer, her chin jutted more determinedly than before and she demanded, "Start by telling me about the ruffian named Bobby—the one in the four-wheeler yesterday."

"Bobby Aguirre. He and Doug Barron are Johnnie Madrigal's sidekicks. I heard about the way you interfered in his business on your drive into town. Don't give him your back," Reies warned her, his worry almost a tangible thing. "He's bad news. His fists don't differentiate between men and women. He's known for extortion like his two pals. He's been suspect in several murders. Vendettas. No witnesses, and so no arrest." Reies paused only slightly before admitting, "He's Pilar's younger brother."

"You're kidding!"

"Nope. And maybe Bobbie's no prize, but Johnnie's got the real mean streak."

She didn't blink when she added, "Johnnie—and the murderer."

"You've ruled out Johnnie? The town's toughest citizen?"

"I haven't ruled out anyone."

"Not even me?"

He watched her expression even more closely as she admitted, "Except you."

If she was lying he couldn't tell. "Why should you make me the exception?"

"Instinct."

"You—a cop?—believe in trusting your instinct instead of facts?"

"In addition to facts—and why not?" Taking her eyes from the road for a second, Libby gave him an annoyed look. "You trust your instincts. Or at least the Apache part of you does."

"I get the feeling you know more about me than I'd find comfortable."

"You may be right." She hesitated before adding, "You respect life. You may be tough on the outside, but you're a person with a heart on the inside. That's why you're helping me. And that's why you'll tell me what you know about my father's murder."

Trying to ignore the discomfort her analysis of him brought about, Reies gritted out, "Only that I found him dead—in my bed."

He should have been prepared for her need to know about her father. Telling shouldn't bother him so much after all these years, but it did. Who, other than someone close to him, could have been responsible for Oliver Reardon's death? And yet, who close to him would have

killed the man and have tried to pin the murder on him?
Or maybe Libby's father *had* already been in his bed, and
not alone.

"I know that much. What I don't believe is that you
don't know more," Libby insisted, as though reading his
mind. "What happened that night, Reies?"

He stared out the window, away from her, glad to see
they were nearing the town limits. "I wasn't there when
your father was killed."

"But you found him. Think about it. What was your
immediate reaction? Who was around? Who did you
suspect?"

Tough questions from a tough lady. A cop. He had to
stop thinking of her as a defenseless woman. She was
anything but. Still, did she really think he would open up
and tell her his innermost thoughts, display his deepest
wounds?

"I'm surprised you don't have the details figured out
already," he said.

She seemed determined to ignore his sarcasm. "You
assumed he was in your bed because of Pilar."

Damn it! The woman could read his thoughts.
"Maybe."

"I don't believe it."

"You don't want to believe it because Oliver was your
father any more than I wanted to believe it because Pilar
was my wife."

"Instinct, Reies, use it. You were young, hot-blooded,
susceptible to a sensual woman. My father was a happy,
satisfied family man."

"Key word—man."

"No. He came here looking for horses, not for a
woman. And whatever Pilar's proclivities, I don't think

she would have gone after a man double her age when she had..."

Now Libby seemed uncomfortable. "Me?" Reies finished for her bitterly.

If only he had been enough for his wild, young wife. Pilar hadn't been faithful to him after the first few months of their marriage. Denial had been easy at first, but it had grown more difficult. At last he'd had to face the truth.

He hated the fact that an outsider—*this* outsider—knew something so intimate about his past.

"So tell me something about yourself that I don't already know," he said. He wanted to see how she liked having the tables turned on her. "You're alone, but are you a loner?"

"Did I want my divorce?" She slowed the vehicle as they approached the town limits. "Yes. Did I want to be single? No."

"Then why?"

"A wife has some rights. She expects more than Jaguars and hand-tooled leather vests and boots from a man. She expects to be a partner. To share. Harry was funny that way. He kept secret everything that would have meant something to me. He hid himself."

With that Libby jerked the car into the first empty space they found and slammed on the brakes. Reies threw out a hand and caught at the dash as he jerked forward. So she had her own vulnerabilities when it came to relationships. He guessed that made her as human as he was.

"We haven't finished the conversation about my father." Though she was breathing heavily, her tone was crisp, no-nonsense, her expression tough. Probably like when she was questioning a suspect. Her eyes held steady.

"If you think we have, then we're wasting our time trying to work together."

"Waste isn't in my vocabulary, lady. We'll just hold off finishing that discussion for the moment."

"Good." A click released both her seat belt and the tough expression that had hardened her eyes. "Because whether or not I like it, I do need you, Reies Coulter."

She grabbed her camera and left the car, and her words echoed through Reies. He needed Libby, too; it was about time this mystery was settled, the murderer brought to justice, the cobwebs of doubt swept clear from over his head.

And yet there was more....

Reies followed Libby Tate as she swept down the street. All the while he wondered why he got the feeling their admission of need, his unspoken still, held a deeper meaning than either of them might care to acknowledge.

"THINK REIES has made the woman yet, or what?"

Johnnie Madrigal raised his eyebrows at the words of his sandy-haired companion, who was leaning out of the back of the pickup watching Libby Tate take a photo before she entered the post office with Reies. Johnnie took a slug of beer. He stretched out legs that jiggled with nervous energy.

"Why? You thinkin' of going after Red yourself?"

"She could be a sweet thing," Doug Barron said, his expression knowing. "Under expert direction." He raised his beer and downed it, then used the back of his shirt-sleeve to wipe the moisture from his mouth. "It's her eyes. That's where you can read the potential. Never saw a pair of green eyes quite like those before."

Johnnie remained silent, trying to remember. "Maybe I have. Maybe you'd better leave her to our friend for the moment."

"Friend? Reies? You must be getting old and sentimental, Johnnie boy. That was a long time ago."

"He can still be useful to the cause." Johnnie's head twitched slightly. "We were best buddies once upon a time. I know the right strings. All I gotta do is pull them. In the meantime, we're gonna learn more about the reporter. She could prove useful, too."

Doug grinned and winked. "Ready and willing, amigo."

"Not that way, you moron. Pilar has her instructions."

"And if she doesn't come through as promised?"

Johnnie crushed the half-empty can in his hand. Ignoring the beer that foamed down his arm and onto his dust-covered jeans, he tossed the squashed aluminum container at the growing heap in one corner of the truck's bed.

"DANIEL, DID YOU KNOW that young state patrolman who was killed on the road out of town?" Reies asked the postmaster as soon as the only customer left the government office.

"I keep to myself, Reies. You know that."

Kilkenny might have been talking to Reies, but he was staring at her, Libby realized. Pretending indifference, she wandered away from the men to study the wanted posters on one of the walls. She almost expected to find some of the locals on the board.

"Come on, Daniel." Reies had lowered his voice. "You know you can talk to me."

"All right, but you aren't going to like this. The kid was in here once. He asked dozens of questions about your whole family, especially ones about you and your brother."

So Wayne had been pursuing his investigation none too subtly. Libby had to strain so she didn't miss a word of the low-toned conversation.

"What kind of questions?" Reies urged.

"Like, when you left town, when you came back. Whether or not I knew where you got the money to fix up the ranch. Whether you or Nick were mixed up with the Coalition. He was the law, Reies, so I couldn't ignore him, but I tried to say as little as possible. Honest."

Libby heard the whisper of fear in Kilkenny's assurances.

"Don't get scared of me, Daniel. I'm not Johnnie."

"Sure, Reies, I know that. Of course I know that."

But by the time Libby and Reies left a few minutes later, the postmaster was sweating.

In the grocery, Libby roved through shelves of goods she didn't need while Reies had a friendly conversation with Sal Zuno.

"That cop was real interested in the Coalition, Reies."

"What did you tell him?"

"Nothing at first, but he kept after me. Finally I gave in and told him the time and place of the next meeting—two nights before the cop was murdered."

"Do you remember if anyone else was in the store at the time?"

Sal shrugged. "No one but your brother, Nick."

They left quickly after that, Reies so stiff and silent that Libby decided to let her questions about the Coalition wait until later, when they were alone—after they resumed the conversation about her father.

Their last stop was the gas station. Angel Lopez owned the place. His dark eyes filled with suspicion at Libby's presence, yet he seemed eager to talk to Reies, giving him more than he asked for.

"You know what I think, Reies? I think Johnnie and his two lapdogs, Bobby Aguirre and Doug Barron, probably did away with the cop just for kicks."

Reies nodded and started to turn away. "Thanks, Angel."

"Hey, Reies, you want me to help you prove it, just say the word."

They were barely out of earshot when Libby asked, "Why do you think Angel is so eager to implicate Johnnie and his pals?"

"Vendetta. He hates Bobby. The Aguirres and Lopezes have been killing each other for decades."

"Or stealing their women," she murmured. He didn't disagree.

Entering Ada's Cafe was like taking a breath of fresh air. Hot and greasy maybe, but welcoming. Libby worked her shoulder muscles, willing away the tightness that had been nagging her upper back and neck for the past hour. They'd gotten little factual information, but at least they had a few leads—more than she'd have gotten alone.

"Hi there, honey!" Ada said boisterously as they chose an empty table opposite the cash register. The lunch rush was just starting. "Didn't expect to see you back so soon." In an aside loud enough for Reies to hear, she added, "See you've corralled the most sought-after man in town. Thought you weren't interested."

Libby smiled. "Right now, what I'm interested in is something tall and cool."

Ada winked. "He's tall, all right, but I see what you mean about the other. He's a hot one."

"Ada, you'll turn my head with all that nonsense of yours," Reies said with a genuine laugh.

Libby realized he really liked the woman—one of the few things they had in common.

"My head's been turned before, handsome, and it's still glued to my shoulders. So, what'll you have?"

"Same as the lady."

"Iced tea?"

At Libby's nod, Reies said, "That'll be fine." He took off his hat and hung it from a corner of the table. "And a set of your specialties."

"Two iced teas, two burgers coming up."

Ada sashayed her pink-clad body back behind the counter and tossed the frozen patties on the grill.

"The two of you been talking about me?" Reies asked Libby, his smile natural, his expression interested.

Leaning back in her chair as far as she could, Libby studied Reies. His hair hung free to his shoulders today, a thin strip of rawhide keeping the long strands off his high forehead. His rugged features couldn't be classed as handsome, but he was, without doubt, all male. Not a man a woman would turn down without due consideration.

Uneasily Libby was beginning to realize she was thinking in those very terms.

"Ada says the women around here see you as the catch of the town. They're amazed because you prefer the company of your horses."

"A good horse is more loyal than a—"

"Don't finish that unless you want a bruised shin," Libby warned him.

"Okay."

But obviously what he'd said was heartfelt. "Pilar must have done a job on you." From the instant scowl in response to her statement, Libby wondered if he still cared about his ex-wife. That would make Rancho Velasquez a living hell for Reies, since Pilar was married to his brother. "I couldn't imagine having to see Harry on a day-to-day basis, even though my love for him died long before the official end of our marriage."

"Were you married a long time?"

"Long enough. Four years. He tried to blame my job for our problems, but even if I had quit, it wouldn't have made a bit of difference in our relationship. He didn't know how to be open. Said he'd lived too long and was too set in his ways to learn." She didn't know why she added, "He actually was quite a bit older than I. Seventeen years. Maybe I was trying to replace my father rather than find a husband."

She thought Reies was about to exchange a confidence in return when three men chose to sit two tables away. That stopped their private conversation cold. She and Reies sat there staring at one another, and Libby began to wonder anew what she'd gotten herself into. They weren't together to share personal experiences or problems. They had a pair of murders to investigate.

Libby was lost in thought when she saw the young woman named Nina huddled over a cup of coffee in a corner of the cafe.

"You have that determined set to your jaw again."

"What?" She flipped her gaze to her companion.

The scarred eyebrow rose when Reies explained, "The point juts out just a little and looks hard as granite." He turned following her line of sight. "You thinking of going over . . ."

"I'll be back in a minute."

Ada was on her way to their table now, balancing their burgers and iced teas on a tray. With a wave, Libby slipped purposefully from her seat, sure that Nina was aware of her presence, and just as certain the young woman was ignoring her. An aura of fear surrounded Nina, but Libby didn't hesitate. She didn't know what questions she could ask or even if the woman would respond, but she couldn't let this opportunity pass.

"Nina, may I join you for a moment?"

Delicate features turned toward the window as a soft voice pleaded, "Please, go away."

"Are you afraid of me?"

In answer, Nina turned back so that her face was in full view, revealing nervous eyes.

Libby sat and covered the young woman's fragile hand. "You can't let Bobby intimidate you anymore. You don't have to stay with him."

"Then who will see to the needs of my family?" Nina freed her hand and gripped her cup. "Have you ever lived on welfare? Bobby is generous. We don't go without, like so many other families in the area. Our union has not yet been blessed by the priest, but that will come. If my being his woman until we are legally married is wrong, that is between me and my God."

"No, Nina, I didn't mean it that way." Libby reached out as if to touch the woman comfortingly. Nina flinched and Libby dropped her hand. "If you marry him, it will be worse for you. Let me help you. If you come to Santa Fe—"

"Nina doesn't go anywhere without her Bobby, does she?"

The woman's dark eyes widened in alarm, and Libby whipped around to see Pilar's swarthy brother standing over them, his expression menacing.

"No!" Nina said quickly. "I don't go anywhere without you. I am your woman." Her voice rose to a quiet hysteria as she clawed at Libby's hand with frantic fingers. "Tell Bobby, please."

"Yes. That's exactly what Nina was saying."

Libby rose and squared off with the man, who was an inch shorter but a lot heavier than she. He pulled at his belt and puffed out his chest in a show of bravado.

"But you," he said menacingly to Libby, "have a quarrel with our love?"

Before Libby could tell Bobby what she thought of him, her shoulders were grasped tightly. She hadn't even heard Reies come up beside her. She caught the warning in his eyes even as his fingertips pressed into her upper arms.

"Women. Always talking when there's work to do." He punctuated the statement with a sharp, direct push toward their table. "It's time we got back to the ranch."

Tight-lipped, Libby allowed him the lead. Reies didn't slacken his grip, not when they stopped at their table where he threw down several bills, not when he picked up her hamburger and shoved it into her hands.

It wasn't until they were out the door and halfway down the street that she thrust the messy burger in front of his face. "What the hell am I supposed to do with this?"

"It's your lunch. Eat it or get rid of it. I couldn't care less." He let go of her in front of the car and held out a demanding hand. "Keys."

"This is my car!"

"Tough, because I'm driving."

Pulling the key ring from her jeans pocket, she slapped it as hard as she could into his waiting palm. He remained stone-faced, not even flinching a little. "I resent your interference."

Reies's dark eyes flashed with an anger equal to what she was feeling. "And I resent your making more trouble for Nina. She's a good kid."

"Then why don't you help her instead of letting Bobby treat her so badly?"

"To begin with, she would have to be willing to take my help.... Oh, forget it." He opened the passenger door with a jerk and stalked around to the driver's side, muttering, "You're not from these parts. You wouldn't understand."

Ticked off at the reminder that she was an outsider, Libby sank into the passenger seat and bit into the burger wishing it were Reies Coulter's head. They drove in silence, what had been the important subjects of the day forgotten for the moment.

By the time they arrived at the ranch, Libby's mood hadn't improved. She followed Reies to the corral, yet left a safe distance between them; Reies's backside made her booted foot itch to make solid contact, and gentleman that he was, Reies would undoubtedly return the gesture!

Two horses, Incendiaria and Zanaton, were saddled and waiting in the shade of the barn. In contrast to Incendiaria's bright chestnut coloring, Zanaton was a dark sorrel, with a star on his forehead and a single white foot. He was a magnificent animal, as impressive in his own way as Sangre. The word must have spread that Reies was going to give Libby a lesson in the Mexican style of riding, because an audience was waiting for them as if no one on the place had anything more important to do than play spectator.

Dressed in gray pants, a loose black blouse, black boots and hat, as if she herself might have been riding, Inez stood between her father and Victor at one end of the corral. "Well, you've finally found your way home, Reies." Her tone relayed her impatience. "Maybe you can hurry this demonstration so the rest of us can get on with other things."

"Emilio refused to sit for me until he was satisfied you weren't going to endanger his guest," Victor explained.

"I would not care to see Miss Tate hurt riding one of our horses," Emilio said.

"She'll do all right." Reies's lips quirked and turned up the tips of his mustache. "She's an adequate rider. Luis, would you bring the horses into the corral?"

Adequate? Refusing to appear annoyed in front of an audience, Libby merely smiled and looked the other way—into a pair of pale brown eyes that sparked with fury. As if daring her to ride Incendiaria in spite of her warning, Pilar was glaring at her from the shelter of her husband's stiffly set arm, giving Libby the feeling Nick was keeping his wife in place by force.

Libby entered the corral right behind Reies and in front of Luis, who led the two horses as instructed.

"First," Reies said, taking Zanaton's reins while Luis looped the mare's reins around a post near the gate, "I will demonstrate the *cala de caballos*," the first event of a Mexican rodeo in which riders exhibit the control and precise training of their mounts. Standing at the stallion's head, Reies twisted the stirrup toward him. The instant he put his foot into it, Zanaton moved forward, snapping Reies into the saddle.

"Then you may try on Incendiaria—if you wish."

"I wish," Libby said, refusing to leave the center of the arena.

She had her doubts about the wisdom of her wish when, after Reies circled the sorrel away from her, he sent the horse into a gallop straight at her, the way he had that first day he'd found her on the range. Her heart picked up in tempo, but this time she held her ground. Zanaton stopped in the same manner Sangre had—crouching and sliding forward in three sets of braking actions—leaving a distance of a mere foot between them.

"The *rayar*," Reies told her. He lowered his voice as the horse stood erect, perfectly still. "Did I mention that Zanaton is not yet fully trained?"

Libby locked knees that threatened to go weak on her, but she didn't move. She crossed her arms over her chest.

"What next?"

"The *cabriolas*."

Reies signaled his mount to begin a series of dancing maneuvers, first to the left, then to the right, then in a complete circle. Then he dismounted and remounted while the horse remained absolutely still. Beast and master were magnificent.

"*Cejar*," Reies called.

Zanaton paced backward in a straight line to his starting point as smoothly and swiftly as if he were moving forward.

"Your turn now, Libby. I'll lead you through step by step, explaining how to use the reins and your legs."

Libby nodded and walked toward Incendiaria. The mare seemed almost as excited as she was, probably because of the spectators. Libby led her to the center of the ring. Copying what Reies had done, she held the reins in her left hand and turned the stirrup halfway around and in position.

"Good," Reies said, edging Zanaton closer. "But shorten the right rein so the horse will move under you as you rise."

Libby made the adjustment, took a deep breath, and attempted the unfamiliar mount. She and Incendiaria managed to dance around each other without success.

"You're wasting your time with this one, Reies," Pilar jeered. "Want me to show her how it's done?"

"Reies," Emilio called, "perhaps this is not a good idea."

Trying to shut out the added protests of Inez and Victor, Libby stroked the mare's nose, spoke to her softly and got herself in position once more.

"Get a good grip on the saddle horn when you throw those reins over," Reies instructed.

Libby nodded, tried again, and this time rose in the stirrup. Victorious, she swung her right leg over the horse's back, and as the mare moved into her, slid into position. Libby's triumph was short-lived, however, for the moment her bottom touched the saddle, Incendiaria went berserk. She lowered her head and began bucking and twisting, trying to dislodge her rider.

"What the hell—!"

Libby barely registered Reies's reaction or that of the spectators, who were all yelling at once. Every muscle in her body was being twisted and pummeled. Concentration alone held her on the thrashing horse. What was wrong?

Luis threw himself in front of the mare and tried to grab the reins, but was almost kicked in the process.

"I'm going to pull you off!" Reies yelled as he made a close pass. "When you feel my arm around you, let go!"

Somehow she hung on for several precious seconds before Zanaton came alongside Incendiaria and Reies reached for her. Libby let go of everything at the first touch of his arm.

"Use my stirrup!" he yelled as she came flying off the mare and into the bulk of his body.

Breathing heavily, she faced Reies, her right foot in his stirrup, her legs straddling his thigh tightly. Her breasts pressed into his chest and their heads were so close that she could see the irises in the black pools of his eyes. For a moment, she forgot everything but the whipcord-hard feel of him. He'd lost his hat in the rescue and his long black hair swirled around his rugged bronzed face. She breathed in his scent—male, sweaty and sensual.

An eternity seemed to pass before her heart stopped pounding.

Reality in the form of Victor Duprey broke the moment. "Are you all right, Libby?" He was running into the arena. "Let me help you get down."

Feeling strong hands on her waist, Libby let go of Reies and let herself lean into Victor as he helped her dismount. "I'm fine." Even when the artist's elaborate necklace pressed into her back, she couldn't disconnect her eyes from Reies's.

An explosion of Spanish made her turn finally. Luis was yelling while Incendiaria stood docilely, her head lowered as if in shame. What had gotten into the horse?

"She must be injured," Reies said, dismounting.

Luis was already undoing the mare's cinches. He'd barely lifted the saddle when the problem became obvious: a slender stalk of cholla cactus was stuck in the mare's back. It had drawn blood, which blended with her chestnut coloring.

Libby was shocked. Someone had wanted to hurt her! Someone who didn't want her to ride the horse. Fury rose in throat as she turned and stalked to where Pilar stood in the shelter of her husband's bulk. "How dare you!"

"Me? I didn't do it!" Pilar looked at Nick pleadingly, but he was frowning down at her. "I didn't, I swear."

Fists balled at her sides, Libby said, "If anything— *anything*—like this ever happens again, Pilar, I'm going to forget I'm a lady. I can guarantee that I'm a lot tougher than you are."

The sable-haired woman's face reflected real fear. "I am innocent!"

"Don't lie."

Libby grabbed the other woman by the wrist and forced her toward Incendiaria. Luis was setting down the saddle and Reies was inspecting the damage done by the cactus, which had not yet been removed.

"Look what you did to this helpless animal, Pilar, and remember what I said."

With that, Libby freed her prisoner. Pilar backed off and wildly looked to the others for support, which was not forthcoming. Emilio was flushed, his eyes hard. Inez looked white and shaky. Victor glanced from woman to woman in surprise. Nick's expression was blank.

Chapter Six

"You all right?" Reies asked a short while after the others had dispersed. He was genuinely concerned.

Libby looked a little grim around the mouth. And for some reason, she was having trouble looking him straight in the eye. He wondered if both were aftereffects of the scare... or of something else.

"I'm sure I'll have a few sore muscles." She stared down at the metal point of her boot, which she dug into the ground, loosening a plug of red-brown earth. "A hot shower will do wonders for my back."

"Go ahead and take one, then," Reies suggested. He had to resist the urge to pull her into his arms and tell her that everything would be all right. He didn't know if it would be, and touching her would certainly be a mistake. "Afterward, get some rest."

That made her head whip up, her eyes snap. "I don't need to be pampered—"

"No one said you did. But you went through a tough couple of minutes there, and your body will admit that easier than you want to. I'd put money you won't have a bit of trouble catching some extra sleep. I have some things to take care of, but I'll bring dinner to you later."

"That's not necessary."

"How else are we going to find enough privacy to talk?"

"Oh." The flash of annoyance in her eyes softened. "I hadn't thought of that."

"And I haven't forgotten our unfinished discussion."

Nodding, hands dug into her jeans pockets, Libby backed away. "I'll just go take that shower now."

"See you in a couple of hours."

She turned stiffly, but Reies knew that for once her rigid stance wasn't due to anger with him. At least she didn't appear to be hurt, although she seemed to be walking a bit more carefully than usual. But she could have been hurt. As a matter of fact, she could have been killed. Reies's protective instincts rushed to the fore, without his thinking about why. Damn the person who did that to Libby. Maybe it was Pilar, maybe not.

He used to be an expert at sorting through Pilar's lies and half-truths, but that had been a long time ago. His ex-wife really was a selfish woman, yet she'd sounded genuinely frantic that no one would believe she hadn't tampered with Incendiaria's saddle. Reies didn't know what to believe. Pilar certainly had the motive to hurt Libby, and who else would have reason to do such a thing?

The answer wasn't one he wanted to go looking for.

Reies wrestled with himself for an uncomfortable moment. If not arranged by a spiteful, jealous woman, the incident could have been designed by someone else, who wanted to frighten Libby into leaving the ranch.

But no one knew who Libby was or why she was there.

No one but Reies.

And he was no more guilty of trying to injure her than he was of murder.

Though he talked a tough game, he would never physically harm anyone except in self-defense—not even someone who threatened to hurt his family as Libby did; he felt very strongly about protecting his loved ones. Ironically that very fact of his personality was what drew him to the woman.

Since he'd learned Libby's true identity, he'd felt a bond with her he hadn't wanted to admit. He respected her, liked her, was attracted to her—even while he hated those feelings, hated being vulnerable, hated knowing he would be forced to open up to an outsider.

But, in some primitive way, Libby's inner pain had become his own, because he understood it so well. Just as he felt the need to protect those he loved, he knew her need to seek justice for the murders of her father and brother was even greater. He couldn't fault her for what she was trying to do. He could only help her and hope that their investigation wouldn't lead to the destruction of a member of his own family.

Honest with himself at last, Reies faced the real reason he'd left Sidewinder all those years ago: he'd been afraid he might stumble across the murderer's identity.

Now he wouldn't rest until he did.

"I WASN'T HERE when your father died," Reies told Libby while she literally attacked the dinner he'd brought her. "I didn't return until late that night, when I found his body in my bed."

Libby digested the information along with a piece of mesquite-grilled beef. She sat on the couch, feeling more than a bit uncomfortable in his presence even though a thin, cotton, brightly colored, Navajo-designed caftan draped her, covering her completely including her toes.

Reies had been correct about at least one thing: she had slept, and so soundly that she hadn't wakened until he'd arrived with the tray of food. Then she'd been so hungry she hadn't even excused herself to dress properly—simply threw the caftan over her nakedness. Now she was glad he was pacing the length of the living area. For wherever he chose to sit would be too close for her comfort.

Forcing her mind back to the conversation, she said, "Johnnie Madrigal swore you were at his place."

"I never saw Johnnie that night."

"What? Johnnie lied? Why would he give you an alibi?"

"I wondered about that myself. I thought maybe he had something to do with the murder and was using *me* as *his* alibi. But that didn't make sense. Both Bobby and Doug would have sworn to anything he told them to say. So I figured he was protecting me because we used to be buddies."

"You and Johnnie? But you're nothing like him."

Reies shrugged. "We were cut from the same mold. But, sometime during the growing-up process, I began to see the difference between right and wrong. Nick was mostly responsible for keeping me on the right track. My little brother always kept his nose clean. His father's influence, I guess. Frank was a good man who didn't deserve to die violently."

"What happened?"

"He got caught in the middle of someone else's vendetta."

"That must have been awful for all of you."

"Especially my mother. Frank's death almost destroyed her. She wasn't the strong woman you see now. She was soft, kind, vulnerable. She had so much love to give...well, after she lost her second husband, she lavished all she had on Nick and me. I guess I was lucky I had a mother who cared so much."

"And a brother."

"And a brother," Reies agreed. "Getting back to my shady past, Nick hounded me until I straightened out. Still, Johnnie and I are a lot more alike than you think."

Libby swallowed another bite of steak and shook her head. "I don't believe it. The two of you have nothing more than this town and a rugged background in common. He's self-serving, a bully and a braggart. And there's something innately cruel about him." Remembering Johnnie's nasty smile, she shuddered. "You're none of those things."

"How do you know so much about me?"

"Would you believe instinct?"

"Maybe."

"And observation. That's what I'm trained to do."

She picked at her rice and refried beans and stared up at Reies, wishing they could read one another's mind. Then this awkward conversation wouldn't be necessary.

"So," she went on, "if you weren't here the night my father was killed, where were you?"

"I was alone, thinking, going over everything that was wrong with my life. Ironic. I set out for a place that gave me some peace and came back to even more trouble."

He dropped onto the couch right next to her and ran a hand through his hair, which still hung free. Thick black strands teased his shoulders. And her. Libby figured he would notice if she moved toward the other side of the couch to put some distance between them. He would probably gloat, as well.

"Why were you the one to find my father instead of Pilar?"

"Supposedly she was visiting her family. She came home almost immediately after I did. As a matter of fact, she was the one to find me as I was checking for a pulse to see if Oliver was still alive."

"What a coincidence. Almost as if she'd been waiting for you to find the body before she entered the house."

"That's occurred to me."

Libby paused and concentrated on her food for a moment. Elena was an excellent cook, she thought, stalling.

"We've gone over this part before," she finally said. "If Pilar was unfaithful to you, it wasn't with my father." She raised her eyebrows, challenging Reies to refute the claim. Though he didn't utter a word, his eyes answered for him. "But you were convinced that my father and your wife had been . . . together, weren't you?"

"Yes."

"And that she killed him? Why? It doesn't make sense."

"Pilar wanted out of Sidewinder, out of this rural area. She was looking for excitement. She thought I'd take her to Santa Fe or some other city after we were married. Maybe she thought Oliver was the answer and he disappointed her, too, or maybe . . ."

His words faltered into nothingness, and Libby sensed the importance of what he wasn't saying.

"What, Reies?" When he shook his head, she slapped the table between them, rattling the tray of food. "Honesty, Reies. I need the truth from you. The truth and how you saw things thirteen years ago. If you can't give that to me, what help are you?"

"You're right. I know you're right." He took a deep breath and a break before going on, and he couldn't look at her when he eventually admitted, "I thought someone was trying to protect the family honor Pilar had soiled."

"You mean make up for Pilar's bed-hopping by killing my father?"

"This isn't Santa Fe."

No. Sidewinder was a town without a conscience. A place where two-bit hoods like Johnnie Madrigal could get away with extortion, and macho men like Bobby Aguirre could start a knife fight in full view of an audience. And it was a place without witnesses when murder was committed.

"Who did you suspect, Reies? Your grandfather? Mother? Brother?"

"None of them. All of them."

His voice was so anguished, Libby couldn't stop from reaching out to give comfort. She touched his arm lightly, and when his face turned and his dark, tormented eyes met hers, she felt something surge between them. She removed her hand. This was no time to be thinking about physical attraction.

"Victor," she croaked softly. "What about Victor? Where did he fit in?"

"Why would you suspect him?"

"He was at the burial." The image was clear in her mind once more. "I didn't know who any of you were, but I swore I would commit each of your faces to memory. You, Emilio, Inez, Nick, Pilar, Johnnie and Victor. You were all there, supposedly mourning. What better way to throw off suspicion than to show up at the funeral?"

"That didn't mean anything. Victor came around the ranch a lot." Reies shrugged. "He was new to the area by Sidewinder standards, lived here maybe less than a year.

He said he was committed to capturing the purity and power of the real people and of the real country."

"Hasn't Victor made a name for himself since then?" Libby asked.

Considering her mother ran a gallery, she supposed she should know, but there were so many artists in that area of the country she couldn't be sure.

"My mother says he's very well-known," Reies told her. "Sought after."

"Then why does he stay here? He can't be poor."

"Victor says he prefers remaining unfettered by the conventions of city life. Quite often he makes solitary journeys into the mountains, away from even the smallest villages, to meditate, as well as to sketch. He says his trips renew him spiritually."

"Was he close to your family at the time of my father's death?"

"Close? Well, Grandfather did befriend him soon after he moved into Sidewinder. He agreed to sit as one of Victor's first subjects."

"And of course he had a chance to meet my father when he came here looking to buy horses?"

Reies nodded. "Right. Oliver and Victor seemed pretty friendly. Sorry, but if you're looking for a motive there, I can't give you one."

Libby's head was spinning, and it certainly wasn't from hunger. Their conversation had given her so much to think about. She pushed the tray away and set her bare feet up at the edge of the coffee table. Leaning back, she winced slightly when her aching shoulders came into contact with the high-backed couch. But something was nagging at more than her muscles, and she couldn't pin down what.

"We have a long way to go before we figure this one out," she muttered, rubbing at a particularly tender area at the base of her neck.

A muscle there had been injured in a physical struggle she'd had in making an arrest the year before. In the months since, it hadn't fully healed and didn't need much coaxing to act up. From experience, she knew her neck and shoulders would be as stiff as a board in the morning.

"Let me do that for you."

"What?"

Reies held up his hands and flexed his fingers. "I give a good neck massage."

"That sounds pretty intimate."

The tips of his mustache twitched. "Maybe it was supposed to."

"How do I know I can trust you to keep those fingers where they belong?"

"Why, you're an officer of the law, ma'am." He gave her a quick once-over. "You can turn your weapon on me if I get out of hand."

Libby was no fool. The caftan wasn't capable of hiding anything from his perceptive gaze, much less a bulky, if small gun. Her holster lay under the bed—not that she felt she would need it. She turned her back toward him and placed herself carefully on the edge of the couch so that they were several inches apart.

"Relax, will you?" he said.

Before she could stop him, he had her by the waist and was pulling her toward him, at the same time lifting one of his legs off the floor and arranging it against the back of the couch. He snugged her between his thighs.

Amazing, Libby thought, how they always managed to make intimate contact when there was no intimacy involved.

Or so Libby tried to convince herself as Reies gently probed the muscles in question.

"You're hard as a rock all along here," he said, running his fingers down from the side of her neck.

"You found the right spot," she murmured, the pleasure-pain mesmerizing her into focusing only on his touch.

He warmed the base of her neck with his palm, then worked the length of the muscle with his fingers, probing harder and deeper with each stroke.

"Aah," she sighed.

"Now that sounds intimate."

"Trust me, it wasn't meant to."

"I guess my ear for these things isn't as good as it used to be."

"It's all those horses you hang around with," Libby told him, completely under the spell of his hands. "They've got you confused."

"Not too badly, I hope. I would hate for an intimate sound to pass those pretty lips of yours... and me miss it."

"I'll warn you," she promised, smiling.

Intimacy with Reies Coulter. The thought wasn't at all abhorrent. What a difference a couple of days made! She hadn't even wanted to ride behind him on Sangre when he'd come looking for her out on the range....

The thought startled her into an attempt to move away. Reies slipped an arm around her waist, making escape impossible.

"Where do you think you're going?"

She could feel his warm, seductive breath on her neck when she said, "I feel much better—"

"But I'm not done."

Reies put both hands on her waist and shifted her body partway around. Then he took her chin and turned her face toward his. Libby's pulse surged as she realized he was about to kiss her. She should free herself from his grip and... The only problem was that she didn't want to. The antagonism and tension that had existed between them days ago had turned into something quite different, and Libby couldn't deny she was curious to explore the altered response further.

Her back was now against his leg on the couch. His face drew near. His dark, fathomless eyes didn't close. Neither did his mouth as it covered hers in an act of possession that was as shocking as it was pleasurable. The fingers on her chin adjusted, flexed, splayed along the length of her neck. They moved downward in a slow, syrupy-feeling motion she couldn't begin to fight. His probing tongue and callused hands created exciting sensations, driving every thought from her head except what it would be like to make love with this man.

Her hand slipped easily up his arm where her fingers found and tangled themselves in his hair. She'd never made love with a man whose hair was longer than hers, Libby thought hazily. He deepened the kiss. When his hand slipped inside her caftan and cupped a breast, arousing first her nipple, then the rest of her, she moaned into his mouth, and in contrary reward found her own mouth freed.

"Was that sound meant to be intimate?" Reies's grin was wider than she'd ever seen it.

Feeling herself flush, Libby let go of his hair and whispered, "Your ear for these things is more in tune than I thought."

"You forgot to warn me," he murmured in mock-admonishment.

"Next time."

The grin widened, but the hand withdrew. "I'll remember that if you will."

Libby blinked, amazed that Reies wasn't going to pursue her further, surprised that she both wanted him to and was glad when he didn't. She slid away from him to the other end of the short couch. From that scant distance, he looked invincible and foreign—unlike the vulnerable, smiling man who'd just held her in his arms. And he was vulnerable inside, Libby knew, no matter how tough he acted on the outside.

"Feeling more relaxed?" Reies asked, his expression neutral.

"No."

"Sorry."

"Liar."

Making no such admission, he brought them back to the investigation. "Where were we?"

"I don't know. Somehow...I got lost in the middle of our discussion." But now that they were back on track, the nagging feeling that she was forgetting something important returned, chasing away the last remains of arousal Reies had so easily called up. Frowning, Libby concentrated until it hit her. "The money."

"What money?"

"My father brought enough money with him to Sidewinder to buy your entire herd if he wanted to—he emptied our bank account—but the money was never found. That's why we lost the ranch," she said. "At least part of the reason. No working capital, and my mother and I trying to run the place without enough stock, added up to a major disaster.''

''I really am sorry, but if you think my grandfather took Oliver's money intending to sell him the horses and then 'forgot' to give it back, you haven't taken a hard-enough look at this place. If Grandfather had had the money, he would have used it to keep up the ranch.''

''I wouldn't believe it of your grandfather, anyway,'' Libby assured him, realizing she had eliminated Emilio from her list of suspects. ''But something happened to the money. I want you to be honest with me, so it's only fair that I tell you—'' Libby took a deep breath ''—at first, I thought that might be where you got the money to make the improvements around here.''

She felt terrible when she saw the hurt flash in his eyes before he could conceal it. She reached out and touched his knee, which was still resting up on the couch.

''It's my turn to apologize.'' She felt the tension she'd caused flow out of him.

''I guess we both have a lot of things to apologize for.''

Libby nodded and removed her hand, all business once more. ''Did anyone around Sidewinder seem to strike it rich after my father's death?''

''I didn't stay around long enough to find out.''

''What about Johnnie and his hoods? Nina told me she stays with Bobby because he takes good care of her family, and he drives that fancy four-wheeler. None of those men seem to have jobs. So where do they get their money?''

''I wouldn't look too closely into their activities, if I were you,'' Reies warned her. ''Not unless you want to end up like Wayne.''

"What are you saying? That one of them is the guilty one? Are you sure that's not wishful thinking?"

"Wishful. You bet. Johnnie was my pal, but that was when I was a kid. I don't condone what he does. I would give anything if he was the murderer instead of someone I care about. But you want honesty, so I'll tell you the unholy trio could be making all that money in a lot of different ways—all illegal. They wouldn't like interference from a little thing like you."

"Little?"

"To them you are, not in size, but in importance. And, lady, if you don't understand that, you're a fool. You might think you're some kind of a tough cop, but you haven't come nose to nose with their kind in that city of yours. Believe me, I know what I'm talking about."

Libby might have taken offense if she hadn't remembered the way she'd felt after her encounter with the three men in the diner. The fear she'd felt had trailed her all the way back to the ranch. Even armed, she wouldn't want to be caught alone with any one of them on a deserted road . . . the way Wayne might have been.

"I do believe you."

"Good."

"But that won't stop me from wondering about the money. It may give us the connection we need."

"Promise me you won't do something stupid to find out."

Libby gritted her teeth so she wouldn't say something hasty and regrettable. Reies was worried about her. She should feel glad rather than annoyed.

The best she could manage was, "I never act without thinking, and we're in this together."

He seemed satisfied with the neutral answer. "What next?" he asked.

Libby knew he wasn't going to like this part. "We have to keep on asking questions about Wayne. He's still the key. If possible, we need to trace his steps that last week he was alive. We need to learn who in your family knew anything about him. Only you can find that out, Reies."

His eyes became as cold and closed as she'd ever seen them, and he rose abruptly. "I'd better get going. I still have a ranch to run."

Or the truth to run away from, Libby thought.

Because she knew how difficult this would be for him, and why he'd agreed to help her in the first place—to protect his family—she didn't challenge him, but accepted his excuse and saw him out. Leaning against the closed door, she couldn't stop from worrying.

What would Reies do if they learned that someone in his family was a murderer? Libby had to believe that he would do the right thing, that he wouldn't try to stop her from bringing the person to justice. She was more worried about Reies himself. Though his emotions might not show through that tough facade of his, surely his heart would break.

Lord help her, Libby thought. She just might care about Reies Coulter's heart.

INEZ OBREGON WATCHED through the window as Libby Tate strolled up to the front porch for breakfast. Time for a confrontation. Yet the woman didn't move from the living room when the front door opened. Nor did she greet their guest, who didn't seem to notice her presence.

Guest?

Intruder was more like it.

And the sooner Rancho Velasquez and her son were free of the threat Libby Tate posed the better.

Inez had felt her protective hackles rise the moment she'd met Libby. She'd known the redhead had meant trouble and she was anxious to be free of the constant need to be on her guard.

Libby began filling her plate from the sideboard. Raising her chin, Inez moved to the coffee urn where they uttered low-keyed morning greetings. Inez took her coffee to the end of the table backing the windows. The morning was a brilliant one, she noted with satisfaction, and sunlight would fall on the reporter's face, revealing what shadow might otherwise hide.

"Are you satisfied with your article on Rancho Velasquez, Miss Tate?"

Libby swallowed a mouthful of food and looked straight at her. "It's coming along."

"So you think your visit with us will have been worthwhile."

"Very."

The lack of expression on Libby's face seemed studied, and that worried Inez. It renewed her fear that the reporter was researching more than just a story on Rancho Velasquez.

"This is your fifth day with us, Miss Tate." Inez no longer felt a need for pretense or subtlety. This was, after all, her own home. "How much longer do you to plan to take advantage of our hospitality while you shoot unnecessary pictures and poke into matters that don't concern you?"

Obviously unprepared for such a direct confrontation, Libby stopped her fork halfway to her mouth, her face a picture of astonishment. But when she recovered quickly and politely murmured, "Until I get the information I need," the older woman had to give her credit for unbelievable poise.

Inez persisted. "And that would be?"

"At least through your father's seventy-fifth birthday celebration. After all, the *charreada* will be very color-ful with everyone in costume, and—"

"Only a few more days, then."

Not satisfied with Libby's answer, Inez bowed her head in her most regal manner and sipped her coffee. She wished she could order the reporter to pack her bags and leave now, before it was too late, but she couldn't countermand her father's wishes.

"What did you mean by matters that don't concern me?" Libby asked.

"Perhaps my phrasing was a bit harsh."

The reporter's smile was at once apologetic and false, Inez decided.

"I'm sorry if I'm an inconvenience to you or your family in any way."

"You are not an inconvenience, Miss Tate," Emilio Velasquez stated firmly.

Inez's head snapped up. Her father strode toward them, his posture, as usual, ramrod straight. His face was drawn into a scowl as he stared at his daughter, making it clear he'd heard at least part of the conversation.

"You are welcome to stay for as long as you like," he went on. "My daughter can be an impatient and private woman."

Impatient and worried, Inez thought. And if her father had any sense, he would be, also.

LIBBY TURNED her outward attention to Emilio as the elderly man helped himself to breakfast, but inwardly, she wondered at Inez's hostility, which the older woman hadn't tried to conceal.

Why did Reies's mother want her off the ranch?

What was she afraid of?

What did she know?

That Inez quickly made her excuses and disappeared into one wing of the large old house didn't surprise her. Libby spent the next half hour entertained by her host, who shared with her some delightful anecdotes of life on a ranch.

"The *vaqueros*, they like to play tricks on each other. I remember one time..."

Emilio always had such a positive attitude, something he might easily have lost over the last decade. Libby found herself growing fond of him.

"The horse was docile when petted," the elderly man was saying, his faded eyes sparkling with good humor. "Even when he was saddled. But the moment anyone tried to ride him—that was a different story. Pedro tricked at least six of the other men before the word spread."

Remembering her own recent experience with Incendiaria, Libby said, "I'm surprised they didn't gang up on him to get revenge."

"I assume they must have, but I do not remember...." He suddenly sobered. "That was just before my oldest son died."

"I'm sorry, Mr. Velasquez."

"As I've already told you, two of my sons died, and within months of each other. And all because of Sidewinder."

Libby didn't say anything. Emilio Velasquez had borne his share of tragedy, as had she, because of the lawless town, and she empathized with his loss. Amazing that he hadn't turned into an embittered old man. For the first time since she'd insinuated herself into his household, Libby felt a stirring of guilt, as if she were betraying the good-hearted patriarch. She only hoped that when the truth was told, he would understand that she had done what she'd had to.

"Well, I must go, Miss Tate." Emilio stood. "I have bills to pay. If you need me for anything, I will be in my study. Reies is taking good care of you?"

Libby almost blushed. "Yes. Very." She took a quick swallow of coffee. "By the way, would you mind if I made a call to Santa Fe?"

"Of course not. The telephone is at your disposal."

"Thank you."

She made a pretense of finishing her coffee, when, in reality, she was stalling, waiting for Emilio to be on his way before she rose and headed for the living room. Unfortunately there was no telephone in her own quarters, so she hadn't called her mother since her second day on the ranch. She knew Gloria would be worrying, and she only wanted to reassure her that she was alive and well. She dialed the Santa Fe number.

One ring was followed by a click and the words, "Blue Mesa."

"Mom, how are you?"

"How am I? Elizabeth!"

Her mother only called Libby Elizabeth when she was angry. "I love you, too, Mom."

"How could you let me worry like this?"

"So much has been happening." Including things she wouldn't dare tell her mother. She could almost feel Gloria's anxiety through the telephone line. "I'm not done with my business here," she said carefully, "but I'm fine."

Certain the pause at the other end was her mother's way of cooling down, she was surprised that when Gloria spoke, it was in a low, anxious tone. "Can you talk?"

Immediately uncomfortable, Libby looked around at the empty room. Undoubtedly her mother wanted to ask some questions she didn't yet have the answers to. "Carefully."

"Captain Wainwright called just a while ago and asked me to get a message to you. I was debating on whether or not I should chance calling you myself, but I was afraid I might blow your cover."

Knowing Libby's circumstances, the police captain wouldn't have tried to reach her unless it was urgent. "Mother, what did he say?"

"That you must contact police headquarters as soon as possible. I asked if he had some new leads about the murder, but he wouldn't tell me."

"Thanks." Her mind racing, Libby cut the conversation short. "I'll get in touch with him. I'd better go now."

"All right. Bye, honey."

Libby went to hang up the phone, but her mother sounded so forlorn, she put the receiver back to her ear, about to offer some reassurances. She heard a soft click... and then her mother hung up.

Staring at the receiver, Libby dropped it back into its cradle and looked around. No one. But that click... Had she been imagining things or had someone else in this house been silent party to their conversation? Surely no one would have reason to be so suspicious of her that he or she would listen in on a private conversation. Maybe there'd been some kind of glitch in the phone line.

Still, she didn't dare take a chance on calling police headquarters; she'd go in person. Possibly Wainwright did have some new information for her. Whatever his reason, knowing her situation, he wouldn't have tried to get in touch with her unless it was urgent.

She would leave for Santa Fe right after she found Reies and told him where she was headed.

Now the only thing she had to worry about was whether or not anyone else in this house was privy to that information.

Chapter Seven

"Would you give me some space?" Libby hissed as she strode into into Santa Fe police headquarters, Reies on her heels.

"Why? So you can leave me behind?" Even as he protested, he backed off a bit.

"You made your point. I brought you, didn't I? For all I know, this might have nothing to do with Wayne."

Libby realized Reies didn't believe that any more than she did. That's why they'd skipped lunch and had left for Santa Fe so quickly. She'd told Emilio she needed to check in with her editor. Reies's pretext for going was that he wanted to check out some details for the upcoming Santa Fe rodeo, as he and some of his men would be performing in it.

Now on her way toward Detective Captain George Wainwright's office, she exchanged greetings with a couple of the officers.

"Libby, I thought you were on vacation," Kay York called out, as her blue eyes speculatively roamed over Reies. "Couldn't stay away from work, huh?"

"Just here for a visit."

While her captain knew what Libby was up to, few of her co-workers did. She waved at the woman and kept going.

Captain Wainwright was standing outside his office, talking to one of the other detectives, and he excused himself when he saw Libby. After giving Reies a quick once-over, he inclined his graying head, indicating that they should follow him inside. He closed the door and propped his lanky body on the edge of his desk as Libby made the introductions.

"You sure you want to talk in front of this guy?" the captain asked bluntly. His bushy eyebrows drew together above serious eyes.

"Then it is about Wayne?" Libby grasped Reies's arm. The captain's obvious surprise made her aware of her action. She let go immediately and sat in a chair opposite her superior while an expressionless Reies remained standing. "We're in this together, for better or worse."

George Wainwright pulled a folder from the stack on his desk. "One of the state patrolmen found something that got overlooked when Wayne's car was searched after the murder. A flyer was caught in the springs under the driver's seat. John Hernandez got in touch with me," he said, mentioning the police lieutenant in charge of the investigation. "He sent us an evidence photo out of courtesy to you, even though he hates like hell what you've gotten yourself into."

"At least it's more than he's been doing the past few weeks," Libby muttered.

Though not officially declared closed, the investigation had been put on hold for lack of witnesses and leads. That's why she'd gone undercover herself.

Wainwright pulled an eight-by-ten photo from the folder and passed it to her. Reies leaned over her shoulder, and together they studied the picture of a handbill declaring a meeting of the Coalition of Citizens for Free City-States that had been held in Sidewinder a few days before Wayne had been shot. Centered at the bottom of the page was a familiar looking logo made up of an intertwined C and S. Someone—her brother?—had circled it several times. Libby handed the photo to Reies.

"I thought the Coalition was dead to all intents and purposes," Wainwright said.

Reies spoke for the first time since entering police headquarters. "Not to the citizens of Sidewinder, or to the people in adjoining towns. Unrest is growing again." He handed the photo back to Libby. "Johnnie Madrigal seems to be the man who's stirring up all the trouble."

Libby's eyes were drawn back to the circled logo. "Johnnie must the one," she said, remembering where she'd seen the unusual combination of letters, "if that expensive piece of jewelry he wears is any indication. It's a chain with a heavy gold medallion that bears this logo. What exactly is this Coalition?"

"One of the organizations that's been trying to regain communal lands that the government has stolen from the people," Reies explained. "The U.S. Forest Service claimed those lands, despite grants given to the towns and villages when this area of the country was under Spanish rule."

Knowing New Mexican lands had only been governed by the United States since 1846, Libby said, "More than a hundred years ago. Why has it taken the people so long to try to get them back?"

"The people protested for decades," Wainwright answered. "But the land-grant movement didn't really start up until the early sixties, when economic conditions worsened. Their farms couldn't compete with the larger ones in California or the Midwest. And at the same time, the U.S. Forest Service and the New Mexico Game and Fish Department started coming down hard on anyone who hunted, fished or let their livestock graze in the national forests."

"So the people in the surrounding villages were pushed into an economic trap," Libby said.

Wainwright nodded. "Can't say as I blame them for fighting back. The problem is that they don't always do it peacefully. I remember that bloody incident—"

The telephone's shrill ring interrupted the conversation. While the captain took the call, Libby studied again the unusually rendered letters in the photo. "Why C and S? Coalition and Sidewinder?"

"That would be my guess," Reies replied. "I've seen the symbol a few times, but never really thought about it."

Their business finished, Libby waited until Wainwright got off the telephone. Then she rose and slipped the photograph back into the manila folder, which she planned to take with her.

"Thanks, Captain. I have a feeling this is going to lead us to something important."

"Be careful, Libby. I don't want to lose my top detective sergeant."

"I'll remember you said that around promotion time."

As they prepared to leave, Wainwright fixed his gaze on Reies. "Both of you be careful."

"Like the lady said, we're in this together, for better or worse. We'll watch each other's back. In my opinion, we make one hell of a team."

As LIBBY HEADED the car toward the Blue Mesa gallery, where they would bring her mother up to date, Reies thought about the words he'd spoken so easily: one hell of a team. The conviction went beyond this investigation.

Though he'd never consciously ruled out the possibility that he might fall for another woman someday, that he might even marry and have a couple of kids, putting Libby Reardon Tate in the likely category was ridiculous. She was an outsider, he reminded himself, and that was trouble. Well, he'd been in trouble before and had always made it through all right. What made him think this time might be different?

He glanced at Libby and saw a woman who was at once vulnerable, tough, compassionate and brave.

The answer was obvious.

They approached the Canyon Road address. The dust-colored facades and the low skyline of the oldest capital in the country were constants. City ordinance prohibited buildings more than three stories high. Santa Fe's architecture was unique to the area—a combination of Spanish influence and Indian pueblo. Practical builders had devised a weatherproof adobe imitation of steel, brick and cement for new structures.

They pulled up in front of Blue Mesa. Without a word, Libby left the car and raced into the gallery ahead of him. A man was browsing through the shop, a pretty, blond saleswoman on his trail. Standing next to a counter, Gloria Reardon looked up from some brochures. Libby flew into her arms for a hug, then introduced Reies and quickly and quietly explained his presence.

Gloria eyed him uncomfortably, her gaze immediately settling on the knife he wore strapped to his belt. "Let's go in the back. Holly, take over for a few minutes, would you?"

The blonde waved. Reies followed the two women into an office cluttered with paper and files. While Gloria cleared stacks of folders from a couple of chairs so they could all sit, Libby brought her up to date on the investigation—minus the cactus incident.

"Mother, I know you can't help worrying," said Libby when she'd finished.

Reies wondered how she could reassure a woman who'd lost her husband and son that her daughter could take on the town that had killed them and win.

"But remember I'm trained for this work, and I'm not as impulsive as Wayne was," she continued. "Have confidence in me."

"You're asking a lot," Gloria told her daughter, while she studied Reies with obvious disapproval.

He surprised himself by making the first peace offering. "Your daughter's not alone in this anymore."

That fact clearly agitated the woman. Her breath was shallow, and she clutched and unclutched her fingers as she settled her hands in her lap. Reies could imagine the thoughts whirling under the cloud of gray-dusted dark curls—first and foremost, that her husband had died in *his* bed.

Reies went on. "You're wondering why I agreed to help your daughter, considering who I am."

Eyes of a faded cactus-green reflected wariness. "Why don't you tell me?"

"I'm tired of running from the truth."

While Libby's expression registered surprise, his admission seemed to soften the worry on Gloria Reardon's face.

She took a deep breath and asked, "What if you don't like the truth you find?"

"I won't try to change it," he promised, "no matter how I feel personally."

"I would like to believe that."

"Believe it, Mother," said Libby. "I do."

Hearing those words from Libby's own lips made Reies feel as if a warm wave of Gulf water had washed over him. She had given him the gift of her trust. He wouldn't let her down.

Libby smiled as she noted a glow in Reies's eyes. She'd said the right thing then, had convinced him of something she'd been sure he would never accept from an outsider. She thought he might even be willing to give her his trust, as well. Suddenly aware of her mother's close scrutiny, she grew uncomfortable and rose.

"We have to get going, Mom, not that I wouldn't like to spend more time with you."

"When this is over..." Gloria's words trailed off uncertainly.

"When it's over, I'll be back," Libby promised firmly.

They left the office and entered the gallery, which was one of the largest in Santa Fe. Among the oils and prints hung modern fiber art and wool rugs with traditional Navajo designs. Several display cases were filled with smaller, equally interesting works, some sculpture and carvings, but mostly wearable accessories and fine jewelry that integrated native elements with modern ones.

Libby always enjoyed poking through the gallery, finding treasures she would love to own but never could afford. She didn't make enough money for luxuries, and despite Harry's insistence, had refused alimony.

About to hug her mother before leaving, she stopped short when her eyes were drawn to an unusual portrait. It was of a man who looked like a young Bobby Aguirre. Coming close, she checked the identification card:

Tough
Artist: Victor Duprey
1975

"Well, look at that," Reies said. "Bobby made the hall of fame."

"As seen by Victor." Libby was disturbed by the picture.

The artist had seen a repressed violence far more savage and frightening than she had seen in Pilar's brother. The man on canvas looked capable of anything... even murder. While the portrait and the immediate background were realistic, the more distant background became increasingly abstract. The edges of a boarded-up jail behind Bobby became muted, with desert flora and fauna woven into the picture, so that the effect was a painted tapestry.

"You know the subject?" Gloria asked her daughter.

"Yes. And the artist."

Libby studied the surrounding paintings. The few pieces of Victor's work displayed were also realistic portraits of compelling people: an old woman shrouded in black against a crumbling adobe church; an Indian youth in front of an abandoned pueblo; a grizzled anglo, his broken-down trailer behind him. All had a similar tapestrylike background representing the New Mexican wilderness.

"I've never met Victor Duprey personally, but he's made this gallery some money over the years," Gloria said. "Of course he doesn't sell as well as he used to, but his agent had promised a batch of new works in the near future. If his talent has matured, he'll make us and himself a small fortune."

"Interesting," Libby said, pulling her gaze back to the portrait of Bobby. "Well, we'd better get going. Reies still has some business he has to take care of before we head for the ranch." The women hugged, and Libby followed Reies back out to the car.

"I hope you don't mind if we follow business with dinner," he said, sliding into the passenger seat. "Did I ever tell you I'm mean on an empty stomach?"

"Just because you missed one meal . . ." she teased. "All right. We'll stop for dinner."

Actually the prospect sounded appealing. Libby had to admit that she was looking forward to spending some noninvestigative time in Reies Coulter's company.

KEEN EYES GLANCED around to make sure the grounds were clear, before looking up to the *viga* next to the door. On this protruding wooden surface lay the key that would open the adobe structure, temporary home of supposed reporter Libby Tate. No one else in sight. A gloved hand reached up and felt around. Leather met metal.

Photojournalist—a good cover for a cop.

This one had been as careless as the last.

Unlocking the door and slipping into the bungalow, the intruder carefully placed a leather case on the coffee table and looked around, wondering where to begin. What information had she already secured? What might she have passed on? Only searching the place thoroughly would tell.

There was adequate time for that.

Libby Tate was the one who had run out of time.

NOT ONLY DID Reies persuade Libby to have dinner in Santa Fe, but he talked her into having a drink after-

ward. She didn't take much convincing. She needed to
relax, to unwind from the tension of the past few days.

Aptly enough, they found a place after dinner called
Rodeo Blues that was dark and smoke-filled and decorated like a bar right out of the Old West. Dressed in a
blue chambray work shirt, jeans and broad-brimmed
black hat, Reies looked more like one of the bartenders
than one of the customers, whom she judged to be mostly
tourists.

She and Reies slid into a booth at the back of the
room, away from the stage, where a country-and-western
singer accompanied himself on the guitar. Reies took off
his hat and dropped it onto the padded seat. They'd only
just made themselves comfortable when a waitress in
cowgirl costume showed up and took their order for two
beers.

Listening to the music, they sat in quiet companionship, until Libby noticed Reies massaging his right thigh
with both hands.

"Recovering from a sprain?" She grinned. "Been
thrown off one of your prize horses lately?"

"An old football injury."

"Football in Sidewinder? Hah!" Libby realized he was
trying to make light of the situation. She could tell he
wanted to skip the subject, but she persisted. "What really happened?"

Surprisingly enough, he explained, "A knife fight
when I was a teenager. The doc told me that I would
never walk normally again, that I would limp. So much
for professional opinions."

Sidewinder, a town without a conscience.

She forced herself not to shudder, to keep her tone
light. "You mean," she said, recalling the slight limp

she'd occasionally noticed, "so much for your determination to prove him wrong. Right?"

"You could be at that." The corners of his mustache lifted. "You're right about a lot of things. Sometimes the muscles act up when I've been on a horse all day."

But he hadn't been on a horse more than a couple of hours that morning. "Or when you're under a lot of stress."

The waitress arrived with the beer, giving him an excuse to avoid answering. He didn't have to. Libby knew he was just as human as she. A little tougher, perhaps, and a little rough around the edges, but human. This investigation couldn't be any easier on Reies than it was on her.

She realized they must have been thinking along similar lines when he said, "I appreciate what you told your mother." He took a swig of beer from his mug. "About believing in me, I mean. Even though we made that pact, I figured you didn't trust me farther than you could spit."

Libby laughed. "I can spit pretty far when I really try." She placed her hand over his free one. The gesture felt good, natural. "I didn't trust you completely, not at first. But you won me over. Must be that good-humored nature of yours."

"Sorry if I've been hardheaded."

"Never apologize for what or who you are. Not with me. Not with anyone."

Her hand was suddenly enveloped as Reies cradled it between callused palms. "Thanks. I trust you, too."

A glow of warmth surged through Libby. "Even though I'm an outsider?"

"I wish you could understand about that."

"I can only guess what it must have been like to grow up in a town where you couldn't even trust your friends. Still, you left, and you were gone for a long time."

"But I came back. Some never do."

"Like your mother's sister?"

"How do you know about my Aunt Manuela?"

"Your grandfather told me."

"My aunt found a way out when she was young, and she's never come back, not even to see us. Mother visits Manuela's home often, sometimes spends several days at a time in Santa Fe, but Grandfather rarely comes into the city."

"So it's almost as if he's lost three children rather than two. How sad."

"We all lose someone we love, sometimes brutally, sometimes by neglect. It hurts either way."

Reies let go of her hand and cradled his beer mug instead. His face was in shadow, but from what she could see of his expression, he was in pain. Was he thinking of Pilar?

"Of course I don't even remember my father," he went on, the twist surprising her. "I was only two when he abandoned us and sent some cheap shyster from Santa Fe to the ranch with the divorce papers. Alex Coulter was a drifter who was working for my grandfather when he got my mother pregnant. She was only seventeen. Maybe he figured he had no choice but to marry her—maybe he was greedy for the Velasquez land. But I guess he figured he wouldn't get his hands on it, because one day he walked out on us both and never came back. Maybe he never meant to stay at all. He certainly never gave a damn about me or Mother."

That had probably been the most revealing thing Reies had ever told her about himself. No wonder his trust was so hard won. Libby wanted to touch him again, to hold him, to soften the hurt. Maybe they could do that for each other.

"Even when people stay," Libby said carefully, "it's not necessarily for the best. That's why I left Harry."

"Why did you marry him in the first place?"

"He was...charismatic. I was young, easily charmed. The first couple of years of our marriage was an extended honeymoon. But when the honeymoon was over, there was nothing left. The only thing Harry was willing to share *was* his charisma. And his money, of course. I never cared about that. I just wanted to make a real future with someone who loved me enough to share himself."

"Maybe you were asking too much."

Libby knew Reies might be talking about his own trouble with being open. "Harry thought so." She lifted her mug and took a sip of beer while making comparisons. The two men were so different in some ways, so alike in others. Unfortunately, the alike was the important part. "I thought I deserved more, so I got out while I could." And she didn't need to involve herself in a similar situation. "Let's get back to the ranch."

The brief closeness they'd shared was severed as surely as if cut by a knife. Reies paid the waitress and picked up his hat. Suddenly in a hurry to put some distance between them, Libby started for the door, knowing he would follow.

Libby at the wheel, they drove back to the ranch in silence, occupied by their own thoughts. Libby tried to concentrate on the investigation, on the possible link between the Coalition and the murders. Her failure to do so wasn't surprising, not with Reies sitting so close. She told herself they had been drawn together by unusual circumstances. Emotional circumstances. That's all there was between them.

Why didn't she believe that?

The trip back to Sidewinder and the ranch seemed to take forever. Without thinking, Libby whipped the car past the main house. Three-quarters of the way to her bungalow, she realized her mistake and slammed on the brakes.

"Keep going. I can walk back. I need the fresh air."

Reies didn't sound particularly friendly. Or particularly anything else for that matter. His tone was neutral. Sensing his mood, Libby stepped on the accelerator. He would be wearing that blank expression again—the one she was beginning to hate.

She swung the car off the road next to the bungalow. Stepping out, she said, "I guess I'll see you in the morning."

"Right. In the morning," he agreed tersely, his back already to her.

Trying not to let Reies, or her own feelings, get to her, Libby removed the key from her pocket. She stepped inside the living room, flipped on the light and advanced into the bedroom, shrugging out of her cotton jacket as she did so. She threw it on a chair, then removed her shoulder holster and set it on the dresser next to the camera bag.

Libby continued undressing, removing first her boots and socks, then her pants. Unbuttoning her shirt front, she walked back to the dresser and stared down at the camera bag. The zipper wasn't pulled quite shut. And hadn't she left the case front side facing out toward the bed?

Worried now, she opened the bag and checked inside. Certain she hadn't left the zoom lens upside-down in its protective slot, as it now was, Libby swallowed hard and tried not to panic. Someone had tampered with the camera bag. Someone had been in her rooms, looking through her things. Had that person found what he or she was looking for? She removed the camera, lens and flash unit, undid the Velcro tabs and lifted the false bottom. The envelope was still inside.

But had it been found?

Had her cover been blown?

Knowing that to assume the pictures had been overlooked would be dangerous, Libby decided not to take any chances. She withdrew the Beretta from its holster and moved toward the bed. She probably wouldn't sleep even with protection at hand, but she'd feel better.

Pulling back the covers so she could place the gun under her pillow, Libby froze in shock while adrenaline sluiced through her.

The rattle was distinct and unnerving.

And so was the blast that followed.

HALFWAY BACK to the main house, Reies was stopped by the discharge of a gun coming from the bungalow.

"Libby!"

He was already running, heart pounding in fear. His labored breathing drowned out any further sounds that might be coming from her quarters. Who had fired that shot? No one came dashing out the front door....

Not bothering to find the key, he used his considerable strength to break through the locked door.

"Reies?"

Her voice was faint, weak. Withdrawing his knife from its sheath, Reies ran across the living room without knowing what to expect. He stopped in the bedroom doorway. Gun hanging from a limp hand, Libby stood staring down in shock, her skin white in contrast to the rattler whose blood stained the sheets.

"A diamondback! Thank God you shot it before..."

His voice trailed off as she lifted her head and he saw the truth in her frightened, confused eyes. "Where?" he asked, rushing forward.

"My leg."

Without ceremony, he grabbed the dead snake and flung it against the wall.

"Stay calm. You'll be all right," he said, knowing panicking could kill her. *Or kill her faster,* a small voice whispered. He ignored the voice, took the weapon from her nerveless hand and placed both the gun and his knife on the nightstand. He inspected the bitten area, several inches above her knee on her left thigh. Even now the tender flesh was swelling and turning purple. He could only hope the viper hadn't nicked a major artery. Thank God she wasn't hysterical. The calmer he could keep her, the better.

"Let's get you on the bed where I can take care of you."

Reies helped Libby lie down slowly, making sure the afflicted area remained lower than her heart by keeping her left foot on the floor. He tried to make her comfortable, even though she was almost lying in the snake's blood.

She turned her head away from the sight. "It stings," she whispered.

"I know it does, but we'll get you through this." He brushed the curls from her forehead. Her skin was cool and clammy. "Just hold on and stay calm. It's very important that you're quiet."

"I know." She licked her lips. "I'm trying. But a diamondback..."

"It's dead and I'm here," he murmured reassuringly. "I'll take care of you."

Reies withdrew his belt and used it as a tourniquet on her upper thigh, making sure he left enough room to slide a finger between the leather and her flesh. The venom had to be prevented from flowing to her heart, but he didn't want to cut off her circulation entirely and chance her losing a leg to gangrene in the process.

"Do you carry a snake-bite kit in your car?"

"The trunk. Keys are in my jacket."

"Don't move," he cautioned again as he found the keys and ran for the front door. "I'll be right back."

Thank God Libby had the sense to carry a kit in her vehicle. Not everyone in desert country did. If he'd had to run back to his Bronco... He didn't want to foster anything but positive thoughts. She would come through this. He kept repeating that to himself. But by the time he reentered the bedroom and dropped the kit on the nightstand, he could tell the venom was starting to do its work. Her breathing was shallow, and when he checked her pulse it was rapid but weak.

"Reies—"

"Shh, don't talk. Save your strength to fight the venom." He was already opening the kit, pulling out sealed antiseptic packets. "This will hurt a little," he told her, guessing she'd remain calmer if he kept talking, if she knew what to expect. "First, I'm going to clean the bite."

Ripping open a packet, he lightly swabbed the swollen area with the wet pad. The slight sound of protest she made pierced his heart. Her lids fluttered, shuttering her eyes. He used another antiseptic pad on the razor-sharp tip of his knife.

"I'm going to loosen the belt for a moment." He had to remember to keep track of time so he could release the tourniquet every ten minutes for the next few hours.

"I hate knives," she whispered, obviously knowing what would come next.

He refastened the belt. "Don't watch. Think of something else."

"Heard any good jokes?"

"There's the one about the desperado who fell for a lady."

Libby didn't answer. He picked up the knife and he made a small incision at the first fang mark. He winced at her hissing sound. She grabbed at a pillow with her left hand.

"That's it. Hold on." He made a parallel cut along the other mark. "Now I'll get as much poison out of your system as I can."

But not with the defective syringe he found in the kit— probably a pinhole leak in the bulb. Tossing it, he put his mouth over the incisions. Careful not to swallow any of the venom-tainted blood, he sucked until his mouth was full. He spit out the fluid and repeated the procedure several times, until he was certain that he'd done all he could.

Reies realized Libby had been watching him. The look in her eyes made him feel odd.

"Thanks," she whispered. "You probably saved my life."

Not yet, he hadn't. "You can owe me one."

He released the belt and went into the bathroom where he flushed out his mouth, then wet and soaped a wash rag. Tightening the tourniquet again, he cleansed and bound her wounds. If Libby felt any pain, she gave no indication. Her lids had lowered again and her breathing sounded even more labored and shallow. He could hardly find her pulse, but when he did, its speed alarmed him.

He turned back to the kit for the antivenin, hoping the shot would take care of the venom already in her system. Now all he could do was call the doctor. That meant he had to leave Libby for more than a few minutes, something he didn't want to do at this critical point. If only he'd had a telephone installed in the bungalow.

After giving her the injection, Reies tried to make Libby more comfortable. He found a clean sheet, folded it in half and spread the material over the red stain. Then he helped get her more fully into bed. He propped her left leg in a more comfortable position on a pillow-covered end table that he dragged in from the living room. By the time he pulled the quilt over her to keep her warm, she was shaking with fever—and she was obviously a little out of it.

That had to be the reason she weakly asked, "Heard the one about the lady who fell for the desperado?"

Reies smiled reassuringly, while inside, he fought panic. If Libby didn't make it through this...

Sidewinder would have claimed a third Reardon.

And he would have lost someone he cared about, maybe loved.

Reies renewed his vow to find the murderer.

That diamondback hadn't crawled into Libby's bed by itself. Someone had put it there in an attempt to kill her. But who had seen through her cover? While he cleaned up the end table and got rid of the rattler's remains, Reies went over everything he knew.

He filled a bowl with water and set it on the nightstand. Then he sat on the edge of the bed alternating his time between seeing to the tourniquet and trying to make Libby more comfortable by bathing her face and neck with the cool liquid. Halfway through his vigil she woke up for a moment. Her eyes looked glassy, feverish, as if she didn't know what was going on, as if she didn't recognize him.

Yet she reached out and touched his cheek. Reies couldn't help himself. He covered the back of her hand and turned his face so he could kiss her palm. Her responding smile was heartbreaking. He could see the effort it cost her. As her arm went limp and her lashes fluttered closed, she whispered something so softly he could barely make out the word "love." She didn't know what she was saying, of course, probably didn't even know who he was.

He checked her pulse. It seemed stronger and slower. Or maybe it was wishful thinking.

Reies didn't know how long he'd been taking care of her when he heard a scraping noise at the front door. He grabbed her gun and spun off the bed, but when he cautiously approached the other room, he heard a familiar, puzzled voice muttering in Spanish.

"Luis."

The *vaquero* stood in the doorway inspecting the damage Reies had done to the hinges and the frame when he'd forced his way in. "I was taking a walk and noticed this door was a little crooked. You did this, gringo?"

"Someone left a present in Libby's bed. A diamondback."

"Mother of God! Is she all right?"

"I've done what I could. I think the antivenin is working. But I couldn't leave her to call the doctor."

"I'm on my way," Luis said, moving off. Over his shoulder, he called, "But this time, gringo, you owe me an explanation."

Divulging the whole truth would be a small price to pay for this man's help, Reies decided. Libby needed to be guarded at all times, and sadly enough, Luis was now the only person on the ranch he could trust.

"I DON'T NEED a bodyguard," Libby protested the next afternoon when she realized Reies was moving his things into her bungalow.

"Hell if you don't." He hung up a handful of clothes next to hers in the closet. "The doc said you were to stay in bed today except for the necessities."

Frustrated, if still weak, Libby wasn't in the mood to be coddled. "He also said that, except for having a sore leg, I would probably be back to normal by tomorrow."

"How do you know? You were still out of it when he got here in the middle of the night."

"I even remember *when* he said it—between the tetanus and antibiotic shots he gave me. All right. I'll take the day to recuperate without making a—"

"At least two days," he insisted. "And after that, you're going back to Santa Fe."

"No!"

"I won't let you take a chance with your life."

"That's not your decision to make. Besides, I put my life on the line every day I do my job."

"But not where I have to watch."

He couldn't quite hide the emotion accompanying his words, though he tried. Finally he pulled the blank mask into position. Why? If he cared . . .

"I'm not leaving, Reies."

He cursed loudly and whipped away from her. "I'll be back in a while. Don't get out of bed before then. Keep that gun out of sight, but where you can reach it if necessary."

He strode through the living room and outside, slamming the newly repaired front door behind him. If he wasn't more careful, he would break the thing off its hinges again.

Libby sighed. Why couldn't Reies just admit he loved her? She was sure that's what he'd been trying to tell her the night before. And he'd been so gentle—smoothing the curls from her forehead, kissing her palm, whispering encouragement. Or maybe the fever had made her imagine those things. But she knew for certain that she'd told him she loved him.

Feeling her face flame, Libby tried to sink farther under the covers, as if she could hide from her own self. The change in position made her groan. Though the swelling had abated somewhat, the abused flesh throbbed every time she moved. At least that pain was purely physical.

It hurt far less than the suspicion that she might have made a fool of herself in Reies's eyes.

VICTOR DUPREY WAITED until Reies was inside the house before he approached the bungalow. For the past several hours, the artist had been walking around as if he was ready to explode—as if Libby Tate was something more than a reporter to him. Victor wanted to keep out of Reies's way. Far better to see the woman alone.

He knocked loudly at the front door.

"Who is it?"

"Victor."

Libby hesitated a few seconds before saying, "Come in."

Entering, he noticed the repairs to the doorjamb. And the top hinge had been moved a few inches higher. The original holes where the screws had been ripped loose were still ragged. He raised a surprised brow. He hadn't known whether or not to believe the story that Reies had literally broken down the door. Seeing the evidence, Victor wished he could have been there.

"Victor?"

"I'm here to bring sunshine into your day." He quickly joined Libby. "That is, if some of the local flora will cheer you up." With a flourish, he presented a bouquet of wildflowers.

She smiled. "How thoughtful. I'm afraid I can't get up to find a vase or put them in water."

"Doctor's orders?"

"Dr. Coulter's." She looked at the nightstand. "Hmm. You could use this water pitcher."

"Great improvisation. Shows a creative streak."

"If I have one, it's well hidden. I barely passed my required art classes in school."

Separating the small handful of flowers, Victor began arranging them in the pitcher, one at a time. "What happened last night must have changed your plans about finishing your article."

"Not really. But since I'm slowed down, I'll have to stay longer than I first thought."

So either Libby wasn't afraid, or she was hiding it well. He had to give her credit for guts. "I've just put the finishing touches on Emilio's portrait." As an artist, he couldn't help but be drawn to a fascinating, challenging subject, no matter how dangerous. "Does that give me the opportunity to start that painting of you?"

"I'm afraid not. I'm supposed to rest, and as soon as I'm up and around, I have to finish my research. But I'll be looking forward to seeing the portrait of Mr. Velasquez at his birthday celebration."

"You think you'll be well enough to attend?"

"The doctor says so."

"Which one?"

Libby laughed. "The one with the degree in medicine. Dr. Coulter thinks I should pack it in and go home."

"Maybe you should." Having finished the flower arrangement, Victor faced Libby and watched carefully for her reaction. "Santa Fe is much more civilized—and safer—than Sidewinder."

Her smile froze. "Are you trying to give me some kind of warning?"

"A friendly one. Snakes don't usually crawl into people's beds any more than cactus grows under saddles. Someone around here doesn't like you and has been expressing that fact rather eloquently."

"You wouldn't know who, would you?"

Fingering a silver charm that hung from his neck chain, Victor wondered if Reies really had shot the rattler as he'd claimed. Libby seemed quite capable of doing the job herself. "If I knew, don't you think I would have told you or Reies?" And before she could pursue the subject, he added, "I'll leave you to rest now."

"Thanks for the flowers." Her steady gaze was speculative. "I'm pleased you stopped by."

"So am I."

Victor smiled as he turned away. He'd gotten what he'd come for, hadn't he?

Chapter Eight

"Waiting for me, Mother?" Reies asked, overnight bag and rifle in hand. He'd just gathered the last things he wanted from his bedroom in the main house.

Inez stopped pacing the length of the living room and stared at her son, her expression odd. "Yes. Waiting..." Her black eyes lowered to the rifle in his hand. "You're determined to be this woman's watchdog?"

"Someone has to be with Libby. What if something else happens to her?"

"Take her back to Santa Fe. Do it now." Her hands were clasped together unnaturally, her lovely face set in a worried frown, so that she appeared closer to her true age. "Let her own people protect her."

"It sounds as if you finally believe that rattlesnake didn't wind up in her bed by accident."

She didn't look at him directly. "No one here would do such a wicked thing."

Then why had the incident happened directly after someone had listened in to Libby's telephone conversation? She'd told him about the click she'd heard.

"Why do you think Libby needs protection?" Reies asked.

"I didn't..."

Inez's voice dropped off and she twisted her hands even as she drew herself into the rigid stance so like his grandfather's. "Why are you so nervous, Mother?"

"I have a feeling . . . it would be better for everyone if Miss Tate left."

"Be more specific. Better for who? You? Grandfather? Nick—"

"For the family," Inez interrupted. "This woman will bring us trouble." As if she'd said too much, she backed off. "But as usual, your needs come before ours. Go, then. Make your bed guarding the outsider."

Since there was no use continuing the argument, Reies left the house. His needs. His mother's way of reminding him that he'd abandoned his family. She'd pleaded for him to stay all those years ago, but he'd been determined. Sometimes he felt she still hadn't forgiven him.

This situation was different, and so was the way his mother was acting. Disturbed. As if she knew something she wasn't telling. She'd been quick to interrupt when he'd mentioned Nick. His half brother had seemed easily irritated lately, but Reies had assumed Pilar had been getting to Nick with her restlessness and constant demands. Now he wasn't so sure.

Not Nick. Please, not his brother.

But who? Which of those he loved was capable of murder?

Feeling as if his stomach were filled with lead, Reies kept on toward the bungalow, just as he'd keep on looking until he found the murderer.

DESPITE HER SPEEDY RECOVERY Libby found herself a virtual prisoner for the rest of the day. Reies and Luis took turns playing jailer. At least she enjoyed Luis's shifts. The cheerful man kept her entertained with wild and humorous anecdotes.

Reies, on the other hand, had been unpredictable from the moment he'd walked into the bungalow carrying his overnight bag and rifle—not that she'd helped him relax. As edgy as he was, Libby found herself taking her frustration out on him, the one person who least deserved that kind of treatment from her. She realized she had to get away from her self-appointed bodyguards or go crazy.

And so, early the next afternoon, she encouraged Luis to leave her alone long enough to get them both lunch. Without Reies's knowledge or approval, she intended to continue this investigation on her own. She waited until the *vaquero* was out of sight, then she got up and left the bungalow. She jumped in her car and set off for Sidewinder, with hopes of finding Johnnie Madrigal for that "interview" he'd promised her.

Afraid that someone might try to stop her before she could get to town, Libby put the Jaguar through its paces and didn't slow the vehicle until she could see the two-block main street. Johnnie's truck was nowhere in sight, so she stopped in the cafe hoping Ada would know where to find him.

Luckily for her, the cafe was nearly empty, and she was the only customer at the counter. They could talk in relative privacy. Ada seemed shocked to see her.

"I thought you tangled with a rattler the other night."

"I did. I'm surprised you heard about it."

"Are you kidding, honey? Everyone in town has heard about it."

Wanting to change the subject, Libby said, "How about a cup of your coffee?"

"Sure." As Ada poured, she peered suspiciously at Libby. "Does Reies know you're out and around?"

"Forget about Reies. I'm interested in finding Johnnie Madrigal."

The blonde lowered her voice to a tense whisper as she pushed the coffee at Libby. "Honey, are you crazy? You don't want to get anywhere near that slime."

"He'll make interesting copy."

Ada's blue eyes glared at her. "I get the feeling you're not being straight with me."

"Why would you think that?"

"That bad luck you've been having—"

"Everyone gets their share sooner or later."

"When a person gets more than their share, it starts to look planned."

Libby made a final plea in a low, but firm, voice. "Ada, I've got to find Johnnie. Can you help me, or should I ask elsewhere?"

The blonde's eyebrows rose, and from the way she shook her head, Libby didn't think she would help her. She dug in her pocket to find change for the coffee, then flipped it on the counter.

"All right, Libby, but you be careful." Ada looked around furtively before bending close to her. "Johnnie is probably over at Victor's place having his portrait painted. Been bragging about it all week."

Two for the price of one. Maybe three if Bobby was with his warped companion. *Three against one* was probably a more apt way of putting it. Libby's mouth suddenly went dry, and she wondered if she was being a clever cop or a dumb one. There was safety in numbers, she assured herself. If one of the men was guilty of murder, he wouldn't want to tip his hand in front of the others. Then again, maybe he wouldn't care.

Disregarding the possible danger to herself, she asked, "How do I get there?"

Reluctantly Ada gave her directions. Libby thanked her and left, all the while aware of the woman's heartfelt concern and burning curiosity. With any luck, she would have some answers soon . . . and be alive to share them.

Victor's place was located in an isolated area a couple of miles outside of town. Libby hesitated when she got to the gravel road that would take her southeast up into the hills. Her palms were damp on the steering wheel despite the cool weather. Maybe she should go back and find Reies and bring him along. Pride prevented her from turning the car around. She went on alone.

After traveling a mile or so, she found the rutted dirt track Ada had told her about. It led straight to Victor's modest home, which looked much like the abandoned adobe buildings overlooking the road coming into Sidewinder. Only this house had been well cared for, from the aqua walls with turquoise trim to the ornately carved front door, decorated with a traditional string of dried red chilies.

Stopping the car next to Victor's truck, Libby took a good look around. No satellite dish. No poles and lines for telephone or electricity. A generator-operated pump at an outdoor well. So, the artist did live the simple life.

As she got out of her car, she realized no other vehicles were in sight. But beyond the house, a saddled palomino was hitched to a split-rail fence, while inside the pasture, an Appaloosa ran free. A movement from the corner of her eye caught her attention, and she turned to see Victor dressed in paint-spattered jeans and shirt waving her over from the front of a small barn.

"Why, Libby, so that was you driving up," he called as she approached his outdoor work area. "To what do

I owe this pleasure? Have you changed your mind about sitting for me?"

"Actually I came to find Johnnie."

She limped slightly as she moved toward him, all the while trying to see beyond his easel. Neither Bobby nor Doug was in sight, a fact that allowed her to relax a little. She surreptitiously dried her palms on the back of her jeans. Posed on a stool, Johnnie's black silk shirt open almost to the waist, her quarry displayed several gold chains, the most prominent of which was the one with the Coalition medallion.

"Johnnie suggested I might like to interview him," she explained, pleased that her voice sounded natural, even friendly. "Since I had some free time—"

"Victor's doin' my portrait."

"So I heard." Stopping next to the artist who resumed mixing paints on his palette, she told him, "I've seen some of your work besides the portrait of Mr. Velasquez. I was impressed."

"Thank you, and welcome to my humble home, Libby. If you can be patient a moment, I'll get you a cool drink."

"No, thanks. I'm not thirsty." Libby glanced back at the house that was indeed humble. "Your place is charming, Victor. But since you're so successful, why in the world would you choose to live so primitively?"

"I'm one of the people, Libby, not an outsider," Victor told her with considerable pride. At the moment, he was working on flesh tones, adding contour and depth to his subject's face. "The natives have accepted me, made me one of them, a privilege few other anglos have earned in this area. I don't need a fancy environment. Nature is my element—a harsh but beautiful land with vital people, who make exciting subjects. What more could an artist ask for?"

"I stand corrected."

"Hey, Red," Johnnie called impatiently, shifting on his stool. "I thought you came because you wanna interview *me*."

"So I did. The portrait—whose idea was it?"

"I choose my own subjects," Victor stated.

"I thought Inez commissioned you to paint her father."

"I make certain exceptions. For friends."

"My portrait's gonna make Victor famous," Johnnie boasted, moving again.

Libby wondered how Victor could get him to hold still long enough to capture him on canvas. She studied the work in progress. The entire piece was lightly sketched in down to the last flower and lizard, but so far, only the likeness of Johnnie had felt the artist's brush.

"It'll be a fine work," she said.

"But it's me that's gonna sell it." Johnnie thumped his chest for emphasis and jumped up. "When the Coalition is the number-one story in the news, everyone will know Johnnie Madrigal and want a copy."

"Johnnie, sit on that stool and don't move!" Victor's tone conveyed his annoyance. His blond brows pulled in a frown, he faced Libby. "I'm sorry, but could I ask you to postpone your interview? You get him wound up about this Coalition business, and he'll never settle down for me."

"Of course. I understand."

She studied the portrait more closely. Victor had captured not only the cruelty of Johnnie's mouth, but the ruthlessness she'd seen in the hoodlum's eyes as well. Victor Duprey was truly a brilliant artist.

"I'm sorry I bothered you, Victor, but I'm delighted I had the opportunity to see your new work. This reveals amazing depth of character." Shifting focus, she inspected the background. "By the way, what's the building you've sketched behind Johnnie? That doesn't look like your barn."

"That's the county courthouse," Johnnie volunteered, in motion once more. "Victor and I figured—"

"Johnnie!"

"All right, all right. I'm sitting still."

"Interesting," Libby murmured, wondering why Victor had chosen the background. "I'll leave you to your work, Victor."

Already concentrating on the canvas, the artist didn't reply.

"Another time, Red," Johnnie called, for once sounding gleeful rather than threatening.

Libby climbed into her car, frustrated that she hadn't been able to get more concrete information, yet satisfied that she'd at least made a start without Reies's help. She'd get back to Johnnie within the next day or two. While speeding back toward town and on to the ranch, she admitted the physical effort had tired her and she was glad to return.

Until she realized Reies was waiting for her, that was.

He was sprawled across the couch facing her, as she entered. Two trays of food sat on the coffee table in front of him. Her stomach growled, reminding her that she'd skipped lunch and it was now closer to the dinner hour. She eyed the food longingly, doubting she'd have a chance to eat without a lecture.

Reies confirmed the fact when he said, "I thought you agreed to rest."

"I did. Yesterday."

Libby tried to minimalize the limp, but her struggle didn't escape his attention. Gaze pinned to her leg, Reies rose from the couch, swearing softly.

"I told you one day wasn't enough—"

"Well, you can stop telling me what to do, Reies. I'm capable of making my own decisions!"

"So was your brother! If he hadn't been so sure of himself, so hell-bent on solving your father's murder alone, he might still be alive."

The stinging reference to Wayne was enough to set off Libby's temper. "He might have been unwise in his approach, but at least I can be sure that neither he nor my mother is a murderer!"

No sooner were the words out of her mouth than she was sorry she'd said them. Reies's expression would have been enough to tell her that the discussion was finished, and his turning his back on her only reinforced the fact. The tension in the room was almost tangible.

Libby picked up one of the food trays and swept into the bedroom, slamming the door behind her. She ate quickly, barely tasting the cold food. When she finished, she lay back on the bed to rest for a while. Maybe she should apologize....

She awoke hours later. It was dark. Though she switched on the table lamp, the light didn't dispel the gloom that enveloped her. Wanting Reies's company— wanting a lot more from him if she were honest—Libby fidgeted. She wasn't going to get back to sleep for a long time until she brought down the barrier her words created between them.

She opened the door to a darkened living room. Soft light from the bedroom fell across Reies's still form. He was stretched out, not on the couch that he'd claimed was too short, but on the floor. Libby thought his preference for the harder surface was part of the stoicism that was his Apache heritage. Reies would rarely choose the easy path if there was one more difficult to travel.

Instinctively, though she couldn't see his face, she knew he wasn't asleep. She sensed his dark eyes staring at her disheveled form. Her turquoise cotton sleep shirt was large enough to cover all but her legs. It might not have been glamorous, but it was comfortable.

Without waiting for permission, Libby joined Reies on the floor, sitting gingerly so she wouldn't make her wounds throb. Barely able to see his face, she recognized a yearning in his expression she was sure he didn't know showed. If he did, he'd hide it from her. She tried to apologize.

"I'll say I'm sorry if you do."

Silence.

Only half-teasing, Libby said, "We could kiss and make up."

"It wouldn't stop at a kiss."

"How do you know that?"

"I know."

Libby knew, also. "I'm out of ideas."

That was a bald-faced lie. She had plenty of ideas. She yearned for soft words, gentle touches and wild love-making from Reies Coulter, even though she knew that she was in too deep already, that getting attached to him would be a mistake. She'd never have everything she wanted from a man who fiercely guarded his emotions, and Libby was afraid she wanted it all.

"I can't believe you would give up so easily," Reies said.

"Maybe I would try harder if you'd tell me what's been bothering you."

Silence again.

Libby touched a shoulder left uncovered by his sleeping bag. The warm flesh seemed to caress her hand. "Reies, we're in this together, remember? Try to forget I'm an outsider."

For a moment, she thought he might actually open up to her. Instead he unzipped his sleeping bag, found his shirt and pulled it on. Her interested gaze traveled down his smooth broad chest, stopping only when it came to the waistband of the jeans he still wore.

"I think I'll get some fresh air," Reies said. "I could use a smoke."

"You do that. Avoid talking about anything that might be painful." Frustrated, Libby leaned back against the couch and watched him pull on his boots. "Keep everything locked up inside until it eats a hole through your heart!"

Surprisingly Reies kept his temper. "You ought to get back into bed and rest that leg if you want to help my grandfather celebrate tomorrow."

"What if I don't feel like it?" she asked, stubbornly remaining right where she was.

"I could pick you up and put you in bed."

"Try it," she dared him, half-hoping that he would.

At least he wouldn't escape so easily. She could try to make him open up to her. He moved away instead.

Stopping at the door, his back still to her, he said, "Someone at Rancho Velasquez is a murderer. You know that as well as I do. I'm the one who keeps trying to deny it to myself." He left quietly.

Grabbing a cushion off the couch, Libby flung it at the door. She was almost tempted to follow Reies, demand he talk to her about what he was feeling.

She could only hope that his tense mood wasn't caused by some knowledge he chose to keep to himself.

THE MORNING CAME far too slowly for Libby. But when the sun rose, the morning sky dazzled her with its blue brilliance. She dressed quickly, pleased that her leg felt normal. It only hurt if she pressed on the bandaged area directly, and even then the fast-healing cuts barely twinged.

She wasn't quite so pleased to find Reies waiting for her on the living-room couch. "Morning."

"How are you feeling?"

"Good as new." She was thinking he'd better not try to stop her from going out when she realized he was smiling at her. He seemed more relaxed than he had in days. "You're in a better mood than you were last night."

"I did some thinking about what you said." He shifted, as though he were uncomfortable. "I'll try to be more direct with you from now on. I can't promise I'll be good at it."

"Practice makes perfect."

They smiled at each other, and Libby felt as close to Reies as she had when he'd tended to her snake bite. She couldn't be more surprised at his sudden turnabout.

"I only ask for this day," Reies went on, the smile fading. "One day that I can spend with my family without having to think about the way it's going to be destroyed . . . with my help."

"Agreed." Even as she said the word, Libby knew Reies wouldn't forget the imminent blow to the family. The knowledge would fester deep inside him. Sympathetic to the pain he was already feeling, she would let him pretend. "After all, this is a day to celebrate."

Reies nodded. "Everyone on the ranch is already preparing for Grandfather's party."

"I'll help."

"Good. Then I can keep an eye on you."

Surprised that he didn't object, she was happy to agree.

They spent the morning together, Libby doing more loafing and observing than working as the *vaqueros* used bales of hay to set up a temporary *lienzo*, a pan-shaped amphitheater composed of a ring and wide alleyway for the *charreada*.

Shortly after noon, the temperature skyrocketed to the upper nineties, half a dozen degrees hotter than normal. Libby napped, grateful to escape the sun, in her adobe bungalow. She awoke with barely enough time to get ready for the party. The sounds of cars and trucks arriving was unmistakable. She quickly dressed in a long-sleeved embroidered and ruffled blouse that laced up the front, tan chinos and the ever-present vest that hid her shoulder holster.

Everyone in Sidewinder had been invited to the party. By the time Libby put film in her camera and walked to the area north of the main house, the sun was already setting. More than a hundred people had gathered around the tables of food and drink. Among the guests, Johnnie, Doug, Bobby and his woman, Nina, were drinking, and being entertained by Pilar. Emilio, Inez and Victor were the center of another noisy knot of people. Libby looked for Reies or Luis. Neither, it seemed, had joined the party yet.

But Ada Fry was about to. Libby rushed to meet the blonde, who sashayed toward the group from her car, her face wreathed in a smile.

"Honey, you don't know how glad I am to see you alive and well." She lowered her voice. "You had me scared when you set off to find Johnnie yesterday. He can be more dangerous than any old rattler."

"I'm sure you knew I was fine the moment I drove through town yesterday," Libby said with a laugh. "News around here sure spreads fast."

"You've got that right." Ada hooked an arm through Libby's and turned toward the refreshment tables. "Why don't we have a drink to celebrate your good health?"

Ada had a beer while Libby stuck to soda. She needed to remain clearheaded, just in case.... She looked around, keeping tabs on all her suspects, a task that grew difficult with the arrival of more trucks and cars filled to capacity. She noticed Nick had finally shown up. While nursing a beer, he aimed a dark glare at Pilar, who remained in Johnnie's company.

"Honey, you sure you're all right?"

"Fine." Libby tore her gaze away from Reies's brother. "I'm sorry. Did I miss something?"

"I don't know how you could miss a sight like that one."

Libby turned, as did many of the other guests. Coming toward the group, led by Reies, were the handful of men who would later, as *charros*, show off their riding skills. Their audience cheered. Though all the men were dressed in some form of *charro* costume, Reies outshone the others. Wanting to remember him like this always, Libby raised her camera and shot.

Black suede pants were fastened down the sides, waist to ankles, with silver buttons. Beneath a short jacket with silver embroidery and trim, his white shirt was pleated and embroidered in silver and black. He went without the low-crowned, broad-brimmed sombrero worn by the others. Instead, his long hair was parted in the middle and the sides were braided, exposing his ears. A black silk bandanna was tied around his head and knotted in back.

"He sure is adorable in that getup, isn't he," Ada said with admiration.

"Reies—adorable?"

Ada laughed. "I meant Luis. He's such a nice fella. Comes into the cafe when he's in town. Keeps me entertained."

Eyes lighting on Luis, who did cut a fine figure in spite of the paunch that hung over his chaps, Libby hid her amusement. So Ada was stuck on him. She wondered if the middle-aged Romeo knew it. Thinking he and Ada would make a great pair, she was delighted when Luis followed Reies toward them, all the while giving the blonde the eye.

Reies smiled at Libby. "I hope you remembered to focus."

"So do I. Let's eat. I'm starving."

"And you, lovely one?" Luis asked Ada, his dark eyes seeming to melt as they roamed up her yellow-clad body to her flushed face. "Are you hungry, too?"

"You'd better believe it, honey."

Thinking that Ada was agreeing to more than food, Libby held back a chuckle. Reies placed his palm square in the middle of her back and urged her toward the buffet, and the other couple followed. They filled their plates with regional specialties, but before they could do more than sample the food, Inez asked for everyone's attention. Dressed in a full-skirted, silver-trimmed black dress, she stood in front of a draped easel, which had been set to the side of the refreshments, a few yards from Libby and the others.

"As you all know," Inez said, "this party celebrates the seventy-fifth birthday of my father, Emilio Velasquez. To honor him, I commissioned Victor Duprey to paint his portrait. Victor, would you like to unveil your newest masterpiece?''

Looking every inch the successful artist, a bright turquoise shirt with silver trim showing off an incredible southwestern jewelry collection, Victor took his place beside the portrait. He raised the drink he was holding.

''Emilio, my good friend,'' the artist began, ''a toast to your birthday, and to your continued good health.''

With a flourish, he removed the cloth and revealed the portrait to enthusiastic applause. Although done in the same style as those Libby had seen in the gallery, this portrait showed Victor's talent even more, capturing the very essence of the patriarch who sat in front of his hacienda. Emilio's inner strength seemed to reach out from the canvas. Even the abstract background tapestry was more powerful, each symbol pulling her eyes to the next—cactus, pronghorn antelope . . . sidewinder.

Shivering, she turned from the image of the small, pale rattlesnake of the region and looked up at Reies, who said, ''Victor has magic in his brushes, doesn't he?''

''If his new works are all this good, Mother will be pleased. Blue Mesa will make a fortune.'' Thinking she should take a photo, Libby glanced back at the portrait. People were herding around the work, blocking it from view.

''Everyone eat,'' Inez shouted over the noise of the crowd, ''so we can begin the evening's entertainment.''

''That's us, eh, gringo?'' Luis said, pulling himself up proudly. To Ada, he added, ''I will make this my finest performance and dedicate it to you.''

''I'm sure your performance is always something to behold.''

Unable to help herself, Libby laughed at the obvious flirtation. Reies's deep-throated rumble joined in. Seeming surprised, Ada blushed, and Luis stood even taller.

Reies cleared his throat, almost choking. "We'd better chow down so we have enough energy to ride the wild mares."

Though she knew he referred to an upcoming rodeo event, Libby imagined a different meaning and broke into renewed laughter. Reies took a forkful of chicken in mole sauce and stuck it in her mouth. For once, his expression was completely open. As she chewed, Libby's laughter drained away, but inside, she was still smiling.

Within half an hour, the guests had all made their way to the *lienzo*. Most found room to sit on the bales of hay, and others stood behind the temporary barrier. Ada had coaxed Libby away from the men ahead of time so they would have prime seats.

The first event was the one Reies had demonstrated the day someone had put the cactus under Incendiaria's saddle: an exhibition of control over the animals.

While she watched and enjoyed the display, her mind wandered. Cactus under her saddle. A diamondback in her bed.

Libby had assumed Pilar perpetrated the first incident, but she wasn't sure the sable-haired woman was capable of the second. Someone was making an eloquent statement, Victor had told her. She looked straight across the arena to where he sat between Emilio and Inez. Reies's mother leaned toward the artist as she whispered in his ear. There was something about Inez's manner.... Was the woman capable of handling a snake? Could she commit murder? Or was she covering up for Nick?

Libby spotted Inez's younger son with his wife. Pilar appeared sulky, Nick grim. Could they be working to-

gether? Her eyes traveled a few yards farther, to Johnnie
and pals. Having seen Pilar with them earlier, Libby
found it more likely that she would turn to Johnnie or
even to her brother Bobby to do her dirty work. Or perhaps they all worked together. She was back to Pilar
again.

Libby's head spun with the possibilities as the audience cheered the end of another event. Luis had just
thrown a bull to the ground by the tail using his bare
hands. She quickly took a photograph as he looked toward Ada, swept off his hat and bowed.

Ada waved and threw him a kiss. "He's a real
charmer."

Libby smiled. "That he is."

As the spectacle continued, Libby relaxed and tried to
banish anything negative from her mind that might spoil
her evening. She wanted to have a good time. She'd
granted Reies his one day. Didn't she owe the same to
herself?

All the *charros* were fun to watch and photograph, but
Reies dazzled her with his superior skills. His final event,
paso de la muerta, the ride of death, began as dusk settled over the valley.

Mounted, Reies circled the ring waiting to come parallel with an unsaddled wild mare. He leaped to her back,
grabbed her mane and used his rope to make an im-
promptu noseband. He led her down the alleyway where
she bucked and twisted, then rode her back into the arena
where he executed a faultless traveling dismount. The
crowd went wild with approval, whistling and shouting
their appreciation for the danger Reies had conquered.

As he remounted Sangre and picked up the mare's
rope, the other *charros* rode back into the arena to take
their bows. Libby yelled herself hoarse by the time the

hoopla died down. She only hoped the pictures she'd taken were worthy of the performance.

Ada climbed off the bale of hay and brushed loose strands from her yellow dress. "I'm going to find Luis and tell him what I thought of his presentation."

"Good luck," Libby called after the other woman. A few seconds later, as she was dusting herself off, Reies found her. She straightened and sighed loudly. "I have to admit I'm impressed."

"Enough to grant me a whim assuming your leg can stand some serious riding?"

"That depends. No *paso de la muerta* for me, thank you."

"I was thinking of a moonlit ride to a spot that's had special meaning for me since I was a kid. We could both use a couple of hours away from this place."

Agreeing with that idea, Libby was touched that Reies would want to share something so personal with her. "I'd love to, but won't your grandfather be disappointed?"

"He'll never miss us. He's having a great time with some of his cronies. On the rare occasions they see one another they hash over the good old days. Besides, as soon as the band starts playing, everybody will be dancing. They'll be at it for hours."

Though she wouldn't mind feeling Reies's arms around her, even if only on the dance floor, Libby said, "I'm convinced."

"Good. Meet me back here in fifteen minutes."

"Deal."

He walked off into the spreading gloom, his spurs jingling. Since Ada hadn't returned, Libby wandered away from the noise of the party. She caught a movement from the corner of her eye. Johnnie. Now what was he doing sneaking off so furtively? Deciding to find out, she fol-

lowed. He headed around the bunkhouse where he disappeared. Libby was nearing a small stand of cottonwood trees when she heard a familiar female voice coming from around the corner.

"When, Johnnie, when?" Pilar demanded.

"When the time is right."

"You've been promising to get me out of this hellhole
for years, ever since I told you about Reardon's money."

Libby stopped dead in her tracks.

They were talking about the missing money...about
her father.

Was she about to hear the confession of a murderer?

Chapter Nine

"Keep your voice down," Johnnie growled.

"You think anyone will hear us over the noise of the party?"

"Pilar—"

"Don't touch me."

"But you like the way I touch you."

"Not anymore. Not—"

Her words were cut off. Libby could imagine the kiss Johnnie forced on Pilar. Hardly daring to breathe, she moved into the shadow of a large cottonwood and steadied herself against the trunk. Anxiety made her pulse surge. What about the money and her father?

The sound of a struggle was followed by Pilar pleading seductively, "Please, Johnnie. I can't take it anymore."

"Then you shouldn't have gone from one brother to the other."

"That's an excuse. Even after I helped you get Reardon's money you didn't take me away. I hoped my engagement to Nick would wake you up, convince you to leave this viper pit of a town. But you cared more about your precious Coalition than you did about me, so I married Nick. He's loved me since we were kids."

"But Nick wouldn't take you away, either, and you couldn't leave me alone forever, could you?"

"I was faithful to Nick for eleven years. I cared for him in my own way. And what did I get out of the marriage? Nothing but my husband's suspicion and jealousy. Not even his babies. I want more than this barren life, Johnnie. I hate it! When I came back to you, you promised it would be on my terms. Now this Coalition business is starting all over again."

"I always find time for you."

"Not enough. Listen to me, Johnnie Madrigal. I've wasted thirty-one years of my life in this Godforsaken country, but it's finished!"

"Be patient awhile longer. When the Coalition strikes again, my name will be known across the state. This is the opportunity—"

"Don't kid yourself! You'll accomplish nothing. More will die, maybe you this time. Leave the risk to your partner and take me away from here, or I swear I'll find a way to do it on my own."

"Before you go, let me show you what you'll be missing."

Libby heard another struggle that was soon aborted. A short silence was followed by Johnnie's whispered words of seduction. Pilar was no longer arguing. Knowing she would hear nothing more of importance, Libby left the security of the tree and noiselessly made her way through the dark toward the sound of music and voices.

So she'd been right about the money. But did that mean Johnnie had murdered her father? Or had Pilar somehow lured Oliver Reardon to her own bedroom on some pretext while Johnnie had searched for the cash? Had something gone wrong to make Pilar pull the trigger? Where did the Coalition fit in and who was the partner Pilar had mentioned?

Questions were whirling through her mind when she approached the *lienzo*. Reies was already there, waiting with the horses. Libby rushed to his side, practically bursting with what she'd learned.

Then she saw his face silvered by the moonlight, and she knew she couldn't tell him. She couldn't bear to see a grim expression replace his welcoming smile. One day was all he'd asked for. She'd promised. Telling him now rather than later wouldn't speed things up. Tomorrow. She would wait until morning.

"There you are," Reies said. "I was wondering if you were going to chicken out."

"Me? You ought to know better. I'm a woman of my word."

"So you are."

Libby realized Reies had saddled Incendiaria for her. She took the reins and stroked the horse's velvety neck. "Are you sure *she* can take some serious riding?"

"She's good as new—just like you. Or are you? Need some help getting on her?"

"A boost wouldn't hurt."

Not that she really needed one. Libby couldn't resist the prospect of feeling his hands on her waist. As he helped her up, she could feel his breath ruffle her hair. Distracted, she almost fell back. Somehow she managed to mount the mare.

"Sorry. The leg muscle twinged a little," she fibbed.

His brow pulled in concern, he asked, "Are you sure you—"

"I'm positive." She wrapped her camera strap around the saddle horn and tied the equipment down for safety.

He swung into his own saddle. "Let me know if you get too tired or sore. We can take a rest stop or come back."

"I doubt it'll be necessary."

"And in case you get cold, I tied an extra poncho behind your saddle."

"Stop worrying about me and let's get started."

They rode away from the noise of music and people up out of the valley and into the quiet of the high desert. A full moon lighted their way.

"Where are we going?" Libby asked.

"It's a surprise. Less than a two-hour ride if you feel up to a gallop where it's safe."

"I told you to stop worrying about me."

"I'm finding that harder and harder to do."

As they made their way through the low scrub and onto a partially grown-over back road, which looked as if it were rarely used, Libby savored those words. Reies must really care. They urged their mounts into a smooth gallop. Exhilarated, Libby felt as if she were leaving her troubles behind. If only life were that easy.

REIES AND LIBBY hadn't escaped the ranch unnoticed. Their observer had slipped away long enough to determine their direction and then had returned to the party without being missed. The couple's destination had been obvious to anyone who knew of its existence. A romantic interlude? If so, they wouldn't plan on leaving before morning.

That left plenty of time to make plans.

Now there would be more than one reason to celebrate.

AS THEY MADE THEIR WAY higher into the foothills where they crossed what looked like virgin terrain with no signs of human habitation, Libby noted they were heading straight for a mesa. She could make out several flat-topped, sheer-walled hills in the area. To the south, the land rose and became more forested. She pointed to the first and largest mesa.

"Is that your surprise?" she asked.

"It is and it isn't."

Reies didn't explain the mysterious statement as he took the lead directly up to the hill and circled around to its north side, where they came to a narrow opening in the rock.

"Give the mare her head," Reies warned as Sangre entered the passage. "Let her pick her own way through."

A hundred yards or so into the dark, winding channel, they came to a moonlit clearing in the center of a box canyon. When Reies dismounted, Libby did the same. She flexed her leg, which had grown stiff though not painful.

"Can you see it?" Reies asked, pointing halfway up the other end of the canyon to what looked like a structure built into the hillside.

"An abandoned pueblo?"

"A small one and too far off the tourist route to be of interest. Or else the place is so well hidden the government has overlooked this tiny part of our native history." He tied Sangre's reins to a juniper branch. "We'll have to leave the horses down here."

Libby secured Incendiaria several yards from the stallion. She and Reies removed the cumbersome saddles, and deciding the horses needed to cool down, gave them water from one of their canteens. Reies then indicated the half-empty container and said, ''We might as well bring that with us. I don't think we'll need the other one.''

From a saddlebag, he procured a flask and a flashlight, both of which he handed to her. Then he removed his rifle and the bedroll, which he tucked under one arm.

''You two be good,'' he told the horses as they started to cross the canyon floor. ''Don't get into any mischief.''

So Reies was whimsical enough to talk to his horses the way some people spoke to their pets. The longer Libby knew him, the further removed he seemed to be from the terse, sarcastic man who'd wanted her off his land.

''Have you known about this place for long?'' she asked, keeping pace with his long-legged stride.

''Yep.'' Reies switched on the flashlight and pointed the beam upward. ''Nick and I used to climb to the top when we were kids. We'd play Indian and pretend we were on watch. Grandfather's the one who discovered the place. He brought us out here whenever he got too restless at home. He probably figured it was a way to keep us out of trouble.''

''Did it?''

''Temporarily.'' As they approached the hillside, Reies bathed the way with the flashlight beam. ''Step carefully. The path's not clear.'' After seeing she was all right, he went on, his spurs jingling cheerfully. ''The three of us thought of this canyon and the pueblo as our secret place, because we never found signs of anyone else having been around.''

''Is it still secret?''

''As far as I know. I've been out here several times since I came back from Mexico, and I've never seen evidence of trespassers.''

''Trespassers? You'd think you owned the place.''

"In a way I should. Or *we* should. The citizens of Sidewinder and other local villages, I mean. This area is part of the communal grazing lands the government stole from us."

"You sound resentful, and yet you're not part of the Coalition."

"I might be if the Coalition was trying to get the land back through the courts, though God knows that would take years and, chances are, would be futile. But the organization espouses separatism and violence. A few months after I left Sidewinder, people were wounded and killed in a Wild West sort of showdown. I could never be a party to such destructiveness."

More will die, Pilar had warned Johnnie. Libby clamped her mouth shut so she wouldn't spill everything to Reies. Tomorrow would be time enough to face grim reality. Tonight would be theirs to enjoy.

They arrived at the base of the pueblo, which was perched on a cliff about ten feet high. The ancient, apartment-style building was small, only fifteen units on three levels, doors leading into them around the three sides not backed by the hill. Time had taken its toll on the adobe walls—chunks of mortar were missing from many places—but overall the long-abandoned building looked as if it were structurally sound.

Reies set down the bedroll and rifle and swept the flashlight's beam over some brush and cactus to one side of the cliff's base. He dragged a ladder crudely constructed of twisted piñon trunks and branches tied with rawhide from the underbrush and set it against the side of the pueblo under the middle, first-floor apartment. Then he picked up his rifle.

"Give me a minute to go up and check things out. I wouldn't want to be surprised by unfriendly hosts," Reies said.

Knowing he didn't mean the human kind, Libby shivered. The last thing in the world she wanted to think about tonight was another run-in with a rattler. Reies was up the ladder and inside the abode in seconds. Through the doorway, she could see the light sweep through the enclosed space, become dimmer, then disappear altogether. Libby knew Reies would be thorough about checking the inner rooms. Still, she was relieved to spot the light moving back through the apartment toward her. Reies stopped in the doorway.

"All clear." He placed the rifle barrel against the wall. "Can you toss the bedroll up here?"

"I think I can manage it."

Libby picked up the roll and heaved. Reies caught it with his free hand. Canteen slung over one shoulder, flask tucked into her waistband, she climbed the ladder carefully, thankful it proved more sturdy than it looked. When she got to the top, Reies took her hand, helped her onto the ledge and guided her into the room. He'd already opened the bedroll and had spread it a few feet back from the door. Already fantasizing about what might happen there, she took a calming breath and turned around for a look at the view. Reies's hand settled lightly on her hip as he turned off the flashlight.

Bathed by the light of a full moon, the small canyon presented a picture of ageless serenity and unspeakable beauty, a haven in a violent land.

"Magnificent," she whispered.

"You can see why I brought you here. Have you ever been in a pueblo before?"

"Several of the large, inhabited ones where Harry took me when he needed items to sell in his gift shop. And I've been out to Pecos and Bandelier National Monuments," she said, referring to the large ruins that were now part of the national-park system and within an hour's drive from Santa Fe. "But this is different. Cozy. No noisy haggling over price. No tourists. It's as if we were alone and set loose in history."

"Tonight, we are."

Reies tightened his hold on her and pulled her closer. Wanting his kiss, Libby raised her face. Moonlight silvered his strong, rugged features. His was a face of the people. And of the land. A face carved by history, representing all three cultures of New Mexico. She wondered if Victor had ever captured Reies in a portrait. Surely his image would explode off the canvas.

Their breaths mingled, lips touched, and Libby was sure she would burst with passion. She suddenly grew nervous with that thought, and shivering, she withdrew slightly.

"Cold?" Reies asked. "I can go back and get the poncho."

"No! I mean, I'll be fine." Libby looked back out at the canyon. "Why do you think they left? The original occupants, I mean. If this place is so well hidden..."

"Their water supply must have dried up. Man can't live on beauty alone." His tone softened as his hand lightly massaged the square of her back. "Although he could try."

Reies turned her more fully into his arms before kissing her again. Libby knew that what would come was inevitable. She snuggled against him, and would have tried to get closer if not for the flask pressing into her stomach. Frustrated, she pulled away.

"What's in the flask?"

"Mescal. Liquor distilled from the leaves of the agave plant." Stepping back, he removed the flask from her waistband. Her stomach tingled where his fingers grazed her flesh through the thin cotton blouse. "I developed a taste for mescal in Mexico after drinking three other men under the table on a bet."

"Sounds like wretched stuff."

"You're about to find out for yourself."

He led Libby to the bedroll. Opening the flask, he took a long swig, then handed it to her. Though she could barely see his face, she sensed his spirit of challenge. Even knowing she was going to regret meeting it, she tilted the flask and took a healthy swallow. The mescal burned its way down her throat.

"Whatever you do, don't light one of those damn cigars," Libby croaked. "The fumes from this stuff must be flammable."

"We'll soon find out, since I intend to make a fire." Removing the flashlight from where he'd hung it on his knife, Reies aimed the beam at a pile of wood neatly stacked next to a round fireplace in the corner. "Just the way I left it."

Libby replaced the top on the flask and lowered herself on the bedroll. "We don't need a fire. My nerves are already roasted." A delightful jingle echoed through the empty room as he crossed to the fireplace anyway. "Did you get those musical spurs in Mexico, too?"

Reies laughed as he crouched next to the stacked wood and set down the flashlight. "That I did. Actually, they're called singing spurs."

Singing spurs. Libby liked the name. The more she learned about Reies, the less she seemed to know about him. Raised in a more conventional environment, he might have been so different. But she had to admit that she didn't want him different. She wanted Reies just as he was—and as soon as possible.

As if he could read her mind, he said, "You know why I brought you here, don't you?" His back to her, he lit the kindling.

"Tell me."

The fire caught and flared. He poked it with a stick, added a few larger pieces at the proper angles so air could flow through the mass and keep it burning. He snapped off the flashlight and stood. Ringed by firelight, he came toward her. He stripped off his jacket, dropped it on the edge of the bedroll and began unbuttoning his shirt.

"We're going to make love, Libby, before anything can come between us."

"Don't I have a vote here?" Her voice sounded odd to her ears.

"You can say no." His fingers stopped at the last button above the black suede pants. "Tell me that I've made a mistake."

"All right. No." When his hands actually began moving back up, she quickly added, "You *haven't* made a mistake."

So that her consent was absolutely clear, she shed her vest and the gun holster, then began to work off her boots. Reies was quicker than she. His spurs still singing on discarded boots, he lowered himself over Libby and nudged her onto her back. His shirt was open, his chest hard and smooth under her questing fingers.

"You're trapped, Desperado," she whispered as he tugged the bottom of her blouse from her pants.

"Are you going to become my jailer now?"

"Interesting idea. For starters, you can undo my blouse."

Sliding down so that her legs settled around his waist, Reies unlaced the ties with his teeth. Libby removed the knotted silk scarf from his forehead and loosened his braided hair. Reies moved up, white string dangling from his mouth. She caught the end with her teeth and tugged his head closer until their lips met, his hair tenting their faces.

Libby began undoing silver buttons on both sides of the suede pants, darting her fingers in and out of the gaping leather. When Reies slid up further, her fingers found the scar on his right leg. Imagining the flesh and muscle exposed by a knife made her shudder.

Sidewinder had done this to him.

She wanted to cry at the reminder of the pain they'd both suffered. Saying nothing, Libby allowed him to take the lead, to touch her where he would, to undress her. Reality had intruded with a harsh bang, killing her whimsy. Panicked, she tried to forget everything but Reies, to pretend . . .

He stripped off his own clothing, the reddish glow of the fire outlining his fit male body. Yet her eyes were inexorably drawn to its one imperfection. The scar was a tangible reminder of the futility of her being with him, of loving him. Even as she accepted his mouth over her own, she knew they were in a no-win situation.

"Lady," he whispered, "where have you gone? Don't, please. Free yourself from shadows and memories. Love me tonight."

Her heart ruling her head, she could not deny him . . . or herself. She *did* love him. Libby slid her hands to his hair. Tangling her fingers through the long, thick strands, she pulled Reies closer. He slid into her easily and she wound her legs around his thighs.

Reies whispered love words into her hair. While she had the opportunity, she would grab not only with both hands, but with everything she had. If, as she suspected, this was to be the only night they would share, then she would help create an experience that neither of them would ever forget.

LIBBY WOKE ALONE to daylight. Wrapped in the bedroll, she was stiff and sore from the hard floor. Her mouth was dry, its taste wretched. Finding the canteen and drinking the last few swallows of water that remained, she wondered if Reies had gone to fetch some food. She decided to get dressed. The fire was out, yet the room was too warm. Another scorcher of a day.

She drew on her hiphuggers, socks and blouse, then hunted for the string, which she finally found dangling from a boot. Her lips curving in a happy smile, she threaded it through the eyelets of the blouse until Reies's spurs sang right through her nervous system. His head appeared over the top of the ladder. One look at his tight, closed expression made her heart drop.

"Reies?"

"The horses. They're gone."

Libby rushed to the doorway and looked out to where they'd left the mounts. "Maybe they wandered off—"

"Someone took them purposely to strand us."

"What are you talking about?" Aware that he was making no move to touch her, that his eyes were as emotionless as she'd ever seen them, Libby grabbed the doorway for support. "A-are the saddles gone?"

"The saddles are there—but the other canteen of water isn't. Someone left us to die out here. *Both* of us."

Chapter Ten

"Dead? Both of us?" Libby echoed uncomprehendingly. "But why?" How could she be so naive—this wasn't the first attempt on her life. "All right, why you?" she amended. "And who?"

Reies avoided answering directly. "I thought you would want to know about the horses. I'm going back down to the canyon to find some usable cactus."

"Cactus? Wait a minute. I'm going with you."

"No. Stay here and don't go out in the sun."

"What difference will my being in the shade a few minutes longer than you make?"

"We're both going to take shelter here at least until the sun is low in the west. It's still morning, and the temperature must be in the mid-nineties already. We'd fry out in the open for sure. I'll be back as soon as I can."

"Why chance going out there now at all?"

He glanced down at the container at her feet. "Any water left in the canteen?"

"No," she said guiltily.

"That's why."

"Reies, wait a minute...."

Libby hadn't finished before he was out the door and on the ladder. She dropped to the bedroll, upset that

Reies was treating her like this after what they'd shared. She was equally stunned that someone had obviously followed them all the way out into the desert to steal their horses.

With his heightened senses, Reies would have been aware of anyone following them. She figured the theft had occurred long after they had fallen asleep. Maybe some kids had accidentally stumbled across the place and saw an opportunity to make a few fast bucks selling the horses. But then they would have been insane to leave the saddles, especially Reies's. Of tooled black leather and inlaid with silver, his tack was worth a small fortune.

So where did that leave them? In the middle of nowhere, with no way to get home. Libby thought harder. What if someone from the party saw them ride out in this direction, someone who knew about the place . . . ?

Nick. And Reies had to have come to the same conclusion.

Other than Emilio—and he certainly wouldn't have set off in the middle of the night—who else but Nick would have known where to find them?

Libby wrapped her arms around her knees and tried to understand what Reies must be feeling. He had to be ripped apart inside. And despite his promise to be more open with her, he was keeping everything to himself—just as her ex-husband would have done.

She was still absorbed in her thoughts when Reies returned, the saddlebag over his shoulder, two large chunks of cactus pulp speared on his knife. About to plead with him to talk to her, to open up, she refrained from doing so when he handed her the cactus pulp.

"No, thank you," she said, making her plea through her eyes.

If he recognized what she was trying to tell him, he didn't let on. "Take one."

"I don't want anything. I'm not hungry."

"But you must be thirsty—or you will be soon."

He was correct, of course. She took the pulp and began to suck the milky juice. "Ach! Forget it," she said, pulling a face. "It's bitter."

Reies backed up against the wall and slid to his haunches. "I'm not going to argue with you. Drink it!"

He was serious. Libby figured he might force her if she didn't comply. "Give me a minute," she said sarcastically. "So I can properly savor this treat."

"It's not meant to be a treat. It's meant to keep you from dehydrating. The mescal we drank last night didn't help any," Reies went on. "Alcohol uses extra body water to get through our systems."

Realizing she was being foolish, that he was looking out for her welfare, even if in an impersonal manner, Libby complied and sucked the bitter juices from the pulp. Reies did the same from the piece on the knife.

If only he would talk to her....

"There's more where that came from." He rose and set the saddlebag in front of her. He speared another piece for himself and backed off. "We'll finish this while we wait. Before we leave, I'll cut up as much of the plant as we can carry."

Not exactly the words she'd been waiting to hear.

She said nothing, watched him pace, but after a while even that grew uncomfortable. "I don't see why we have to wait so long before leaving. We can't be that far from the ranch."

"Six or seven hours on foot, maybe more if we lose our sense of direction."

So many hours in open country without shelter of any kind. Libby voiced her worst fear. "We'll be easy targets out there for anyone who wants us dead." She decided she would leave specifying who to him.

"We're both armed." Reies took more pulp and sat several yards from her. "Besides, I'm sure the idea was to let the desert take care of us, which is exactly what might have happened had we set out early this morning. Getting lost is easy under the midday sun. You lose your sense of direction and the desert all looks the same then."

They lapsed into silence, staring at one another. Libby willed him to open up to her. Either he didn't get the silent message or he was ignoring it again. "I'm not your enemy, Reies," she said softly. "Don't treat me like one."

"Or what?" he asked tersely. "You'll think badly of me? I'm already doing enough of that for the both of us. I'm sorry as hell that I brought you out here."

There was nothing more she could say to him.

A FEW HOURS LATER Libby fell asleep, and Reies stilled the urge to touch her. She might wake up and he wanted a few more minutes to think. If anything happened to her...

As much as he wanted to deny Nick had anything to do with the murders and the things that had been happening to Libby, Reies couldn't. Everything was falling into place—not that it made any sense to him.

Reies realized Wayne's death and the repeated attempts on Libby's life had to have been meant as coverups. He thought back to the time of the first murder. What reason would his brother have had to kill Oliver Reardon? Could Nick's dance with violence have begun because of their youthful rivalry over Pilar that Reies had won? Assuming Pilar had lured Oliver into her bed, had

Nick killed the man out of jealousy rather than to protect the family honor as Reies originally feared?

The fact that he knew his own brother so little shocked him.

Though more than three years had separated them in age, they couldn't have been closer as kids. Reies had hung around with Johnnie as a teenager, but that had brought him nothing but trouble, had almost gotten him killed. The scar on his leg was a permanent souvenir of that episode. Through it all, Nick had been his conscience.

What had happened to make his younger brother change?

First Oliver, then Wayne, now Libby. And he mustn't forget about himself. If Nick was the guilty one, that meant he was willing to kill his own brother to cover up his crimes. That was the worst betrayal of all.

Lost in anguish, Reies suddenly realized Libby was awake and staring at him. She was flushed from sleep and the heat. Droplets of sweat gave her skin an unnatural sheen. Her expression was cautious.

"It's time to go," he said softly.

"How long have I been asleep?"

Shrugging, Reies rose and stretched. "Hours."

He was aware that she hoped for some closeness from him, but he dared not give it to her. A cynical realist, Reies saw no happy ending for them. Not now. He'd been trying to fool himself into believing they could make it happen for themselves, but that daydream had been shattered with the morning's discovery.

As for his inner turmoil, he was sure she would want—no, expect—him to talk about Nick, but he couldn't. Not until he had his conflicting emotions unjumbled.

"I'll go down and fill the saddlebag with more cactus pulp," he told her. "Bring the bedroll. And maybe you'd better get that poncho I tied to your saddle. We'll need both tonight."

Nodding, Libby lowered her head as she reached for her boots, but not before he saw the disappointment in her eyes.

Gathering his rifle, the flask, canteen and flashlight, Reies left her to her privacy. He tried not to think about what had passed between them such a short time ago.

Filling the saddlebag with wet pulp, Reies remembered the Coalition flyer found in Wayne's car. The logo had been circled several times. There had to be a connection to the murders. And yet, when the group had been formed, Nick had been as against it as he was. What about now? As far as he knew, Johnnie was the big honcho, running things.

If that flyer *had* been a clue...

Maybe it was time he joined the ranks of the organization and found out what was going on.

When the saddlebag was full, he slung it and the canteen over his shoulder, tied the flask and the flashlight to his belt, and picked up his rifle. Libby was waiting for him by the saddles. She clutched the bedroll and poncho under one arm. The camera strap dangled from the opposite shoulder.

"I'm ready," she called.

"Let's get started then. We'll travel nice and slow. Don't push if your leg starts bothering you. We have all night if we need the extra time."

"The wounds are almost healed, and as far as I'm concerned the sooner we get back, the better," she muttered.

The sun hung low in the west and the temperature seemed to have dropped about ten degrees. Reies kept the waning sun to their backs until it vanished. They continued on, taking short breaks to rest their feet and chew on cactus pulp. Luckily they were within hours of their destination. That entire barrel cactus hadn't held more than a quart of liquid. One person needed three to four quarts a day to prevent dehydration in the desert, Reies knew. What he'd found would barely keep their mouths and throats wet.

By the time dusk settled over the barren landscape, the temperature had dropped considerably. Reies was weary, and he was afraid Libby was beyond tired and was well on her way to being exhausted.

"Let's stop over there." He pointed ahead to a sprawled dead juniper whose grizzled limbs bore witness to the uncertainty of life in the high desert. "We can take a longer rest, maybe an hour or so."

"I can go on," she said defensively.

"I can't," he lied. "My leg is acting up."

She looked instantly contrite. "I'm sorry. I wasn't thinking of that."

"Besides, the stars will be out soon. They'll keep us from getting lost in the dark."

Libby spread the bedroll on the ground, and set the poncho and camera on the covering. Surreptitiously, she rubbed her stomach.

"Hungry?"

She shook her head. "A little nauseous."

Reies held out the saddlebag. "You get the rest of the pulp."

"We'll split it!" she snapped, ignoring his offering. Then, looking around the dead juniper, she added, "But first, I need some privacy."

Reies sat and stretched out on the bedroll. "I'll keep my eyes closed," he promised.

That Libby set off with far less energy than she'd had an hour before worried him. Lack of appetite, nausea, irritability, economy of movement were all beginning signs of dehydration.

He'd barely had his eyes closed for minute when he heard her yell, "Reies, come quick!"

Flying to his feet, he grabbed the rifle and ran. "What's wrong?"

"Nothing. I'm fine. We're fine! I found water!"

Reies picked her form out of the deepening twilight just as she got down to her knees. He squinted, took a thorough look around. She was cupping her hands to dip them in the pool.

"Wait!"

Her hands sliced through the water as he descended on her and forcibly pulled her up and away from the water. She tried to free herself, but merely managed to knock the rifle from his other hand.

"What the hell is wrong with you now?" she demanded. "I just wanted some water."

"Not this water. You've stumbled on an arsenic spring."

"You're crazy. You're trying to make me crazy!"

"Look, Libby. Do you see any vegetation? Think. Plants thrive around good water." He freed a hand and grabbed the flashlight. Switching it on, he swept the beam around the barren water's edge. Several animal carcasses lay rotting in various stages of decay. "They died drinking this water. You want to join them?"

Libby sank against him, her body trembling. Unable to help himself, he wrapped his arms around her back.

He held her close and stroked her hair until she stopped shaking and pushed herself away.

"Sorry." Her voice was gruff, and she was staring down at her toes. "I guess the tough cop isn't as tough as she likes to think she is."

"None of us are, lady, and don't you forget that."

Reies found his rifle, then hooked an arm loosely around her shoulders until they reached the bedding. Without prompting, Libby found the saddlebag and sucked on a piece of cactus pulp. They rested until the muted sky was transformed into a canopy of stars.

They set out once more, Libby wearing the poncho for warmth, since the desert was chilly at night even in summer. Reies carried the rest of the gear. Consulting the stars, he got his bearings and set their course. They continued in short stretches, stopping more often than they had earlier. He blamed his leg, but he knew she saw through his excuse to let her rest. Libby couldn't hide her fatigue, nor the fact that her wounds weren't quite as healed as she'd claimed. She was limping. His own feet were sore and blistered. With her higher-heeled boots, her feet had to be worse.

Eventually they arrived at the edge of ranch property, but Reies was too tired and tense to rejoice. He judged the time to be after midnight.

"Another half hour at the most," he told Libby.

She didn't answer, only gave him a half smile before plodding on. The half hour stretched into forty or more minutes. But finally, they crested a hill and looked down into the valley where they spotted the hacienda, its windows glowing, a sight at once gratifying and dreaded. He knew a welcome party awaited, one that would undoubtedly include his brother.

They were yards from the porch when the door burst open and Inez came flying out and down the steps. Ignoring Libby, she threw herself at Reies.

"You're alive." His mother held his face between trembling hands. Tears made rivulets down both her cheeks. She looked older than Reies had ever seen her. "Oh, my son, we were so afraid when the horses found their way back..."

"Thank God you found your way back," Nick said heartily from the shelter of the porch. "We were just making plans to take a posse out at first light."

Reies pushed past his mother. With eyes as cold as the night, he stared at his smiling half brother, wondering if Nick really wanted him dead. The younger man's welcoming expression gradually faded. The night seemed to grow still as Reies's tension reached out to hold Nick fast.

"We were at the pueblo in the box canyon," Reies said. "Someone took our horses and water supply and left us to...fate."

Nick's face mirrored shock, which intensified as he grasped Reies's implication. "Reies, what the hell are you trying to say?"

Before Reies could decide whether or not to confront his brother directly, his grandfather stepped out of the doorway.

"What is going on?" Emilio demanded. "Why are you not inside? Inez, help Miss Tate before she faints. Nick, take those things from your brother. Elena," he yelled, "a pitcher of water. And make a pot of tea. And hot food."

As Nick dutifully took the bedroll and rifle from Reies, the patriarch clasped his older grandson to him. His mother was helping Libby up the steps. Reies closed his eyes momentarily, thankful for the short reprieve. But now or later he was going to have to face and solve this nightmarish mystery.

FED UNTIL SHE WAS UNABLE to swallow another mouthful, Libby headed for her quarters, Reies at her side. She was bone weary and ready to drop. That didn't prevent her from confronting him when he followed her inside— as if he actually expected to stay the night.

"We need to discuss a few things, Reies."

He moved around her toward the couch where he picked up a pillow. "Not now. We're both exhausted."

"What about your promise? You had your day. Two days really."

"I can't even think straight."

Libby pulled the pillow from his hands and looked him directly in the eyes. "You haven't been thinking straight since you found the horses missing, or you would have talked to me like you promised. We need to discuss *everything*," she stated. "Even unfounded suspicions."

"I can't change a lifetime habit overnight."

"That's a convenient excuse to treat me like I mean nothing to you."

Reies looked away, avoiding her again. "Give me time to think things over," he said.

"You've had time. We've run out of time, or hadn't you noticed?"

"I need more."

"I don't have it to give you, Reies. I gave you everything I had less than twenty-four hours ago. But that doesn't seem to mean anything to you." Libby threw the pillow back down on the couch to express her frustration. "You can't do it, can you? You can't be open with me. You never intended to."

"That's not true."

She marched to the door and reopened it. "Just get out."

"I'm not leaving you alone."

"I don't want your company, not unless you're willing to come through with your end of the bargain. Until you come to your senses and let me share what's bothering you, I won't let you come any further into my life."

"All right. I'll leave," Reies said grimly. He started to go, stopping only inches from her. "But I'm posting Luis outside your door."

"Post your mother for all I care." Libby deliberately unsheathed the Beretta. "But I'm warning you, I'm sleeping with this in my hand. I'll shoot anyone who tries to take one step inside. Even you."

Reies backed off, whirled around and stalked into the night. Locking the door, Libby throbbed with fatigue and disappointment. The least he could have done was to have assured her he cared. But maybe he didn't care. And maybe she couldn't think straight, either. A good night's sleep would do her wonders, but it wouldn't change the fact that the killer knew who she was and why she was there. If she wanted to bring the murderer to justice, she would have to work fast, keep her mind from distractions.

In the morning she would speed up her investigation—on her own.

Chapter Eleven

The morning had come and gone without her by the time Libby woke up. More determined than ever to nail the killer before he, or she, could strike again, she tried to make sense of the facts and impressions she'd been collecting over the previous week. That she was missing something—a vital clue—kept bugging her, but she couldn't put her finger on it. Maybe a full stomach would help.

On her way to the main house, she opened the front door of the bungalow and almost tripped over Luis. He was sitting on her stoop, back slumped against the adobe wall, eyes shut, mouth open. "I'm so glad you're guarding me."

Startled awake in the midst of a snore, he flew to his feet. "I was merely resting my eyes against the morning sun."

"Past noon and there's no sun." The sky was a gloomy gray, the air far cooler than it had been the past few days. "Looks like rain."

"Not until late tonight."

"Good." She didn't want anything slowing her down today. "I'm going to get some lunch."

Flushed with embarrassment, Luis picked up his hat. "I thank the Mother of God that you were not harmed yesterday."

"Me, too. Thanks, Luis," Libby said, her mind working.

How to proceed?

From her first day as a detective, Captain Wainwright had driven home the concept that her job could only be done with the right combination of investigation, intelligence, and intuition.

So far, her investigative techniques had resulted in a bag of jumbled puzzle pieces that didn't fit together. Her intelligence made her peg Nick as the killer because he knew about the canyon; it hadn't given him a motive. And intuitively she ruled out not only Nick, but Inez, because of their obvious relief at seeing Reies alive and unharmed the night before.

That left Johnnie, Victor and Pilar. And Bobby? She'd witnessed his violent nature firsthand. Pilar could have overheard her telephone conversation and passed the information on to her brother. Could she have been wrong about the killer being at her father's gravesite?

Instinct, Tate, instinct, she chided herself.

Any one of them could have found out about the pueblo. A four-wheeler could have made it out there, but she'd looked in vain for tire tracks when they left the canyon, so the guilty one must have been on horseback. Since horses outnumbered people in the area, that fact didn't help.

These thoughts were going around and around in her head when she entered the house.

"Miss Tate." Emilio Velasquez was standing in front of the living-room window. "I hope you have suffered no ill effects from your unfortunate adventure."

"Just a few blisters on my feet."

The elderly man shook his head. "Who would do this thing?"

"I don't know, but I intend to find out."

"Yes, I thought so."

Libby fell silent. Emilio Velasquez wore the air of a defeated man. His stance was less upright and his shoulders seemed to slump. Quite a contrast to his portrait, which had already been hung and dominated the room behind him. She walked toward the canvas, fascinated as always by Victor's work, and wanting to find some way to comfort the patriarch who, in twenty-four hours, seemed to have grown truly old.

"I didn't get the opportunity to tell you how wonderful your portrait is. It reveals a man of great strength and endurance. A man I wish I had known years ago," she added softly.

"Years ago, I never would have let certain things happen on this ranch...in this town."

The way he looked at her made Libby feel uneasy. Guilty. "You couldn't have prevented what happened to Reies and me yesterday."

"Perhaps I could have had I looked deeper into the reasons for your coming here. I did not do so until it was almost too late."

His gaze locked with hers and she could have sworn he knew the truth. She caught a glimmer of recognition in his faded brown eyes before he turned toward his portrait.

"But now my only strength lies in my legacy to my family. This ranch. Even Victor saw that."

Puzzled, Libby asked, "What do you mean?"

"The background in my portrait—the only thing of significance left to an old man. The hacienda and a rocker on the porch."

About to protest, Libby stopped with her mouth open. The only thing of significance . . . She thought about the portrait of Bobby, with its background of a boarded-up jail. That, too, had been of importance to the subject. But what about Johnnie and the county courthouse? An exception to Victor's rule? Or was it?

The nagging feeling that she was missing something returned stronger than before.

"Will you join me for lunch?" Emilio asked.

Libby blinked and faced the old man. Her appetite was gone. "Some other day. I promise." She was already backing toward the door. "I have a few errands to run."

That was the truth. Things were finally falling into place. She had to get to Santa Fe and police headquarters where she could run some computer checks and try to call up the missing piece of the puzzle.

Even though she knew that Reies had been the one to renege on their promise to tell one another everything, and so she owed him nothing, a small voice told her to let Reies know where she was going. But Libby ignored it and left the ranch in a quandary.

SIDEWINDER. Reies was beginning to hate the town. The whole area had long ago been permeated by corruption, and it was difficult to tell the good guys from the bad. Needing to identify with something, Reies, too, had closed his eyes to that fact and had called Sidewinder home. As insular as the wilderness in which he lived, he'd built an invisible fence around himself to discourage trespassers.

And Libby had breached the barrier and invaded his heart. And yet . . . he still couldn't share his feelings with her.

As he headed for the house to clean up, after working with the horses, Reies prayed he was wrong about suspecting his brother of murder.

Nick had seemed so glad to see him the night before, so shocked at his silent indictment. Clearheaded now, Reies knew he wasn't justified in assuming anything until he heard his brother's side of the story. There was only one thing to do: voice his doubts straight on and give Nick the chance to defend himself.

After showering and dressing in a pair of jeans and a freshly ironed white shirt, he tied his hair back from his face with a strip of rawhide. He heard movement in his brother's room next door. Now was as good a time as any.

Reies knocked at Nick's door. Pilar answered. She leaned against the woodwork, her loose sable hair sliding to cover a cheek, but not before Reies noticed the shadow of a nasty bruise, one she'd carefully tried to conceal with makeup.

"You're staring," Pilar said in a throaty, seductive voice. "Come inside."

She moved back, but Reies remained fast. "Tell Nick I need to talk to him in private."

"This bedroom is private."

"But is Nick here?"

"He will be. Eventually."

"When, Pilar?" Reies asked, unable to hide his impatience.

"After the meeting, I suppose. We're alone in the house, Reies." Pilar stepped closer, ran her hand down his chest, devoured his face with her eyes. "The old man is visiting one of his friends, and Inez has gone to Manuela's."

Reies caught her wrist before her hand could get more intimate. "What meeting?"

"That damned Coalition," she snapped, wrenching her arm free. "It's become an obsession with him, too. I don't understand the fascination grown men have with these stupid war games."

"Nick part of the Coalition? I don't believe it. He was as against its being formed as I was."

"That was more than thirteen years ago. He was a kid. He's a man now. He's changed." Her face darkened, and Pilar turned to a dresser where she snatched up a loose piece of paper that she brandished in his face. "See for yourself."

The logo jumped out at him—the same intertwined C and S that had been in the photograph Wainwright had given Libby. Reies grabbed the flyer and read it. The meeting was to begin in less than half an hour outside the church.

"This doesn't prove anything."

"Then why has Nick been gone each time the Coalition has met ever since you returned to the ranch? You've been so blind you haven't even noticed."

Reies crumpled the sheet of paper in his hand. A thought nagged him that couldn't so easily be crushed. *Since you returned.* He headed quickly for the stairs.

"Reies, come back."

Ignoring Pilar's plea, he strode into the kitchen where the housekeeper was in the midst of making dinner.

"Elena, have you seen Libby?"

The woman shook her head. "Not since lunchtime. She drove off and hasn't come back."

Reies grabbed a flour tortilla, filled it with beans and a strip of steak off the grill. "If she does, tell her I'm at the Coalition meeting in town. Tell her to meet me there."

Reies practically ran out of the house to the Bronco, and ate as he drove. He tried not to worry, but his foot was heavy on the accelerator. Maybe Libby had gotten wind of the meeting and already planned on being there. If so, he would find her and apologize. He couldn't allow her to continue the investigation alone. Despite his self-assurances, his anxiety was high by the time he got to town.

Parking as close to the church as he could get, Reies jumped out of the Bronco and began searching for her. Although dozens of people had already gathered and more were coming, Libby wasn't in sight. And he hadn't spotted her car. Where was she?

Reies joined the crowd in front of the church where the wind played havoc with the flaming torches on either side of the steps. He hung back a little in order to see everything. Furtive whispers and wary looks aimed his way made him feel like an outsider in his own town. But he'd never made any bones about his opposition to the Coalition in the past, and people had long memories.

He searched the crowd for Nick. He couldn't find his brother, either. What he did see among the usual rabble-rousers astonished and disturbed him: many ordinary, peace-loving citizens, including a handful of anglos. This wasn't even their fight. The communal land grants had been given to New Mexican natives—not to anglos.

Before he could mull over the implications, the crowd stilled. Reies looked toward the church steps where Johnnie Madrigal took center stage, Bobby and Doug behind him forming a triangle of power.

"My friends," Johnnie began, pausing until he got the group's attention. "We've come to a crossroad in our search for justice. Pleas for negotiations about the communal lands—the lands that the United States government stole from our ancestors—have all been denied."

An angry rumble rose and grew around Reies. The fact that the citizens were so easily aroused made him shift uncomfortably. They'd been primed for this reaction, and primed well. But had Johnnie, the town's biggest troublemaker, been able to do it alone?

The rising wind tumbled dark hair around his beautiful face, a face suddenly turned evil, and Johnnie held out his hands for quiet. The rumble dropped to a murmur. "Although the people of Sidewinder and other villages of this county have, for decades, protested the loss of our communal lands to the U.S. Forest Service, the government is still disregarding our claims. If we stay on the road of *peaceful* negotiation, the government will continue to refuse to acknowledge its crime against the people." His voice rose and he slowly raised both arms, making tight fists. "But if we take destiny in our hands," he continued, "and change course, they won't be able to ignore us anymore."

To Reies's dread, the crowd cheered. Again, he was struck by a note of discord. Johnnie's appearance was too well-staged, his words too eloquent, his actions too finely orchestrated. Reies's gaze traveled over the roused crowd, examined the intense expressions, sought something that would explain this phenomenon....

Nick. Reies spotted his brother across the churchyard. A sea of angry people separated them. So he'd been there all along. Where had he been hiding? Reies began to move through the gathering toward his brother. Pilar's words echoed through his head: *Since you returned.*

"Are you with me?" Johnnie yelled.

"Yes!" the people cried with few exceptions.

Had Nick resented giving up the power on the ranch so much that he now had to find a substitute? Was he the one behind Johnnie? Did he envy his own brother so much that he would have left him to the perils of the desert?

"Then we must unite with our friends in the neighboring towns!" Johnnie shouted. "I've met with their leaders and they agree...the Coalition *must* strike again!"

That stopped Reies cold in his tracks. More innocent people's lives destroyed. More wounded and dead. And the greatest irony was that the orders for death and destruction were about to be issued from the steps of the church. He had to stop this massacre from happening, but how? If he pushed his way forward to challenge Johnnie now, the aroused crowd would eat him alive.

Nick—where was he? Reies could no longer see his brother. Suddenly a hand closed around his arm. Reies jumped, then turned to see Ada Fry, looking as rattled as he did. Her blue eyes frantic, she indicated they should move away from the assembly. Nodding, Reies followed her into the dusk, darkened further by angry clouds, away from the press of bodies.

"United and armed, we'll storm the county courthouse and take hostages until our demands are met!"

Reies shuddered and looked back, knowing that the picture of Johnnie Madrigal inciting violence in normally peaceful citizens would be forever etched in his mind. Several people were backing off, but most of the town was with him.

"Reies, honey," Ada said, clutching his arm again, "I've been going crazy trying to get hold of you. I called the ranch twice, and both times Pilar hung up on me, so then I drove over there, but you'd already left. Elena told me where I could find you.''

"Has something happened to Libby?"

"No. She's fine. I hope. I have a message—"

"Where is she?"

"In Santa Fe. Now wait a minute, I've got to get this straight. Libby was very particular that I repeat her words exactly." Concentrating, Ada paused, then said, "She said to tell you not to worry, that she's sure you're wrong, but that she's checking on her facts. Does that make sense so far?"

"Not exactly. Is there more?"

"You're supposed to meet her at her mother's gallery as soon as possible." Ada took a deep breath and spoke as if by rote. "She said that there was an important piece of work you had to see again, that she'll wait until you got there, and that you'd better show up...or else."

"Or else what?"

Ada eyed him as if he might eat her. "Got me, honey, but if I was you, I wouldn't wait around here to find out."

"I'm on my way." Reies patted her arm. "Thanks."

He raced to the Bronco as the first drops of rain spattered the windshield. Over the din of voices, he could hear Johnnie stating that the following Monday would be the day to take action. His mind was in a whirl, what with Libby's mysterious message, Johnnie's unexpected command of the people, and his brother's possible betrayal.

Could Libby's brother have found out that the Coalition was planning to storm the county courthouse? Did Nick murder Wayne to keep him from taking action? But what did that have to do with Oliver Reardon's death thirteen years before—the last time the Coalition had been active?

Maybe the pieces didn't yet fit, but even if Nick were only one of Johnnie's followers rather than his mentor, Reies's brother had turned his back on everything he'd ever stood for. As Pilar had said, Nick was a man now. Maybe he had changed for the worse.

Reies drove off into the rainy night as if the demons from hell were on his tail.

FROM THE SHADOW of a cottonwood tree, the brains behind the proposed insurgence watched Reies speed out of town toward the main highway, undoubtedly heading for a rendezvous with Libby Tate.

This cop had been quite a challenge—not the easy target her brother had been. She had overcome and ignored all attempts to get her out of the way. The woman had proved to be a stimulating opponent. She deserved no less credit for her bravery and cleverness merely because she'd gotten help from an unexpected source.

But even challenges became boring after a while.

Sometimes face-to-face violence was the most satisfying solution. Libby Tate would be back, and her reception wouldn't be anything to celebrate.

LIBBY WAS GOING CRAZY waiting for Reies to show. The gallery had closed almost half an hour before, and she'd practically forced her mother to go home before the rain got any worse, making driving dangerous. Flash-flood warnings filled the airwaves.

Standing in front of the glass doorway and staring out into the pouring rain wasn't helping Libby's nerves or her temper. Where was Reies? She was thinking about calling Ada to make sure the message had been passed when she saw a lonely set of headlights coming down the road. Face pressed to the glass, she made out the bulky shape of a Bronco pulling up in front of the gallery.

Relieved, she unlocked the door and opened it as Reies fled his vehicle. The short dash left him soaked to the skin, and his broad-brimmed black hat streamed water onto the gallery floor. Now that he'd arrived, Libby wasn't quite sure how to begin. She took her time securing the door; she was still feeling awkward because of their last encounter. A searching look at his face revealed his gloomy mood, yet relieved some of her anxiety.

"Libby, before you tell me what this is all about, I want to apologize for going back on my word to open up." Reies removed his hat and hung it from the corner of a nearby glass case. "It's not easy changing the habits of a lifetime, but because you're important to me, I'm willing to try."

"Reies, I do understand—"

"No, you don't," he interrupted, his voice anguished. "The reason I couldn't talk to you was that I was sure the killer was someone close to me." He took an uneasy breath. "My own brother. The idea was eating me up inside."

Even while she registered the significance of the admission, Libby shook her head. "You're wrong about Nick. Didn't Ada get the message straight?"

"She didn't mention Nick."

"I didn't want to say too much. I was hoping you would understand. Reies, didn't you realize I would come to the same conclusion you did? You kept telling me how no one knew about the pueblo but your grandfather and brother. I suspected Nick myself until we got back to the ranch. He was overjoyed to see you, Reies, and when he realized what you were thinking, he was hurt. His feelings were written on his face, and I honestly don't think he faked them."

A ray of hope cast away some of his gloom. "Then who?"

"Let me show you."

Libby led him to the wall where Victor's work was hung and she flicked on the track lights.

Drawn to the painting entitled *Tough*, Reies asked, "Bobby?"

"Look carefully at each of them," Libby urged, watching Reies. "Each background is of significance to its subject. Victor's working on Johnnie's portrait now. The building behind him will be—"

"The county courthouse," Reies finished with conviction. His gaze had settled on the painting she'd wanted him to see—the Indian youth. "I looked right at this when you brought me here before and didn't recognize the abandoned pueblo. That's it, all right." He turned to her, his brow creased in puzzlement. "Victor?"

"Victor," Libby echoed more certainly. "From the first, his paintings made me uneasy because he so accurately portrayed the power and violence that was often hidden in his subjects. I wondered how he could recognize and bring to life those qualities with such brilliance. When Johnnie let it slip that the county courthouse would be the setting for his portrait, Victor interrupted quickly. Still, it wasn't until today, when I looked at your grandfather's portrait again, that I began to see the pattern. I started thinking about the paintings I'd already seen. I found even more than I was looking for in the tapestries that illustrate Victor's obvious fascination with the wilderness. Especially," she said, pointing to the lower right corner, "the sidewinder."

The pale rattlesnake of the southwest was repeated in each of the paintings in exactly the same way—intertwined with Victor's name as if it were part of his signature.

"I'll be damned."

"The S that Wayne carved in the earth before he died didn't stand for the town," Libby told him. "He came back to Santa Fe, here to the gallery, shortly before he was ambushed. That must be when he figured it out for sure. And while he lay dying, he tried to identify his murderer—Victor."

"The Coalition's logo," Reies added. "The abstract C is intertwined with his personal sidewinder symbol, rather than an S—Victor's clever way of flaunting his leadership of the Coalition without revealing his identity. He's the one behind Johnnie...but why?"

"I don't know, Reies. I haven't figured that out, and I doubt that he'll tell us anything. Without a confession, we'll need some solid evidence. What we've got wouldn't hold up in a court of law."

"Let's get back to Sidewinder and face the murderer. I'll make him talk. If he knows we're onto him, maybe he'll slip up."

Libby wasn't sure that playing games with such a dangerous man was a good idea. And they had to be careful not to step out of the bounds of the law or a conviction wouldn't hold. Still, she was desperate to nail him.

"All right, but let's try Victor's Santa Fe home first." When Reies stared at her blankly, she said, "With all his talk about being one of the people, his money had to go somewhere. I stopped at police headquarters earlier. In addition to telling Captain Wainwright about the trouble brewing with the Coalition, I checked out Victor on the computer. We came up with a credit history you wouldn't believe, and a Canyon Road address not far from here.''

"What are we waiting for?"

Libby flicked off the track lighting and fetched a plastic, rainproof jacket from the office. She locked up the gallery and followed Reies to the Bronco. She gave him the address and sat staring out into the cold, wet night as he drove.

"We're even," Reies said suddenly.

"What?"

"When I took care of the snakebite, you said I'd saved your life, and I said you could owe me one." He found her hand in the dark. "Clearing Nick erased your debt. You couldn't have made a better trade-off."

"I don't think the two things are quite on the same scale."

"As far as I'm concerned, lady, you've tipped the scale in your favor. If I wasn't in love with you already..."

Filled with a sudden warmth that chased away the night's chill, Libby squeezed his callused hand. Perhaps there was hope for them yet. "I love you, too."

They remained touching and silent until they found the address. Reies stopped the Bronco in front of what turned out to be an estate. Though surrounded by a high, black, iron-grill fence, the gate wasn't locked. Half of the first floor was lit. They entered the grounds, taking the brick walkway to the front stoop. Libby undid the top snaps of her rain jacket so she could get to her gun if she had to. Her hand shook when she pressed the buzzer. The thought of the coming confrontation was enough to make her light-headed. Reies's steady support kept her calm.

When the door burst open with a shouted, "Victor?" Libby stared in amazement and felt Reies stiffen next to her.

Chapter Twelve

Reies couldn't contain his shock. "Mother, what are you doing here?" She was dressed in a billowy, low-cut turquoise blouse, and her long hair was free of the restraining coronet of braids. "I thought you were at Aunt Manuela's."

"I . . . I came to visit Victor, but he hasn't arrived, and I got trapped by the rain." She looked pointedly at Libby. "Why are the two of you here?"

His mother was nervous and trying to hide the fact, Reies realized, as he pushed Libby through the doorway without waiting for an invitation. Undoubtedly Inez wanted to ask how they'd found out about Victor's Santa Fe home. While Libby hung back, he passed the grand flight of stairs leading to the upper story and entered the living room, not caring that he left a trail of water behind him.

He was too busy inspecting what hung over the stone fireplace. A portrait . . . of his mother.

It was of a younger Inez, and Victor had bared a fiery, passionate, defiant nature. The artist had furthered the image by the use of a rumpled bed in the background. Reies couldn't tear his eyes from the suggestive image . . . couldn't believe that he had never guessed.

"Now you know," Inez said, placing herself between the canvas and her son. "Victor and I have loved each other since he moved to Sidewinder fourteen years ago."

"Loved, or been lovers?"

Her head lifted defiantly, reminding him of the woman in the portrait.

"I was lonely without a man. Victor made me happy."

"I can't believe you were happy sneaking around, meeting Victor in secret all these years."

"I lost my previous men. Your father abandoned me. Frank was killed. There was no one else until Victor. Eight lonely years. I thought having an affair while keeping my distance would satisfy my physical needs while protecting my heart. I didn't know I would fall in love with Victor."

"But he doesn't return the feeling?"

"Of course he does, but he loves his art as well. He gives me as much time as he can. I'm grateful for what I have."

"Grateful that you're involved with a murderer?" Libby asked, finally moving forward to stand next to Reies.

Black eyes flashing, Inez whipped her head around. "How dare you defile Victor?"

Reies studied his mother. She seemed desperate, as if she were trying to convince herself.

"Because," Libby said, "he defiled my family by murdering both my father and my brother. Before I married, my name was Reardon."

Inez almost collapsed into a chair. "Proof! Where is your proof?"

"In Victor's paintings. I can show you the abandoned pueblo where Reies and I were stranded the other night. And they all have a unique signature," she said, approaching the fireplace. "Would you like to come here and see the sidewinder woven through his name? My brother carved that symbol into the earth before he died. Perhaps you would like to see the photographs of Wayne. He was shot three times at close range with a rifle—"

"Stop!" Inez screeched. "Stop."

His mother had known the truth instinctively at least, and Reies couldn't pity her. "You knew, and yet you continued sleeping with him."

"You don't understand."

"You're right, Mother. I don't understand how you could have protected him. I thought you were protecting Nick. I thought my own brother was a murderer, while all the time you could have told me the truth."

Face in her hands, Inez began sobbing. "I suspected, but I didn't want to believe the man I loved was a cold-blooded murderer."

"Where is Victor?" Libby demanded.

"I don't know. He was supposed to meet me here after the meeting."

"He must still be in Sidewinder, then," Reies said. "We'll have to go back."

Libby moved to an ornate desk that held a unique copper telephone. "Let me call Captain Wainwright first. I'll have this house put under surveillance in case Victor does show up here." She switched her attention to Inez. "And you had better think seriously about telling us everything you know. Your lover has murdered at least two people. Until I can bring him to justice, nothing is stopping him from killing again. Let it be on your conscience if he does."

Inez wailed and tore at her loose hair. Reies pulled her up out of the chair and held her close to his wet body. He couldn't help her, but he could show her his love.

"Come, Mother. Let's get your wrap while Libby makes her call."

Within minutes the three were driving cautiously through the pouring rain toward Sidewinder. Libby sat in the front passenger seat, Inez in the back. Reies tuned in to a local radio station that was still broadcasting flash-flood warnings. Driving as they were on roads tucked into the foothills of the mountains, they could easily find themselves in a situation more dangerous than facing Victor Duprey.

"Why?" Libby asked softly. "I keep asking myself why Victor would want both my father and my brother dead. The Coalition has to be the key."

Reies agreed. "Maybe he needed money to finance the movement. If he stole the money your father brought with him, and if Oliver caught him—"

"Victor didn't steal the money," Libby interrupted. "Johnnie did the deed with Pilar's help. I overheard them discussing it the night of the celebration."

"And you didn't tell me? Where's this sharing you keep harping about?"

"You wanted your day, remember? I gave it to you."

"And then I reneged on my promise." His fault again, Reies realized. "Johnnie could have stolen the money on Victor's orders, but I doubt it. He wasn't even involved with the Coalition in those days."

"Then there's some other connection. I just know it."

"Instinct?"

"Instinct, and the history lesson Captain Wainwright gave me when I saw him earlier. He told me about the last Coalition raid on the county courthouse. Two police officers and four Coalition members were killed. Other officers and innocent citizens were wounded or beaten. Property was destroyed. Hostages were taken, and the remaining members fled to the mountains. Eventually the leaders were tracked down and arrested, but the two witnesses, who could identify any of them, were found dead in an irrigation ditch. There were no convictions.''

"Six more deaths Victor should be held responsible for," Reies said.

A muffled sob from the back seat made him glance into the rearview mirror. His mother's head was bent, her long hair not quite hiding the tears flooding her cheeks. Reies could think of no words to comfort her. He wasn't sure he wanted to. The woman was a stranger to him.

Another score to even with Victor.

SOME OF THE TENSENESS had drained from Libby by the time the Bronco arrived at the darkened hacienda. No cars or trucks sat in their usual parking spots around the main house. Staying put in a safe place was a wise move when flash-flood warnings were issued. Emilio, Nick and Pilar must have been elsewhere when the rains began.

"What now?" she asked.

"I think we should stick together in the main house. You can check with your captain, let him know we haven't been able to find Victor. Maybe he's shown up in Santa Fe."

Libby sensed Reies didn't want to let his mother out of his sight in case she tried to warn her lover, but she was afraid it wouldn't matter. As in the county courthouse raid, there would be no one to testify to Victor Duprey's crimes. She'd been fooling herself by believing she could bring him to justice. She had no proof. Not unless Inez knew more than she was telling.

"Do you mind if I change first?" Libby asked, disturbed by the latest thought. "These wet jeans and boots feel wretched."

"Tell me about it," Reies said. "All right. We'll all go."

Libby wanted to assure him that an escort wouldn't be necessary, but that would only provoke an argument. He drove the Bronco practically to her front door, then insisted his mother come inside with them. Rain seeped down the back of Libby's neck before she got the bungalow door unlocked. She was already unsnapping the slicker when she entered the room and flipped on the light switch.

"Well, well, what a surprise. A party."

She stopped short. Water dripped down her face into her eyes, making her blink several times. Her unexpected visitor looked dry and comfortable propped on the couch, rifle balanced across one of his knees. The barrel was pointing straight at her.

"Victor," Libby said more calmly then she was feeling, aware that Reies and his mother had stopped in the open doorway. "We've been looking for you."

"Have you? Well, you've found me." He waved his free hand as though issuing a friendly invitation. "Come in and close the door. Nasty night out there."

"Victor, you're not thinking of doing anything stupid, are you?" Reies asked as he followed instructions.

"Actually I'm far from being stupid. I'm only going to finish what the two of you forced me into starting." His cold blue eyes were fixed on Libby. "Too bad you didn't heed Inez's warning, Libby. She tried to spare you."

Libby focused on the rifle, already calculating how long it would take her to get to her own gun. Her palms felt sweaty. Unless he was distracted, she wouldn't have a chance in hell of taking Victor out. "What warning are you talking about?"

"The cactus under Incendiaria's saddle."

"I only meant to scare you into leaving," Inez said. "I swear."

"Inez is telling the truth. From the moment you arrived, her instincts were alerted. She knew you meant trouble. You really ought to thank her for trying to do you a favor before something...permanent happened to you."

"Like the snake?"

"Yes, that was my idea. A clever one, I might add. Too bad you survived, though I admit the challenge was inspiring."

Libby noticed the silver snake wrapped around Victor's wrist. He'd been wearing the bracelet the first time she'd met him. Why hadn't she remembered?

"And the horses at the pueblo?" Reies asked.

"You can thank Nick for taking me out there, oh, a couple of years ago. He probably doesn't even remember."

"Nick wouldn't have to be a genius to put two and two together, Victor," Reies said. "You kill us and he'll add it up, all right."

Inez began to shake. "No, Reies, not you." Disbelief was in her words. "Victor wouldn't kill you."

"He'll have no choice, Mother."

Victor shrugged and rose carefully, so that his rifle never wavered. "I'm sorry, my dear. If Libby had taken her accidents to heart and left, I wouldn't have to take care of Reies, as well."

"No!" Inez screamed, running across the room like a madwoman. Hands formed into claws, she threw herself at Victor and fought him for the rifle. "Not my son. You can't kill my son, not if you love me."

Libby used the distraction to reach for her gun, but by the time she slipped the Beretta from its holster, Victor had caught Inez by the hair and had pulled her in front of him. Her body shielded him, while his rifle barrel kissed her forehead. Libby glanced at Reies, who'd taken several steps forward but now stood frozen, his knife drawn. A stalemate. Though she couldn't chance using her gun now without endangering Inez, Libby refused to lower it.

She thought quickly. If Victor confessed to murder in front of witnesses, and if somehow they managed to come out of this alive...

"Why, Victor?" she asked. "Why did my father and brother have to die?"

His eyes widened with shock, and Libby realized he hadn't made the connection.

"So, you're another Reardon." His lips were practically at his lover's ear. "You didn't tell me that, Inez."

"I didn't know. I only heard...her say she was...going to police headquarters." Inez was taking great gulps of air between words. "Victor," she pleaded, "don't do this. If you kill them, you must kill me also." Tears streamed from her eyes, her puddling mascara leaving black rivulets down her cheeks.

"So that's how it is." He jerked her head back by the hair, making her cry out. "You would betray me after all our years together."

"And you would destroy me if you take my son from me!"

"You didn't answer my question, Victor," Libby prodded. "I know the murders had to do with the Coalition, but how did they fit in? The land-grant movement wasn't even your fight."

"Perhaps not, but I was hungry, my dear. I saw pushing the burgeoning Coalition into action as my opportunity to achieve fame and fortune. I knew that when nationwide media attention was focused on the Coalition and on Sidewinder, my portraits would be in demand. I hadn't counted on your father almost ruining my plans."

"How?"

"He overheard a conversation I had with Inez and put things together. Bright man. Still, I thought another anglo would appreciate the way I was turning useless human beings into saviors. *My* saviors. Reardon said he wouldn't let me exploit these people. He threatened to expose me. Not only would that have ruined my plans, but the citizens of this lawless town would have turned on me, possibly killed me. So, one way or another, your father had to die. If it hadn't been for—"

"And you tried to frame me," Reies interrupted, "because I was opposed to the Coalition."

"You're more clever than I gave you credit for. I put Reardon's body in your bed for that very reason. I was afraid people would start listening to your sanctimonious spoutings about taking a nonviolent stand, so I took away your credibility. Your leaving town when you did was the perfect added touch. Too bad you had to return, and Wayne Reardon had to come sniffing around at exactly the wrong time."

"But you already had what you wanted."

"No, he didn't, Reies," Libby said, never taking her eyes from Victor and his terrified captive. "Don't you remember our first visit to Blue Mesa? My mother said Victor's work was no longer selling as well as it had. Isn't that right, Victor? Your career needed a boost, and so the Coalition was reborn from the ashes."

"Like the phoenix rising. Appropriate imagery. Maybe I'll use it some time."

"You'll have plenty of time to paint in prison," she assured him.

"I won't be rotting in any jail."

Hearing the faint uncertainty in his tone, Libby persisted. "You might as well give up now that we know the truth. You can't kill us all. Either Reies or I will get to you.''

''The hell you will. Reies, get away from the door and over there with your woman before I kill your mother.''

''Victor,'' Inez sobbed, ''don't I mean anything to you?''

Not taking his eyes from Victor, Reies moved toward Libby. The villain inched his way to the entrance, shielding himself with Inez, whom he dragged along like a broken doll.

''Open it,'' he growled in her ear.

Frantically Inez felt for the knob. Her head was pulled back so far she couldn't see it, and Libby thought her neck might snap. Finally the older woman got the door open, and Victor backed through it.

''Follow me out here and I swear I'll kill her!'' the artist yelled as he backed into the sheeting rain.

Reies started to move after him, but Libby grabbed a handful of wet jean jacket. ''Give him a head start, or else he'll kill her right now. He's desperate.''

Reies swore, but stayed put.

Libby tucked her gun back into its holster and ran to the window. Lightning split the black sky, allowing her to see Victor dragging Inez around the bungalow. ''His truck must be hidden by the trees to the north. Now they're out of sight.''

''Let's get to the Bronco. We'll tail them.''

''You read my mind.''

Victor's truck shot out from behind some trees and careened onto the road. Reies started the Bronco and shot after him, following the hazy red of the truck's taillights. Victor would have to stop eventually, Libby told herself. Then they would have their opportunity to nail him.

Only when the truck turned onto a rutted wilderness road that led straight toward the mountain's foothills did she become uneasy about what they were doing. Rain was collecting so fast that the ground couldn't absorb the water. The spinning tires drove great wet sheets away from the vehicle. Libby took a deep, calming breath. The idea of getting caught in a flash flood frightened her more than facing an armed man. Nature didn't make man's mistakes, and could be far more cruel.

Libby broke the tense silence. "Where do you suppose he's heading?"

"I don't think that he knows. He's just trying to get away from us any way he can."

She kept her doubts to herself as Reies pushed on, slowing the vehicle when they got too near the red taillights. Since his truck sat closer to the ground than the Bronco, Victor would have to drive with even more caution than Reies did. She kept herself steady by keeping that in mind. When the truck's taillights suddenly gave way to complete blackness, however, Libby felt as if her heart were bumping up against her ribs.

"Oh, my God," she whispered.

Obviously desperate to lose them, Victor had turned out his lights and was now driving blindly into the storm.

"Damn! He's going to kill my mother one way or another."

Libby couldn't disagree. As a matter of fact, Victor might succeed in killing them all. Holding onto the dash, she pressed herself forward, as far as the shoulder harness would allow. But no matter how hard she tried, she couldn't see anything past their headlight beams.

"Reies, he could turn off anywhere, and we wouldn't know it."

"Then we have to catch up."

He stepped on the gas, making Libby's heart accelerate. They were following a dangerous, winding, hilly road. Seconds felt like minutes. The truck still couldn't be seen. Then, as the Bronco sped up and over a knoll, Libby spotted it sitting in the middle of the road. "Stop!" she yelled, bracing herself.

Reies was already braking. The shoulder harness crushed the air from her chest and her forehead hit the dash, stunning her.

"It looks as if he got trapped by the water," Reies said excitedly. "Come on." Finally seeming to realize Libby wasn't responding, he asked, "Are you all right?"

"Fine." She felt a single trickle of wet slide down her forehead, and she was having trouble focusing. "Just got the breath knocked out of me."

As if she were moving in slow motion, Libby undid her seat belt while Reies reached behind them and pulled out a waterproof flashlight. She put her hand to her forehead, and touched the wetness. It was warm. Blood. She shook her head to clear it, but only succeeded in making it throb. Despite the fogginess slowing her down, she clambered out of the four-wheeler, along with Reies.

"Over there!" He pinned the other couple with the beam.

Stopped from crossing what probably had been a dry riverbed before the rain began, Victor was setting off along the gully away from the truck. The upward path was strewn with boulders and rocks. Rifle in one hand, he held Inez's wrist fast with the other.

Her head cleared somewhat, yet Libby hesitated, transfixed by the eerie sound of the rushing stream. Flash-flood waters could rise ten or more feet in less than an hour. The swift current was deadly.

And she had never learned to swim.

Sweat broke out on skin protected by the rain jacket. Heart pounding in her ears, she was unable to move, and her numb feet remained rooted in the wet earth.

"C'mon!" Reies yelled. He was already several yards ahead of her. "We can catch them."

Then what? Libby neither voiced the question nor looked where the gully tumbled downward into the churning waters, as she ran after Reies on legs that lacked their usual strength. Lightning shattered the blackness, and for a moment she could see Victor and Inez clearly a short distance ahead. Inez was having trouble keeping up. Victor was hauling her along through sheer force.

Spurred on by Inez's desperate situation, Libby forced her legs to move faster, and she closed the distance between her and Reies. She prayed that the bump on her head wouldn't affect her balance and make her clumsy.

A scream of fright pierced the sound of pelting rain. Reies's flashlight picked up his mother as she lost her footing and slid several yards down the incline, dragging her captor with her. Victor tore himself free of her, and with a single glance over his shoulder, he ran. Inez clung to a boulder, her long, wet hair whipping across her face, effectively blinding her.

"Hold on, Mother!"

Reies and Libby descended to her level. Libby clung to rocks as she went. Loose stones scattered and dropped into the water mere inches below, and her stomach somersaulted after them. Still, she kept calm, kept going. Reies reached Inez and made his way around to her other side.

"Stay calm, Mother. Libby, can you get her left hand?"

"I think so." *Don't look down,* she told herself as she took the last couple of steps. *Don't listen to the water.* "I've got her."

"There's a little more room to maneuver over here," Reies said. "We'll all move together . . . now."

Inez clutched Libby's hand and the three moved as one. The beam pitched as Reies clambered upward. He set the flashlight on a rock and used both hands to help his mother. A churning sensation around the soles of her boots made Libby look down to see the undulating water lick her feet.

A mistake.

Her next step, taken too quickly out of panic, threw her off balance. Her left foot slipped out from under her and that leg plunged knee-deep into the cold, swirling stream. Her chest and stomach hit hard against the slick rock, and unable to breathe, she clawed for a hold. The torrent of water continued to pluck at her. She had little strength left with which to fight, and her single toehold was tenuous at best.

"I'll get you!" Reies shouted.

In the process of reaching for her, he sent the flashlight hurtling into the water. Eyes wide with terror, Libby watched the light race downstream, bobbing and spinning before being sucked under and extinguished.

Her life could be extinguished just as easily.

Strong fingers closed around one wrist and Reies held her fast. "You've got to help me, Libby. Steady your weight over your right leg and push up."

"I can't. I'll slip."

"Do it!"

The sheer force of his words impelled her to action. Gathering the reserves of her strength, Libby pushed while Reies pulled, and by some miracle, was able to snatch her left leg from the greedy waters. She paused to take a long, shaky breath and let her head stop spinning.

"Come on. You've got it now," Reies urged.

A few seconds later, she was being pulled into his strong, wet arms. Water was pouring off his hat and down the back of her neck inside her jacket, but she'd never felt so wonderful. She held him tight. Next to them, Inez stood as still as a statue, her arms wrapped around herself.

"Victor." Libby pulled herself free and looked around. The rain had let up to a steady drizzle and the sky seemed to have lightened a bit, yet she couldn't see far enough to spot the murderer. "We have to go after him."

"Libby, no."

"Then I'll go alone."

"I can't let you do that."

But she was already doing it, moving more surefootedly than she had earlier. She sensed Reies following closely. He didn't try to stop her.

"Let Victor go," Inez pleaded. "He'll kill you both."

Libby moved faster, the memory of her father's and brother's funerals driving her forward. She took steady, even breaths and didn't look down. Instead she concentrated on her purpose. She could do it. She would catch up to Victor and bring him to justice.

She had to do it.

Once more, lightning lifted the curtain of night and Libby's gaze was drawn to a spot about fifty feet away. Her quarry was trapped by a smooth, eight-foot bluff in front of him. He couldn't go on. He was cornered!

His only way out was past her . . . or down.

Chapter Thirteen

"Victor, you can't get away. Give yourself up."

Libby shouted the words as she moved uphill toward a large cottonwood. A shot exploded, the whine of Victor's bullet cutting close to where she'd been standing. She was taking a breath of relief when she was thrown up against the tree.

"Stay here and don't say another word," Reies whispered. "I'm going up and around."

Realizing he meant to surprise Victor from above, Libby grabbed a handful of wet jacket to stop him. "You're crazy. You'll kill yourself."

Without another word, he pulled himself free and began working his way uphill. Fear for Reies's immediate safety made her listen intently, but she couldn't hear his footfalls, so silently did he move. She realized the rain had stopped completely, and the clouds seemed to be clearing as if preparing the way for the full moon.

"What's the matter, Libby?" Victor called, taunting. "Afraid of a little bullet?"

She knew then that he didn't suspect Reies was prowling so close. The artist probably assumed he'd stayed back to take care of his mother. Though Libby didn't answer, Victor's baiting continued.

"I thought you were the tough cop—so why don't you come here and show me how mean you can be?"

As quietly as possible, she unsnapped the top of her jacket and withdrew her Beretta. She sensed rather than heard someone behind her. Whipping around, she almost shot out of reflex. Luckily she realized in time that it was only Inez. Reies's mother wore an air of defeat as she stared first at the weapon aimed at her, then at Libby, her black eyes so like her son's. Libby lowered the gun, and without saying anything, the older woman joined her in the shelter of the tree.

"Where are you, Libby?" Victor sounded impatient. "I'm waiting for you."

Libby glanced to the left of the high, steep bank and saw a flash of white—Reies's shirt. He must be getting close and would be in position in another minute. Ducking low, she started to slip out from behind her shelter, but Inez tried to interfere. The older woman shook her head, her eyes wild with fright. Libby put a finger to her lips and crept forward.

"Say something, damn it!" Victor yelled.

He fired blindly, this bullet coming closer than the first. A lucky shot, or had he heard her furtive movements above the rush of the stream? Her pulse zigzagged through her body. A few more steps, and she took shelter behind a boulder. Any closer and he would surely see her. And she would be able to see him.

"Your brother wasn't so tough. He was easy prey."

Libby's chest tightened at the reminder of Wayne's murder. She wanted to curse Victor, to go after him blindly, but that was what he was hoping for.

"Did you see your brother's body, Libby? I mean, before they fixed it up for the funeral?"

Victor's laugh made the hair on the back of her neck stand up. She swallowed the urge to scream a curse, let it echo through her mind until she thought it would explode from her. Her hand tightened around the Beretta. She chanced raising her head a few inches and waited for another flash of movement from the cliff. Her muscles were wired for action.

"I shot your brother three times with this very rifle."

Libby clenched her jaw to keep from answering. Reies had to be in place. She couldn't wait any longer. She slipped from her shelter and, keeping herself well hunched, inched forward. She could make Victor out now, just barely, but she knew he couldn't see her. He was looking too high and too far to the right.

"Your brother looked surprised," Victor sneered. "He thought—"

The spread-eagled body of a man landed on him. The rifle jerked and fell to the ground.

"Reies!" Libby rose and led with her gun. The men were rolling across a narrow strip of wet, sandy earth that ended in a dead fall to flood water. She stopped scant yards away. "Give up, Victor," she demanded. "You don't have a chance."

She could see them clearly now, trading punches. The rifle lay away from her on their other side. Victor scrambled to his feet and went for it, but Reies seized and yanked the other man's ankle. Victor went down cursing and kicking. His boot heel struck Reies square in the forehead. Reies flew backward toward the steep bank, saving himself from falling only by twisting his body and rolling to the side.

The scene played in slow motion before Libby's horrified eyes. Victor bounded to his feet, swept up the rifle and turned to face his opponent, who was struggling to his knees. He would kill Reies if she didn't stop him.

"Drop it!" she screamed, raising the Beretta and using both hands to steady her aim. "I'll shoot!"

Victor ignored her. The rifle moved up and into position, its deadly barrel pointed straight at Reies. She had no choice. Aiming for Victor's shoulder, she squeezed the trigger. His body jerked at the impact of the bullet, and the rifle went flying. At the same time Reies hurled himself full tilt at the artist.

The clouds chose that moment to unveil the moon, illuminating a picture that no painting could ever capture: Reies ramming Victor in the thighs before falling to his hands and knees at the edge of the embankment; Victor flying backward, his features set in a mask of terror, his body turning in the air as he faced his death in the churning flood waters below.

Victor's scream was short-lived. Libby moved to the edge of the embankment and spotted his body, spinning and twisting in the rapid waters, swept downstream faster than she could run. Her hand shook as she replaced the Beretta in the holster. She'd never killed before. Technically, she hadn't killed now, she told herself. Her bullet had only disarmed him. Victor might still be alive.

Not for long.

The man who had incited so much violence would die by violence—nature's own, a fate more horrible than the prison term she'd had planned for him. An ironic form of justice for crimes not only against her family, but against the people of Sidewinder.

Libby thought she might be sick. Bile rose in her throat. She caught movement from the corner of her eye and turned to see Inez standing at the embankment. The woman wailed, a heartfelt cry that shattered the last of Libby's composure. Inez was feeling her way down the rocks toward the water.

"Inez, stop!" Libby shouted, already running.

The older woman ignored her, made the sign of the cross and then leaned forward, about to throw herself into the water. Libby's feet dislodged a handful of stones that sprayed Inez, and she slid to a stop and caught a handful of thin cotton jacket and loose black hair. The rip of material sent a chill through Libby. Their proximity to the flooded stream made her heart pound with fright. She leaned back for balance and hung on, while Inez struggled to fling herself forward.

"Mother!" Reies yelled.

"Let me... die with Victor," Inez begged between heaving sobs. "I don't want to live. I don't deserve to live."

Then Reies was at his mother's side, wrapping her in his strong arms, forcing her back up to safety, while she shrieked and fought him.

"No, Reies, let me go!"

"Victor was a murderer, Mother. I know you cared about him anyway, but he would have been taken from you even if he'd lived. He would have spent the rest of his life in prison. You wouldn't have wanted to go to prison just because he did," Reies added reasonably.

"Yes! Yes!"

Inez wailed again, sending gooseflesh crawling up Libby's spine as she carefully put some space between herself and the water. Feeling helpless, she stopped a respectful distance away from mother and son. The older woman tried to pummel Reies with closed fists, but he grabbed her above the elbows, rendering her powerless. He gave her a sharp shake.

"Mother, please try to calm down."

"I can't. You don't understand. Victor did kill Wayne, but it was to protect me." Hair spilling into her face, eyes glittering as tears fell from them, she plucked at his shirt. "Because *I* killed Oliver Reardon."

The statement rocked Libby to her very core.

Reies shook his head. "I don't believe it. Victor admitted he killed Oliver."

"No, he didn't," said Libby. That conversation had been burned into her memory despite everything that had happened since. She went on, "Victor said that, one way or another, my father had to die. He was about to continue when you interrupted him."

"I was aware of Victor's involvement with the Coalition and his reasons from the beginning," Inez said. "I knew the chance he was taking, but I couldn't stop him. He said no one would actually get hurt. Then Oliver Reardon overheard Victor's plans. Someone would have killed Victor if Oliver had told. I was frantic. I'd already lost two men I loved. Wasn't that enough? How many losses can one person bear? Victor said I shouldn't worry. He would take care of it. That's when I knew he meant to kill Oliver Reardon himself."

"So you did it for him to protect your lover."

The sound of Reies's anguish pierced Libby to the quick, but she didn't say anything. She couldn't. The man Inez had murdered had been her father, after all. She wrapped her arms around herself to fight the nausea pressing in on her once more. She'd thought she'd had it all figured out, but Inez's confession came as a total shock. She wasn't as clever a cop as she had thought.

"It...it wasn't like that. I didn't mean to...kill Oliver." Inez took a great gulp of air and went on. "I was only trying to scare him away before Victor could do something crazy. No one was in the house that night but the two of us. I went to the guest bedroom where he was staying and begged him to forget about what he'd heard." She squeezed her eyes shut for a moment and took another breath. "He...he said his conscience wouldn't let him. I had Frank's revolver hidden in my skirts. I only meant to threaten Oliver with it—to scare him so that he

would leave. He tried to take the gun away from me."
Inez sobbed, and her tears fell freely. "We struggled and
the gun went off. An accident. I swear as God is my witness it was an accident. But the barrel was pressed into his
stomach..."

"Gutshot," Reies said. He pulled his mother close and
wrapped his arms around her shaking body. "How did
Oliver end up in my bed?"

"Victor came...and found us. I was sitting on the bed,
the gun in my hand. I...I don't know for how long." She
pressed her forehead into his chest. Her voice was muffled. "Victor took it from me and brought me to my
room. He told me to sleep, said that he would take care
of everything. I didn't know where he put Oliver until
after you found him."

"And you never wondered why he tried to frame me?"

"He said everyone would assume Pilar had defended
herself against Oliver's physical advances, that no one
would blame her, that everyone would think you were
just protecting her. I wanted to believe him. I thought the
threat of violence from the Coalition was over, but Victor said he'd lost control, that the group was acting on its
own when those men raided the courthouse. I had to believe him." She raised her head and pleaded, "Don't you
see?"

"And what about my brother's murder?" Libby
asked. "What did you believe about that?"

Inez looked confused, as if she'd forgotten that Libby
was there. "That Victor was protecting me."

"He was protecting himself. You heard him." Libby
bit her lip so she wouldn't cry. "He enjoyed himself. Enjoyed killing my brother."

"And I fooled myself into believing Victor's lies all
those years. He would have killed me tonight and I would
have deserved it. Please, Libby, you must see that justice

is finally done." Inez broke into renewed sobbing. "Arrest me. Maybe some of the guilt will go away. I've tried to pay for my sins, but God hasn't forgiven me. Maybe he won't ever forgive me, and that's why I am doomed to spend the rest of my life alone."

Libby felt moisture slip down her own cheeks. Tears for a woman who couldn't live with her self-condemnation. Tears for a father who had been trying to do the right thing, and tears for a brother who had been seeking justice. Tears, too, for her own love, which was now lost forever.

Over. Everything was over. Staring at a bedraggled Reies, who was once more sheltering his mother close in his arms, his black hair mingling with hers, Libby realized how much he cared for Inez, in spite of her misguided deeds.

He would never forgive her for arresting Inez. But she would have to. Theirs was an impossible love, one without a future.

Over.

The word held such emptiness.

HOLED UP IN HER Santa Fe apartment with what she figured must be the onset of pneumonia, Libby was trying to sleep away both her physical and emotional discomfort. Therefore, when her doorbell rang she considered pulling her pillow over her head and ignoring her uninvited visitor.

"Libby, I know you're in there! Either answer this door or I'll break it down."

It was Reies.

"Give me a minute!" she croaked.

Why had he come? She didn't know what to expect. Recriminations? A final goodbye? Wiping her nose with a tissue, she opened the door. Her eyes devoured every disgustingly healthy-looking inch of him.

"I heard you were sick." He placed a warm Crockpot in her hands. "I brought you some chili guaranteed to burn that nasty cold right out of you."

She stood staring down at the pot, not saying a word.

"If you don't let me in, Libby, you'll force me to pick you up and carry you back to bed, where you belong."

His tone of voice made her legs move—and her heart pound. Why was he doing this? She carried the pot into the kitchen where she set it on the counter. He followed close behind, and when she didn't make a move to do so herself, reached round her to plug it into an outlet.

She grabbed the counter behind her for support. "What exactly do you want, Reies?" The words sounded as choked as her insides felt. She couldn't control her voice any more than she could control her emotions.

"That's simple. I want you." His black eyes met hers steadily as he smoothed the limp bangs from her forehead. "If you'll have me."

Libby slipped away from him and placed herself in front of the refrigerator, her arms crossed over her chest. "You'll never forget your mother is in jail because of me."

Reies stalked her, backed her into a corner.

"My mother is in jail because of what she did. She made her bed thirteen years ago. I'll never stop loving her, but I won't let her stop me from loving you, either, Libby. I only hope you won't hold what she did against me. Accident or not, she made every member of your family a victim—including you. My mother has to learn to live with what she's done. I want to learn to live with you."

"But, Reies—"

He put a finger to her lips, stopping her protest. "C'mon, lady, sit down." He led her to the tiny table and pulled out one of the two chairs for her. "Let me get you some of that chili. Where do you keep your bowls?"

"The upper cabinet to the right of the sink."

Not knowing what to say, Libby sat in silence, broken only by her occasional sneeze. Reies moved around her kitchen as if it were the most natural thing in the world for him to be doing. When he set a bowl of chili in front of her and took the other chair, she stared at him. She had thought she wouldn't see him again outside of a courtroom.

"Eat," he said, handing her a spoon. "While I fill you in on what's been going on at the ranch with Nick and me. When I think of the things I thought about him—"

"Don't." Having barely tasted the chili, Libby set down the spoon and covered one of his hands. "We both went through hell. Nick can't possibly blame you, can he?"

"No, but I blame myself. You knew Nick was innocent before I did."

"You were too close, too emotionally involved."

"And you weren't?" Reies paused long enough to load the spoon with chili and place it in her hand. "I had to straighten things out with him and make some other arrangements, or I would have been here beating down your door yesterday."

"Good thing you didn't," she said, choking down the mouthful of food. "Yesterday I was a mess."

Reies grinned, and Libby smiled in return. She wondered if the chili was really as wretched as she thought or if her taste buds were askew because of her cold. Thinking Reies might have made it himself, she didn't want to hurt his feelings, so she continued eating.

"Nick and I talked things through like we should have done long ago. I told him about my suspicions. I wouldn't have blamed him if he'd hated me, but I felt he had the right to know. I owed him the truth. You taught me that."

Libby felt a warm glow that had nothing to do with the jalepeño peppers she was eating. "What did Nick say?"

"That he understood. Nick has turned into quite a man, and I never took the time to get to know him since I've been back. I want to correct that. Pilar told me he was obsessed with the Coalition. Well, he is, but not in the way she thought. He'd heard about the trouble brewing and was going to those meetings to try to figure out how to stop history from repeating itself."

Libby set down her spoon. "Reies, about Pilar. She and Johnnie—"

"I know. So does Nick. I told him what you said about the money. He got the whole truth out of her. She overheard Oliver telling Grandfather that he had the money with him. She helped Johnnie steal it the same night as the murder."

"So that's why Johnnie gave you an alibi, so no one would suspect he'd been near the ranch."

"Right. Nick kicked Pilar out. He told her to come back when she grew up and acted like a woman instead of a child. She probably went straight to Johnnie."

"What about the Coalition?"

"Nick and I are going to work on that together. With Victor gone, Johnnie's lost his edge. We think we can settle the people down, talk them into approaching the problem through the legal system. Nothing may be solved, but we can try."

"You two did have a lot to talk about."

"And so do you and I." Reies ran a finger down her cheek tenderly. "I want us to be together, Libby. We make one hell of a team."

"Oh, Reies." Libby sniffled and blew her nose into a napkin. She couldn't believe the way he'd opened up to her. A week ago, he would have kept his feelings to himself. "I want to be with you, too, but where?" Her voice cracked. "I would never be able to live in Sidewinder."

"I know that. I never thought I could be happy living anywhere else, but I was wrong. I didn't need to belong to a place, I needed to belong to someone—to a wonderful, gutsy, tough lady cop with a stubborn chin. I would live anywhere with you." Smiling wryly, he looked around him. "As long as it's not in some small apartment with no land."

Libby's heart pounded with renewed hope. "You would leave Rancho Velasquez after all the money and work you put into it?"

"Nick spent his entire adult life taking care of the place until I wandered back. I think he deserves to have the reins permanently. I have enough money left for a down payment on a small spread of my own. Maybe twenty or so miles outside the city limits?"

"You would do that for me?"

"I would do it for us. And after I dazzle the locals at the rodeo this weekend, I'll have people beating down our door for our horses. We can make it work, Libby. We can get married next week. All right?" At her happy nod, he went on, "You can stay with the force or work alongside me on the ranch. It's up to you." He took one of her hands and cradled it between his palms. "Luis will be our foreman. I think he and Ada have something serious going, because she wants to come, too, as our housekeeper and cook."

"Ada? Our cook?"

"What's wrong with that? She owns a cafe."

"But her food is terrible."

"She made that chili you're eating."

Libby began to laugh, and once she started she couldn't stop. "Reies Coulter, did I ever tell you I love you?"

"And I love you, lady," he said gruffly.

Before she knew what was happening, he'd lifted her up and into his arms. As he headed toward the bedroom, his mouth took hers in a fiery kiss that left no doubt about his intentions.

When he set her gently on the bed, she protested, "Reies, you'll get my cold."

He leaned over her, tugging free the strip of rawhide that held his hair back. "Woman, there isn't a thing about you that I don't want. And I play for keeps." He held out his hand. "Partners for life?"

She shook on it. "Partners." Then she tangled her fingers in his long hair and pulled him closer. "Come here, Desperado, and show me how you seal a bargain."